THE TREASURE AT POLDARROW POINT

An Angela Marchmont Mystery Book 3

CLARA BENSON

MOUNT
STREET
PRESS

MOUNT STREET PRESS

Copyright

© 2013 Clara Benson

All rights reserved

ClaraBenson.com

Cover concept by Yang Liu
WaterPaperInk.com

Cover typography and interior book design by Colleen Sheehan
WDRBookDesign.com

Print spine and back cover design by Shayne Rutherford
DarkMoonGraphics.com

Chapter One

'WHAT YOU NEED, Mrs. Marchmont,' said Dr. Wilding, 'is a holiday. A bout of influenza like the one you've just had is bound to leave you feeling below par. A few weeks of sun and healthy sea air will see you as right as rain.'

Angela Marchmont sighed.

'I dare say you're right,' she said. 'Perhaps I have been over-exerting myself.'

'There's no doubt about it,' said the doctor. 'Fit and healthy people don't tend to faint all over the place—especially not in the Royal Enclosure.'

'Don't!' said Angela, blushing at the memory. 'You can't imagine what a fool I felt. And to do it in front of Cynthia Pilkington-Soames too! She won't admit to it, but I have it on good authority that she writes the society gossip column in the *Clarion*. Now I suppose I shall be all over the papers again, and just when I was hoping for a little peace and quiet.'

'All the more reason to get away, then. Yes,' he went on, 'you may consider it as doctor's orders.'

'Where do you suggest I go?'

'Anywhere you like, so long as it's not London. What about the South coast? Bournemouth, perhaps? Or if you really want to get away from it all, then Cornwall is the place to go.'

'I've never been to Cornwall,' said Angela thoughtfully. 'A quiet hotel or a little cottage by the sea would be delightful.'

'A cottage, you say?' said Dr. Wilding. 'Ah, now if it's a cottage you're talking about, then perhaps I can help. Another patient of mine, Mrs. Uppingham, was telling me just the other day of a house she has down there. She had been going to spend the summer there, but she broke her leg and so won't be going anywhere for a few weeks at least. I wonder if she'd be interested in renting it to you.'

'Where is it?'

'Place called Tregarrion, near Penzance. I don't know whether you've heard of it. It's a quaint old fishing-village— or used to be, at any rate. The artists discovered it a few years ago, and the tourists followed shortly afterwards. Still, I gather from my patient that it hasn't been totally spoilt yet, and is still pretty quiet by comparison with St. Ives and all those other fashionable places.'

'It sounds the very thing,' said Angela, 'but I'm not sure it will be possible. I am engaged every evening next week, and after that I promised to go and stay with the Harrisons in Kent for a few days. Then, of course, there's Goodwood, and by that time perhaps Mrs. Uppingham will have recovered and want her house back.'

'I should have thought you had had enough of racing after that little exhibition of yours at Ascot. Well, I can't make you do it, but I'll be disappointed if you don't. You can't be too careful of your health, you know. We none of us are getting any younger.'

'By which I suppose you mean *I* am not getting any younger,' said Angela dryly. 'How very tactful of you to put it that way.'

The doctor grinned unrepentantly.

'You are easily in as good a shape as a woman ten years younger, Mrs. Marchmont. If all my patients were as healthy as you I should make no money. But you are not eighteen. You can't simply shake these things off in the same way you should have done twenty years ago.' He glanced at his watch and rose. 'Well, I must be going, but do think about what I said.'

'I shall,' said Angela.

He nodded and went out.

'Shall you go, *madame*?' said Angela's maid, who had been busying herself silently about the room during the doctor's examination.

'I don't know, Marthe,' said Angela. 'I'd like to take a holiday, certainly, but you know what the Harrisons are like. Marguerite goes into such a huff if one cancels a visit. I should have to spend the next two years making it up to her.'

'She is like a spoilt child, that one.'

'A little, perhaps, but she is very good company, and I have been promising to go to them since last year.'

'You do too much, *madame*,' said Marthe. 'Everybody wants you. It is very tiresome. The doctor is right: you have been ill and should rest yourself.'

Marthe had firm ideas as to her own influence and importance which were very nearly correct.

'And I shall,' replied Angela, 'only it may have to wait a few weeks, until I have the time.'

'You must make time. It is foolish to be afraid of one's friends in such situations as these.'

'I am not afraid of Marguerite Harrison,' said Angela with dignity. 'Whatever makes you think I am?'

The girl made no reply but her expression said much. Angela was about to defend herself further but was saved the trouble when the telephone-bell rang. Marthe answered it.

'Mrs. Pilkington-Soames would like to speak to you,' she said.

Angela's heart sank. She took the receiver.

'Hallo, Cynthia,' she said warily.

'Angela, *darling*,' said an excitable, high-pitched voice at the other end of the line. 'I *do* hope you're feeling better now. How simply *awful* for you, to faint in front of the King like that!'

Angela closed her eyes briefly but was given no chance to reply.

'His Majesty was *terribly* concerned for you, naturally, but he had to rush off and present the Gold Cup so he couldn't stay. I did hear that he was asking about you afterwards, though.'

'Oh,' said Angela.

'I understand you've been quite ill, lately. Is that why you fainted? Of course, we all know about that business at Underwood, and how you were attacked. Tell me, was it *very* dreadful?'

'Er—' said Angela.

'It must have frightened you out of your wits. The papers were full of it all. Is that why we haven't seen you very much recently?' Mrs. Pilkington-Soames lowered her voice to a more sympathetic level. 'They do say that you had a sort of nervous breakdown afterwards.'

'That's absolute non—' began Angela, but Cynthia pressed on.

'Oh, come now. You can tell me. Why, everyone knows that I am absolutely the *last word* in discretion. Now, somebody said it was influenza, but you can't fool me, darling. Influenza, at this time of year? Whoever heard of such a thing? But seriously, Angela, I can recommend a tremendously good doctor—well, I suppose one ought to call him a psychiatrist, really. You remember Naomi McNamara, don't you?'

'I—' said Angela.

'*You* know, the one who had that rather unfortunate episode with the gardener's boy? Nymphomania, I think they called it. Well, she saw this Dr. Gambara—or is it Gambetta?—I can never remember these foreign names, and he put his hands on her head and chanted something terribly esoteric and now of course she's left her husband and gone off to Scotland to join the Order of the Sisters of Divine Mercy. So you see, he's obviously an expert in matters of the mind.'

'Er—' said Angela.

'Do remind me to give you his card. Now, darling,' said Mrs. Pilkington-Soames, suddenly becoming brisk and business-like, 'I have something to propose to you.'

'Oh yes?'

'Yes. Let me explain. I was at an evening party the other night and just *happened* to fall into conversation with a terribly clever man, a Mr. Bickerstaffe who, I was quite astonished to discover, turns out to be the editor of the *Clarion*. Naturally, I know nothing about the business—' (here, Angela pulled a disbelieving face) '—but he was quite the gentleman, which surprised me, as I had always understood that newspaper people were rather *rough.*'

'I see.'

'Anyhow,' went on Mrs. Pilkington-Soames, 'you won't believe it, but while we were talking about this and that it *somehow* came out that I knew you. He was terribly excited when he found out, and asked me if there was any chance that I should be able to get an interview with you. Now *do* say yes, darling.'

'Are you quite mad?' said Angela before she could stop herself. Fortunately, Cynthia was not listening, and went on:

'Why, just think what an *enormous* scoop it would be for me! You are one of the most famous women in England today thanks to your recent exploits. The public are simply *dying* to know everything about you. I thought perhaps I could write about you from a more personal angle, with some photographs—you know what I mean: "Mrs. Marchmont relaxing at home," and all that sort of thing. You could give the readers your advice for baking the perfect sponge cake, or something of the kind.'

'*Baking?*' said Angela, aghast.

'Oh yes, our women readers love all that domestic stuff: "When at home, our lady detective puts away her gun and takes up her rolling-pin." We could even have a picture of you in a pinny.'

'*Our* women readers?'

Cynthia was brought up short as she realized what she had just almost admitted.

'Well, the *Clarion's* readers. I was quoting Mr. Bickerstaffe directly,' she said rather feebly. 'Anyway, I've told him that you'd be delighted. It will be easy enough—we can do the interview itself at the Harrisons' next week, and I can send a photographer round after that to take some pictures of you in your flat.'

'I didn't know you were going to be at the Harrisons.'

'Didn't Marguerite tell you? Yes, I shall be there. Anyway, darling, I really *must* dash now, but I'll see you next week. And don't worry about the interview—it will just be a cosy chat between friends.'

She saluted Angela gaily and hung up. No sooner had she gone than Angela rattled the button urgently and asked to make a trunk call.

'Go into the bedroom and start packing my things,' she said to Marthe as she waited for the operator to connect the call. 'I am not going to Kent after all. I am going to Cornwall instead. I am just going to tell Marguerite now. You see, you were wrong,' she could not help adding. 'I am not afraid of anyone.'

'I see nothing of the kind, *madame*,' said Marthe. 'I see only that you are more afraid of Mrs. Pilkington-Soames than you are of Mrs. Harrison.'

Since this was perfectly true, Angela made no reply.

CHAPTER TWO

ANGELA MARCHMONT THREW open the French windows onto the terrace and took a deep breath of bracing salt air. The warm sun glinted on the sea, and the sound of the waves crashing against the rocks beneath was at once uplifting and soothing. Above and below her seagulls wheeled, swooped and shrieked, and the sea was dotted here and there with brightly-coloured fishing boats and pleasure craft.

'This is quite delightful,' said Angela to herself. 'I can't think why I have never come here before. I'm sorry for Mrs. Uppingham and her broken leg but I must say it has all turned out rather well for me.'

As befitted its name, Kittiwake Cottage was perched halfway down the cliff path that led from the former fishing village of Tregarrion to the sea. It was one of a pair of quaint old white houses that sat side by side, maintaining a dignified distance from the bustle of the town itself. The other was named Shearwater Cottage, and was presently inhabited by an elderly woman and her daughter. To Angela's left lay the wide sweep of Tregarn bay, which stretched into the distance and ended in a headland some miles away, its curving shoreline broken only by the town's little harbour. Tregarrion was an undeniably picturesque place, its hilly streets lined with brightly-coloured houses that looked almost like a child's toy building-blocks stacked one on top of the other. It was easy to see why artists had begun flocking here a few years before. Away to the right and far below was a rocky cove, tucked out of sight of the town, its cliffs scarred and pitted from thousands of years of battering by the ocean. The cove was reached by means of the cliff path, which forked in two just before it reached Kittiwake Cottage and descended steeply to a tiny beach of yellow sand. The other branch of the path led along the cliff top to a nearby promontory, where sat a big house in dark stone which stared gloomily out to sea and appeared to be in a state of some disrepair.

Angela sat on the terrace for a while, taking in the sunshine and thinking of nothing in particular. Eventually, however, lured irresistibly by the possibilities of the day, she got up, fetched a parasol and went out through the gate that separated the little garden from the lower cliff path. As she was looking to the left and right, wondering which way to go, she caught sight of a figure toiling up the track from the beach. As it drew near, the figure revealed itself to be a young woman wearing a bathing-dress and cap and carrying a damp towel. She caught sight of Angela and waved.

'Good morning, Mrs. Marchmont,' she said, as soon as she was within speaking distance. 'Isn't it the most splendid day?

The water is simply heavenly down there. I shouldn't have come out at all had I not promised Mother I'd be back within the hour.'

'Isn't it cold?' said Angela.

'A little, at first,' said the girl, 'but the exercise soon warms one up.' Her normally pale, serious face was alight with enjoyment. 'What about you? Do you intend to bathe while you are here?'

'Why, I haven't swum in years,' said Angela, 'but I'll admit it does look very appealing. Perhaps I shall give it a try one day.'

'You must do it at low tide, though,' said the girl. 'At high tide the sea gets very rough and dangerous and can dash you against the rocks. Not only that, but if you're not careful you can get cut off from the path and drown.'

'I shall keep that in mind,' promised Angela.

'Helen!' cried a voice suddenly from the window of Shearwater Cottage. The girl lifted her head and her face immediately drained of all its radiance and once again became pallid and expressionless.

'That's Mother,' she said. 'She gets cross if I leave her for too long, but I'm afraid I was enjoying my bathe so much I rather forgot the time.'

The voice called again, more loudly this time, and Helen smiled apologetically.

'I must go,' she said, and hurried in through the gate and up the garden path. As Angela watched her go, she caught sight of a woman's face at the open window. It was a discontented, querulous face: the sort of face that looked as though its owner liked nothing better than to find fault. The woman caught sight of Angela and her habitual frown disappeared, to be replaced by a wide smile. Angela waved and went on her way.

She reached the fork in the cliff path and, after a moment's thought, took the branch that led back behind her own cottage and towards the big house on the headland. The sun was high in the sky now, and it would have been very warm had it not been for a refreshing sea breeze that was just strong enough to bring relief from the heat without blowing one's hat off. Angela strolled along the path, stopping every so often to drink in the sunshine and the scenery and to look back at the way she had come. Her spirits lifted with every step and she idly pondered the possibility of buying a little holiday house in the area.

The place was quite deserted—or so she thought until she came to the point where the cliff top curved around and jutted out to form the headland. Here a bench had been placed at the side of the path in such a way as to take best advantage of the view. On the bench a man sat, smoking a cigarette and idly drawing patterns in the earth with a malacca cane. He was impeccably dressed in a light suit and straw hat, and was the very picture of ease and contentment.

Angela glanced at him as she passed by and would have thought no more about him had he not happened to look up and give what she was almost sure was a start of surprise when he saw her. Her attention caught, she turned her head sharply to look at him, but in that instant he had recovered himself, and merely put down his cane and raised his hat with an affable smile. Angela acknowledged the salutation and walked on. She must have imagined it; or perhaps he had recognized her—after all, her photograph had been in the newspapers often enough lately.

After a few minutes she reached the end of the headland and stopped to look at the old house which, she now saw, stood perilously close to the cliff edge. At one time it must have had a large expanse of garden, but the erosion of the cliffs had caused a portion of it to be sacrificed to the sea, and what remained looked as though it had once been well-tended but was now in need of attention. The state of the house itself was little better: paint peeled from its doors and window frames, and one of the upstairs windows was actually boarded up. It must have been a handsome building once—perhaps the home of a wealthy farmer or boat-owner—but its glory days were long gone and it sat there forlornly, a sad relic of better times.

Angela was just wondering whether the house was inhabited when a side door opened and out came a frail, elderly lady, accompanied by a middle-aged man. They were dressed for walking, and Angela eyed them discreetly as they came out through the gate and headed in her direction.

As they passed the old lady paused and smiled at Angela.

'Good morning,' she said. 'You are admiring our view, I see.'

'I am,' replied Angela, 'and it is a beautiful one. You are very fortunate.'

'We are indeed,' agreed the woman, 'although of course you are seeing it at its finest today. There is nothing more delightful than taking a bracing walk along the cliff top, but the winter storms we get here may not be so appealing to the less hardy.'

'Yes,' said Angela with a laugh. 'I can imagine that this place would not be for the faint-hearted during a gale.'

'No—there is always the danger that one might be blown out to sea!'

'Or that the cliff will collapse,' Angela said, indicating the garden. 'Don't you worry that you will lose the house?'

'Oh no,' said the old woman. 'One day the sea will surely come to claim its own, but that is unlikely to happen in my lifetime. You see how the garden has been ravaged, but it has taken many, many years for it to reach that state. I believe I am safe for the present.'

'You are more sanguine than I, Aunt Emily,' said her companion with a slight shudder. 'When the winds are battering at the house I confess I do occasionally wonder uncomfortably whether we shall wake up in the same place that we went to bed—if indeed we wake up at all.'

The old lady let out a musical peal of laughter.

'What nonsense!' she said. Turning to Angela, she went on, 'Dear Clifford has always been the cautious one of the family. Odd, since one tends to associate youth with daring and recklessness.'

Since dear Clifford was plump and balding, and unlikely to see forty-five again, Angela did not find this as odd as his aunt apparently did.

'Are you staying nearby?' went on the woman.

'Yes, I am at Kittiwake Cottage.'

'Which one is that?'

'The house just along there. It belongs to Mrs. Uppingham.'

'Oh, of course, Mrs. Uppingham. Is she a close friend of yours?'

'I have never met her. The house was recommended to me by her doctor, who knew it to be available at present.'

'Such a charming lady—I know her very well. Oh, forgive me, I ought to introduce myself. I am Miss Emily Trout, and this is my nephew, Clifford Maynard.'

'How do you do? I am Angela Marchmont.'

As she spoke, she thought she saw Clifford glance briefly at his aunt and raise his eyebrows.

'I am very pleased to meet you, Mrs. Marchmont,' said Miss Trout. Shall you be staying here long? You must come to tea very soon. We have few friends in Tregarrion and we are so isolated up here that it is quite a treat to us to have company. Do say you will. I have many exciting tales to tell about things that have happened at Poldarrow Point over the years.'

'Poldarrow Point? Is that the name of your house?' asked Angela.

'Yes,' said Miss Trout, 'and it has a very interesting history. You know, of course, that this area used to be notorious for smuggling in the olden days? Well, the house has a close connection to the nefarious activities that went on many years ago. But I shan't tell you another word. You must come to tea if you want to hear more. Can you come tomorrow? You may bring anyone you like.'

Angela laughed at Miss Trout's disarming method of getting her own way.

'If you will promise to tell me about the smugglers then I shall certainly come,' she replied.

The old lady clasped her hands together in girlish delight.

'Oh, I am so glad!' she said. 'Then we shall see you at four tomorrow. Don't be late!'

'I shan't,' promised Angela. She said goodbye and set off back to Kittiwake Cottage, leaving Miss Trout and her nephew to continue their walk.

CHAPTER THREE

THE MAN HAD gone from the bench when Mrs. Marchmont passed it again, but she was not thinking about him, as she was turning over in her mind the encounter with Miss Trout and her nephew. She had rather taken to the old woman who, despite her frail appearance and gentle, ladylike manners, gave every impression of being rather a character. Angela was curious to know more about her.

It was almost one when she returned home. Dr. Wilding had told her that the cottage was provided with a cook and a cat, but up to now she had met only the former. As she sat resting on the terrace after lunch, however, she noticed a large tabby sitting on the garden wall, gazing down at her. Angela immediately put down her book and raised her hand in invitation. The cat sniffed at it delicately, then after a moment's indecision leapt down onto the terrace and began winding in and out of the legs of her deck-chair.

'I seem to have passed muster,' said Angela to herself as she settled back into her chair and resumed reading.

It was very pleasant, sitting outside in the sunshine with the cool breeze fanning one's face gently. Angela was gradually overcome by a delicious drowsiness, and the words began to dance on the page in front of her.

'Goodness, I feel as though I could fall asleep,' she murmured, and that was her last conscious thought until she awoke with a start some time later. Blinking, she looked at her watch. It was just after three o'clock, and she had been asleep nearly an hour. She sat up.

'That's quite enough of that!' she said firmly, and rose from the chair. As she did so, she thought she heard a familiar sound, and turned her head to listen. Yes, she could definitely hear music playing somewhere in the distance. It sounded rather jolly, and Angela decided to seek the source of it. As she went out through the garden gate, she met Helen Walters and her mother, who were just setting out for a walk themselves from Shearwater Cottage, and she was invited to join them.

Mrs. Felicia Walters was something of an invalid—or, at least, it suited her very well to say so. Angela suspected that there was nothing much wrong with her that a short spell of having to look after herself would not put right, but of course that was unlikely to happen as long as her daughter was there to satisfy her every whim. She walked with a stick, leaning on Helen's arm all the while, and together the three of them proceeded along the cliff path towards Tregarrion.

Despite—or perhaps because of her physical infirmity, Mrs. Walters had an enthusiastic, nay, passionate interest in the business of others. As soon as she had arrived in the area, she had cast out her net and set her snares among the local populace, and through a combination of artfulness and perseverance had soon learned almost everything that could be told about anyone living or staying in the immediate vicinity. Having drained the well dry, she had been looking about for new sources, and had therefore been delighted when Angela had arrived at Kittiwake Cottage a day or two earlier—all the more so as Mrs. Marchmont's name was familiar to her from the newspapers. As they walked, Mrs. Walters went on the attack. Angela recognized the type, but from her recent fame had become well used to fending off impertinent inquiries by offering up unimportant snippets of information that could hurt no-one. Thus the walk proceeded in a state of amicable compromise, interspersed with occasional bouts of fencing.

Mrs. Walters was most interested to hear that Mrs. Marchmont had been invited to Poldarrow Point for tea.

'Miss Trout and her nephew are very agreeable people,' she said. 'It's such a pity that they don't mix more with the people of the town. They must be very lonely out there in such an isolated spot.'

From this, Angela deduced correctly that Mrs. Walters had been unsuccessful in her attempts to draw them in.

'And Poldarrow Point is such a fine old place,' went on Mrs. Walters. 'Or, at least, it must have been, once. I suppose they can't afford the upkeep any more. It is difficult, these days, to keep a large house running smoothly—and without the help of her brother I suppose it is even harder.'

'Miss Trout had a brother, did she?'

'Oh, didn't you know? Yes, her brother was old Jeremiah Trout. He had lived there for about thirty years before Miss Emily came to stay, but he went away a few months ago, leaving the house in the care of Miss Trout and her nephew. He died abroad shortly afterwards. I believe he was quite ga-ga, the poor old thing, although he kept the garden beautifully for many years, before he lost his mind. In fact, I believe he won prizes for it.'

She stopped to bow a stiff greeting to a gentleman who was just then coming up the path in the opposite direction. The man smiled and bowed in return, and went on past. He was dressed somewhat outlandishly in a pair of knee breeches and a waistcoat, and sported a wide-brimmed hat with a feather in it that looked almost exactly like his moustache. He was weighed down by an extraordinary assortment of knapsacks, glass jars, field-glasses, digging implements and a number of other items that were identifiable only as scientific equipment, and he jangled as he walked.

'That is Mr. Donati,' said Mrs. Walters. 'He is a scientist from Switzerland. I am not at all sure that I approve.'

Angela could not tell whether she was referring to his nationality, his *métier* or his clothing, but forbore to inquire.

Helen Walters had walked silently beside them up to now, but she suddenly looked up and said:

'Mother, you have forgotten your scarf again.'

Mrs Walters gave a click of impatience.

'So I have. Why didn't you remind me, you silly girl? I shall catch my death of cold without it. Well, you will just have to go and get it for me. You can catch us up.'

Helen ran off without another word.

'She is such a forgetful girl,' said Mrs. Walters. 'It is very provoking sometimes.'

They were now coming into Tregarrion itself. On the cliff top at the very edge of town stood a square, modern building that gleamed white and was visible from miles around. The Hotel Splendide had opened a year or two ago and had become immediately popular with the younger, more fashionable set. It offered sun-bathing and swimming, having not one, but *two* swimming-pools, as well as a large terrace from which led a flight of rocky steps that went down to the beach. It also offered cocktails, fine food and daily entertainment in the form of a jazz orchestra.

'Oh, there is the music again,' said Angela as they approached. 'That must be what I heard earlier.'

The hotel terrace was set out with tables and chairs, many of which were occupied by holiday-makers dressed in their summer finery, laughing, talking and enjoying the sunshine while harried waiters ran to and fro carrying trays. As the two women watched from the path, three girls in bathing-dress ran up the steps from the beach, screaming with laughter. The whole scene was very gay and lively and Angela was tempted to stay a while.

'Suppose we stop and have tea,' she suggested.

Mrs. Walters looked a little doubtful, but at that moment the band finished with a flourish the exuberant dance tune it had been playing, and struck up a gentler, more soothing number.

'Very well,' she said.

Once they were seated, she became more animated as she eyed the people sitting at the tables nearby. She was particularly interested in a young couple who were sipping cold drinks and looking bored. The woman had fair hair, dark eyebrows and red lips and was rather pretty, while the man was handsome enough, with dark hair and eyes and very white teeth. He lounged carelessly in his chair, not looking at his wife, except when he threw an occasional remark at her.

'Do you know that couple?' whispered Mrs. Walters. 'I don't suppose you do. They are the Dorseys. Lionel and Harriet Dorsey. They arrived a week or two ago. They're terribly glamorous, don't you think?'

'Oh yes,' said Angela, glancing at them. In reality she had not been paying much attention, for she had spotted someone she recognized. The elegantly-dressed man she had seen on the bench near Poldarrow Point earlier was sitting at a table a little way away, reading a newspaper and drinking tea. There was something out of the ordinary about him, and she wondered who he was.

Just then they were joined by a breathless Helen, carrying her mother's scarf.

'At last, my scarf!' exclaimed Mrs. Walters. 'How slow you are, dear. I have been absolutely freezing cold without it. I shouldn't be at all surprised if I am unwell tomorrow.'

'I'm sorry, Mother,' said Helen colourlessly.

Angela looked at her in curiosity. Helen Walters was young and healthy, and should by rights have been forging a life of her own, dancing with young men and having fun. Instead she seemed a slave to a selfish old woman. 'It can't be much of a life for her,' she thought, 'running around after her mother. I wonder whether she is happy.'

She remembered the radiance in the girl's face that morning as she returned from her bathe. Perhaps the occasional moment of pleasure made up for the long hours of servitude.

'Oh, good afternoon, Mr. Simpson,' said Mrs. Walters suddenly, and Angela looked up to see the man from the bench passing their table. He stopped.

'Good afternoon,' he replied in a rich, pleasant voice.

'Have you met Mrs. Marchmont? She is staying in Kittiwake Cottage at present.'

The man turned to Angela and his deep blue eyes twinkled.

'We met this morning on the cliff top, I believe,' he replied. 'How do you do, Mrs. Marchmont. I am George Simpson.'

The introduction was acknowledged and they exchanged pleasantries about the weather and the scenery, then he bowed and passed on. Angela was surprised to feel a pang of disappointment at the stolid Englishness of his name. From the looks of him she had half-expected something a little more dashing.

Mrs. Walters shortly afterwards announced that she was tired and wished to return home, so they paid for their tea and left.

'You must tell me all about your visit to Poldarrow Point,' said Mrs. Walters as they said goodbye at the gate of Shearwater Cottage. Angela promised to do so, and returned to her own house.

She was greeted by Marthe, who was in a state of some agitation.

'Oh, *madame*, I am so glad you have come back,' she said. 'The gipsies have come and they want to steal everything! I have hidden your jewel-case but these people are cunning—they stop at nothing. Perhaps they will creep into the house while we are asleep and cut our throats!'

'What is all this nonsense?' asked Angela, half-laughing. 'Marthe, have you taken leave of your senses? There are no gipsies around here.'

'But I tell you there are, *madame*,' said Marthe, throwing up her hands. 'They sent a little ragamuffin before them to beg for food and a bed, but I am not a fool. I know their tricks. She will let them all in and then we are done!'

'Someone was begging for food and a *bed*?' repeated Angela, puzzled. 'Why, that's—'

She was interrupted by Marthe, who looked out of the window and gave a little scream.

'There she is now! Did I not tell you? We shall all be murdered! Oh, why did we come here?'

There was a knock at the door.

'Don't be absurd,' said Angela. She went to the door and flung it open, then started at the sight before her. A girl of about twelve stood there, covered in grime from head to toe and with bits of straw sticking out of her clothes and hair.

'Barbara!' said Angela in astonishment.

'Hallo, Aunt Angela,' said the girl. 'Why on earth did you have to go all the way to Cornwall? I've had the devil of a job to find you.'

CHAPTER FOUR

BARBARA WELLS SAT on the terrace wolfing down bread and butter and scones as though she had not eaten for days—which in fact was almost the case. Angela sat opposite, gazing at her with an expression that was something akin to terror.

'Are you going to eat that scone?' said Barbara.

Angela pushed her untouched plate over to the girl.

'I say, thanks. Did your cook make these? They're simply topping. She and I shall be friends, I'm certain of it.'

'Barbara, why aren't you at the Ellises'?' said Angela.

'Scarlet fever,' said Barbara with her mouth full. 'Ginny got it, and then Tom, and now they're all dying, or something. They sent me a telegram two days before the end of term to tell me not to come. I tried to call you but nobody answered so I just decided to turn up at your flat. Of course, you weren't there but then the porter told me that you'd gone to Cornwall and gave me the address. I had no money so I had to get here as best I could, walking and cadging lifts. I've spent the last two days in a hay-cart. I dare say I'm a bit grubby.'

'But why hadn't you any money?'

'I lost it all on a horse.'

'*What?*'

'Delectable, for the Gold Cup. I thought it was *such* a dead cert. I had it from Jim at the stables, who had it from Delectable's trainer himself. Jim said not to bother going each way as it simply couldn't lose, so I stuck the whole lot on to win at fifteen to one and the dratted thing came in second. Then I found out that Jim had gone each way after all. I shall kill him when I see him, the sneaky rat.' she finished darkly.

'Perhaps that will teach you not to bet in future,' said Angela.

'I certainly shan't be taking any more of Jim's tips, at any rate,' said Barbara. She sat back with a sigh and licked a stray blob of jam from her finger. 'So,' she said, 'where am I to sleep?'

'You can't stay here!' said Angela, aghast.

'Don't be silly,' said Barbara. 'Where else can I go? I can bunk in with Marthe. She won't mind. I shan't be any trouble. I say,' she went on, jumping up and running to peer over the back gate, 'this is an awfully nice place, isn't it? That little cove down there looks marvellous for bathing. I believe I shall forgive you for running away.'

Angela knew a *fait accompli* when she saw one—and indeed, it was true, the girl had nowhere else to go. She sighed and called Marthe.

'Miss Barbara needs a wash,' she said, trying not to laugh at Marthe's disgusted face.

'No, *madame*, what she needs is a bath,' said Marthe. 'I shall prepare one immediately.'

'Look here,' said Barbara in alarm, 'there's no need for that. I can get clean just as well by having a bathe in the sea. I was just thinking of doing that now, as a matter of fact.'

'Nothing but hot water will get that dirt off you,' said Angela, 'and besides, it's high tide now so it's not safe to swim. Remember that.'

'What should I do with her clothes, *madame*?' asked Marthe.

Angela stared at the little scarecrow before them.

'I should suggest burning them, but we have nothing else to put her in.'

'Of course I brought a change,' said Barbara with dignity. 'I'm not a complete idiot.'

She allowed herself to be conducted into the house by a scolding Marthe, leaving Angela to adjust her thoughts. She was not enthusiastic at the idea of having a schoolgirl on her hands for the next few weeks, but consoled herself with the reflection that Barbara seemed fully capable of amusing herself. And indeed, that looked as though it were the case: after emerging from Marthe's ruthless ablutions, face shining clean and hair washed and tamed, Barbara announced that she was going out to explore. She returned in time for dinner and went to bed without fuss since, truth to tell, she was extremely tired after her journey from London.

'I am going to Miss Trout's for tea today,' said Angela the next morning as they sat on the terrace.

Barbara's eyes opened wide.

'Miss Trout!' she exclaimed in a kind of ecstasy. 'What a glorious name! How I wish I had a friend called Miss Trout. Although Kipper or Haddock would be even better,' she said thoughtfully, and went on with her breakfast.

'You may come if you like,' said Angela, ignoring this outburst. 'She said I might bring someone. But you must behave as other children do.'

'How *do* other children behave?' asked Barbara with interest.

'I'm not entirely sure,' admitted Angela, 'but I'm fairly certain they don't lose all their money on the horses then run about the country dressed as a tramp.'

'I don't do that *every day*,' said Barbara. 'Of course I shall come, and I promise I shall be an angel.'

The sun was still warm, but the sea breeze was much stronger than it had been the day before, and it whipped at their skirts as they walked along the cliff top. At four o'clock sharp they presented themselves at Poldarrow Point, and were admitted to a large, gloomy drawing-room which was decorated in the style of sixty years ago. Its furniture was elegant but shabby and worn, and the paper was peeling from the wall here and there. Altogether the place looked as though it had seen better days.

Miss Emily Trout was sitting with her nephew, their heads bent over a book whose pages were yellowed and ragged around the edges. She looked up as they entered and rose to greet them with a beaming smile.

'Mrs. Marchmont, I'm so glad you could come,' she said. 'And who is this young lady?'

'Barbara Wells,' said Barbara, holding out her hand politely. 'How do you do, Miss Trout?'

'Barbara is my god-daughter,' said Angela. 'She arrived yesterday and is staying with me at the cottage.'

'I don't have any parents,' explained Barbara helpfully, 'so I have to go to whoever will have me. It's Angela's turn now.'

Clifford Maynard laughed.

'Then we have something in common,' he said. 'It is Aunt Emily's turn to look after *me* at present.'

'Don't you live here all the time?' asked Angela.

'I do now, yes. I had spent the last few years in London, attempting—unsuccessfully, I might add—to make a living on the stage, but I came down here a month or two ago to visit Aunt Emily and have somehow ended up staying for the present.'

'Dear Clifford is always so kind,' said Miss Trout. 'I have few relations still living, and even fewer who are prepared to come all this way to see me, so it is a great comfort to have Clifford with me here all the time. I had not seen him for many years—since he was quite a child, in fact, so I was most surprised and delighted when he turned up here.'

Angela, perhaps uncharitably, wondered whether Miss Trout had any money to leave, then almost immediately dismissed the idea, since the state of the house made it highly unlikely.

'I say,' said Barbara, who had made a bee-line for the window, 'you have a corking view here.'

'"Corking" is the very word,' said the old lady, her eyes twinkling as she joined the girl. 'Do you like it?'

'Oh yes, it's simply splendid. I should like to live in Cornwall always. I go to school in Hertfordshire, which is deadly dull—no sea or lakes or mountains, or anything like that at all. But look, there's our cottage, and the little cove where I went for a bathe this morning.' She beamed. 'How lucky you are!'

'What should you say if I were to tell you that this house has a secret passage leading down to that very cove?' said Miss Trout.

Barbara stared.

'A real secret passage? Here in this house?'

'Oh yes.'

'May I see it?'

'You shall certainly see it after we have had tea,' replied the old lady. 'Shall we?'

They all sat, and Miss Trout poured tea from a china teapot with a chip in the spout.

'As you can see, most of the things in this house are in a sad condition,' she said. 'My brother was unlucky enough to lose most of his money in an unfortunate speculation, and so was unable to afford the upkeep. I have even less money than he did and so the place has rather been left to fall to rack and ruin.'

'Have you never thought of leaving?' asked Angela.

Miss Trout looked shocked.

'Oh no! I could never do that,' she said. 'Why, this house has been in our family for a hundred and fifty years or more.' She drew herself up. 'I am the last of the Trouts,' she said (here

Barbara stifled a giggle), 'and I am quite determined to stay here until the bitter end.'

Angela glared at Barbara, then said, 'Your brother is no longer alive, I take it?'

Miss Trout gave a mournful smile.

'Unfortunately not. Jeremiah could no longer stand the Poldarrow winters and their effect on his health, so a few months ago he went abroad to Italy, where he sadly died only a few weeks later.'

'He ought to have stayed here,' said Clifford. 'At that age the journey was bound to kill him.'

Miss Trout took out a handkerchief and dabbed at her eye, and Angela tactfully changed the subject.

They finished their tea and Barbara immediately said, 'Please may we see the secret passage now?'

Clifford smiled and Miss Trout gave her tinkling laugh.

'Why, of course!' she said. 'But first I must tell you a little of the history of the house. A hundred and fifty years ago Poldarrow Point was nothing like the big, rambling building you see today—at that time, it was merely a large, comfortable farm-house. It was owned by my ancestor, a man called Richard Warrener, who was better known in these parts as Preacher Dick.'

'Was he a pirate?' asked Barbara breathlessly.

'No,' said Miss Trout, then paused dramatically. 'He was a smuggler.'

Chapter Five

A T THAT MOMENT there was a loud banging noise from upstairs that made them all start.

Clifford Maynard grimaced impatiently.

'The fastening on the shutter must have worked loose again,' he said. 'I had better go and fix it or it will keep us awake all night.'

He went out, and Miss Trout said, 'This place is all very well when the weather is calm, but as soon as the wind gets up then you can be sure that something or other will need mending. Now, where was I? Oh yes, I was telling you about Preacher Dick.'

Angela had been listening with interest.

'Was he really a preacher?' she asked. 'I shouldn't have thought that a man of the cloth would be embroiled in illegal activities.'

'Oh, but it was quite common in those days,' Miss Trout assured her. 'Taxes on goods were so high that many people considered them to be immoral in themselves, and anything that could be obtained without paying duty to the government was considered fair game. Whole villages were involved in the business at times. Richard Warrener was a gentleman farmer and Methodist lay preacher—and also the source of much of the smuggling activity in the area in the late eighteenth century.'

'Did he dig the tunnel?' asked Barbara.

'So the story goes,' replied Miss Trout. 'You will, no doubt, have noticed that Poldarrow Cove itself cannot be seen from Tregarrion, and that it is also sheltered from the strongest of the winds. That made it the ideal spot for landing illegal cargoes. Ships would drop anchor a little way out and the booty would be brought ashore in skiffs. Warrener's men would be waiting on the beach for the goods, and would haul them up through the tunnel and into the house. From there they could be distributed for sale. I understand it was an extremely profitable business.'

'How thrilling!' said Barbara. 'I should have liked to have been there to see it. I don't suppose it still goes on today?' She seemed almost regretful, and Miss Trout laughed.

'No, I'm afraid not. Eventually, the government reduced excise duties and almost immediately the practice all but disappeared. Shall we go and see the secret passage? Barbara, my dear, there is an electric torch in the top drawer of that chest. Could you fetch it out for me, please?'

Barbara did as she was asked and handed the torch to Miss Trout, who rose and led the way out of the room and into the gloomy entrance-hall. Under the stairs a little door was set unobtrusively into the panelling. Miss Trout turned the key that was in the lock and opened the door, just as Clifford joined them again.

'Have you fixed it?' she asked.

Her nephew nodded briefly.

'Let me go first, Aunt,' he said.

He took the torch and descended, followed by Angela, Barbara and Miss Trout. At the bottom of the stairs was a large, square room that was empty apart from a few boxes and old bits of broken furniture.

'It's just a cellar,' said Barbara in disappointment.

'This is where the contraband was stored once it had come up from the beach,' said Miss Trout. 'The tunnel is over here.'

Clifford led the way under a beam and into a smaller room. This one was completely empty.

'There,' he said, indicating a square trap-door set in the middle of the floor. It was bolted shut. He bent and drew back the bolt with a little difficulty, then pulled up the heavy door by a metal ring. It rose and fell backwards with a clatter, and they all peered down as Clifford shone the torch into the hole.

'I can see a ladder!' said Barbara in excitement. 'May I go down it, please?'

Before anybody could reply she sat on the edge of the hole and lowered herself into it, feeling with her feet for the metal rungs that had been set into the rock. Angela felt a pang of concern for Barbara's frock but said nothing.

'Do be careful,' said Miss Trout, as Barbara disappeared into the depths of the earth. They heard the *clunk* of her feet on the ladder as she felt her way down it.

'It's pitch-black down here,' she said, her voice echoing from below. 'May I have the torch, please?'

'There's not much to see,' said Clifford, 'and you wouldn't want to leave us in the dark up here, would you? But I shall try and shed a little light on things for you.'

He crouched down and directed the torch farther into the hole.

'There's a tunnel here!' exclaimed Barbara. 'Oh, *do* let me see where it goes.'

'Not now,' said Angela. 'That's enough. Come up now.'

There was a clanging and a thumping as Barbara climbed back up and emerged once more into the cellar.

'I should have liked to follow it all the way down to the beach,' she said wistfully.

'It wouldn't be possible at this time anyway,' said Miss Trout. 'The entrance to the tunnel is completely blocked at high tide.'

'Then I shall go down to the cove tomorrow and look for it,' said Barbara with decision.

It was cold in the cellar and Miss Trout shivered.

'Shall we go back upstairs?' she suggested. 'Clifford, would you shut the trap-door for us?'

'Please, may I do it?' asked Barbara eagerly.

'Certainly,' said Clifford. 'Don't forget to bolt it, too.'

They returned to the welcome warmth of the ground floor and the drawing-room.

'What became of Preacher Dick in the end?' asked Barbara. 'Was he ever caught?'

'No,' replied Miss Trout. 'He lived to a ripe old age and died in this house, I believe. But I have something else to show you.'

She picked up the book that she and Clifford had been poring over when the others arrived and handed it to Angela.

'These are his memoirs,' she said. 'He wrote them when he was an old man and had long since given up the smuggling trade.'

Angela looked at the book in her hands. It was a slim volume, bound in calf leather, and bore all the signs of having been well-used. She opened it up and saw that each page was closely-written in an old-fashioned hand.

'"Being A Faithful Record Of The Life Of Richard Warrener Of Poldarrow Point In The Parish of Tregarrion, Written By His Own Hand,"' she read. 'He must have had some very fascinating tales to tell,' she said as she handed back the book.

'Oh, nobody more so,' said Miss Trout. 'One of his exploits in particular has passed into legend within the family. It concerns a priceless treasure which was lost but may still be in the house to this very day.'

Barbara's eyes grew round.

'A treasure?' she said in excitement. 'What was it?'

Miss Trout lowered her voice.

'It was a diamond necklace that was supposed to have been made for Queen Marie Antoinette,' she said. 'It is a most mysterious story. Should you like to hear it?'

'Yes please,' said Barbara.

'Well, then,' said the old lady. 'This necklace was made many, many years ago by a firm of Parisian jewellers, and was said by all who saw it to have been the most fabulous ornament ever to have been made by man. The jewellers used only the finest diamonds and gold, and poured all their skills as master craftsmen into its production. It cost them a great deal to make, but they hoped to sell the necklace to King Louis the Sixteenth and so make the money back ten-fold. However, to their dismay, when the King suggested to his wife that he buy her the necklace, she refused it, saying that the money would be better spent on building a man-of-war for the navy.

'Now, the Court of King Louis was a place of politics and intrigue, and was full of people wishing to curry favour with the Queen. One such person was the Cardinal de Rohan, who had displeased Marie Antoinette and was anxious to get back into her good graces. Another was a woman who called herself the Comtesse de la Motte. She was a thief and an adventuress who was determined that she and her husband should become rich by hook or by crook. Seeing her opportunity, the Comtesse became Cardinal de Rohan's mistress, at the same time convincing him that she was a confidante of Marie Antoinette and was willing to act as a go-between to help him regain the Queen's favour.

'Her real aim, in fact, was to get her hands on the necklace. To this end she produced forged letters that she claimed were from the Queen, in which Her Majesty indicated that she had forgiven the Cardinal. She also arranged a meeting between him and the Queen—although in reality the woman he met was an actress who merely resembled her closely.

'A short while later, the Comtesse produced another forged letter from the Queen, requesting that the Cardinal procure the diamond necklace in secret for her, with the Comtesse de la Motte acting as her agent. Rohan, who was only too anxious to remain in favour, complied. He obtained the necklace from the jewellers and handed it over to the Comtesse who, far from presenting it to Marie Antoinette, immediately gave it to her husband, who left the country with it.

'Of course, very soon the jewellers wanted payment and approached the Queen, who announced that she knew nothing of the matter. In this way the deception was discovered and a great scandal ensued. The Comtesse de la Motte was tried and convicted of the theft, while the poor, foolish Cardinal was acquitted but exiled.' She paused.

'What happened to the necklace?' asked Barbara.

'It was never seen again,' said Miss Trout significantly. 'It had been thought that the Comtesse's husband had taken it to London and broken it up in order to sell the diamonds singly, but this was never proved—and according to a legend that has been passed down through the Warrener family for the last hundred and fifty years or so, the necklace met quite a different fate. Look here.'

She picked up Richard Warrener's memoirs and turned the pages carefully, as though searching for something.

'Ah, here we are,' she said, and handed the book back to Angela. 'It is a little difficult to read, and your eyes will surely be better able to see than mine. His spelling is a little erratic, after the fashion of the time.'

Angela squinted at the page and read aloud:

'"Now, in the spring of 1785 a sloop of sume 25 tons came in close to shore that had taken a cargo from a privateer. The men bringing in the goods, I was much surprized to see a French gentleman brought ashore besides in a state of fever and close to death. I calling for my wife to tend to him, since his strength was allmoste exhausted, we carry'd him to bed where he did most earnestly beg for absolution as his life was drawing to a close. I taking pity on him promised to hear him, being that as I told him, there were no Catholick priest near by, but that we did worshipp the same God and so I believed there were no harm in it. At once did he produce from about his person a pacquet which he said held a treasure of great value, dishonestly taken. He could not he said go to his grave with the matter weighing on his conscience so he earnestly desir'd that I should take the pacquet and do with it as I did see fit. I asked hime what it was and he said it was a thing of great price thatt belonged to a French lady but was then stolen. I heard him confess his sins and bade him be at peace and shortly afterwards he died. When I returned to the shore the sloop was already departed and I ask'd the men to tell what they had heard about the gentleman, but all they knew was that he had come aboard the sloop at Guarnsay in great secresy and was thought to have come from the Court of Paris. I returning to the house took the pacquet and opened it, to my greate surprize finding within—"'

Angela faltered and peered more closely at the page, then looked up.

'Oh,' she said. 'The next page has been torn out.'

CHAPTER SIX

WHAT?' CRIED BARBARA in dismay. 'Are you quite certain?'

'Quite certain,' said Angela.

'Oh dear,' said Miss Trout. 'That is a pity. But it is a very old book, so I am not surprised that it is in bad condition. I imagine the page was torn out accidentally some years ago, and got lost.'

'But we were just about to find out what was in the package. Was it Marie Antoinette's necklace?' asked Barbara.

Miss Trout shook her head.

'It is some years since I looked at the book, and I don't remember clearly what it says,' she replied. 'Is the page really missing? That is unfortunate, as those memoirs are the only evidence we have in writing. However, as you see, Preacher Dick says that he received the mysterious package in 1785— the same year in which the necklace disappeared, and in this family it has always been understood that that and the contents of the package were one and the same.'

'But what did he do with it?'

'He is supposed to have hidden it somewhere safe in this house. I don't know what he intended to do with it—he was a smuggler, not a thief, after all, and perhaps he did not relish the thought of selling stolen goods taken from a dying man whose soul he had just commended to God. At any rate, there are no stories of his becoming suddenly wealthy, so there is every reason to believe that he kept it.'

'I wonder who the French gentleman was,' said Angela. 'I know something of the story and the Comtesse's husband died many years after the theft, so it can't have been him. Perhaps he handed it to someone for safe-keeping.'

'Yes,' said Barbara impatiently, 'but that's not important. What I want to know is: where is the necklace now?'

'I don't know,' said Miss Trout, 'but I should dearly like to find it.'

There was a wistful tone to her voice that spoke of more than mere curiosity as to the fate of a long-lost artefact. It was not lost on Angela.

'I dare say something like that would be of immense value today, even more so than it was at the time,' she said. 'Should you be allowed to keep it if you found it, I wonder? I suppose by rights it belongs to the descendants of the Parisian jewellers who were so unscrupulously robbed of their diamonds.'

'I don't think that would be fair at all,' said Barbara stoutly. 'What have they done to deserve it? Finders keepers, I say. It has been in Miss Trout's family for over a century and I think she should be allowed to keep it. Or if not, then she should get a reward for finding it,' she added as an afterthought.

'You are very kind,' said Miss Trout with a sad smile, 'but this is all immaterial since we have no idea where it is and are unlikely to find it in time—' she was about to go on but stopped herself.

'In time for what?' said Angela.

'Now, Aunt,' said Clifford, 'there is no need to bother Mrs. Marchmont with our troubles.'

'You are right, of course,' said Miss Trout, with some reluctance, it seemed.

'Of course, I shouldn't dream of prying,' said Angela.

'Do you need the money?' said Barbara, prompting another glare from Angela.

'I'm afraid I do,' replied Miss Trout with a laugh. 'There is no use in denying it.'

'Lots of things need fixing in this house,' said Barbara. 'If you found the necklace then you could afford to do it.'

'If that were the only problem, I should be quite happy,' said Miss Trout, 'but I'm afraid there is more to it than that.' She looked half-apologetically at Clifford and went on, 'Unhappily, it looks as though we shall have to leave this house altogether unless something turns up in the next week or two.'

Angela and Barbara made noises of concern then Barbara said, 'Why?'

Miss Trout sighed.

'The Warreners had always been a well-to-do family,' she said, 'but some time in the middle of the last century they found themselves down on their luck. I suspect that the end of smuggling also meant the end of the family's wealth. In addition, my grandmother, who was the last of the Warreners, married a clergyman—my grandfather Trout—who, while a good, kind man, had no money of his own at all. At any rate, fifty or sixty years ago, finding themselves in desperate need of funds, my grandparents sold the freehold of this house and entered into a lease that would allow them to stay here for a modest rent. That lease is shortly due to expire and, if it cannot be extended, all connection between the Warreners and Poldarrow Point will end.'

'Why don't you extend it, then?' asked Barbara, who was not entirely sure what a lease was, but pictured it as a sort of invisible indiarubber band that attached Miss Trout to the house and prevented her from leaving it.

'That would be far beyond my means, I am afraid,' said Miss Trout.

'Who is the freeholder now?' asked Mrs. Marchmont.

'He is a wealthy man who lives in Penzance. I have already heard from his solicitor, Mr. Penhaligon, who says that his client invites me to renew the lease—otherwise, he must politely remind me to vacate the house at my earliest convenience on or before the fifth of August.'

'Why, that's only about two weeks away!' said Barbara. 'Miss Trout, you simply must find the necklace, then you can sell it for thousands of pounds and stay here forever. Angela and I will help you, won't we, Angela?' Before Angela could speak, she went on, 'Aunt Angela is a terribly famous detective, you know. She's solved all kinds of horrid murders, and her name has been in all the newspapers. And I can help too—I'm good at finding things and I'm small enough to get into holes and places that grown-ups are too big for. *Do* let's, Angela,' she finished pleadingly. 'It'll be frightfully exciting, just like a treasure-hunt!'

Angela's heart sank as she saw her prospects of a peaceful holiday receding even further.

'Now, Barbara, I don't think it's quite fair to impose on Miss Trout like that,' she said.

'Oh, but—' began Barbara in disappointment, but Miss Trout was nodding in agreement.

'Your godmother is quite right,' she said. 'You are here on holiday and I shouldn't dream of bothering you with my little problem. I should feel far happier knowing that you were outside enjoying yourself in the sun, rather than grubbing about in this gloomy old house looking for something that might not even be here. If nobody has found the necklace in the last hundred and forty-odd years, then it's hardly likely that we will find it in the next two weeks.'

'Have you searched for it?' asked Angela.

'I am rather frail these days,' replied Miss Trout, 'and to be perfectly truthful it had not, until recently, occurred to me to try and find it, since there seemed little use in looking for a mysterious object that was known about only by legend. Other than making the most cursory of investigations, therefore, I have done nothing.'

'Did Preacher Dick leave any clues?' asked Barbara eagerly.

'Not as far as I know.'

'Oh, but he must have,' said Barbara. 'What would be the use in hiding something so well that nobody could ever find it? I'll bet he left a secret message somewhere in those memoirs.'

She picked up the leather-bound book and turned the pages carefully.

'It's awfully difficult to read,' she said, frowning, 'but there must be a clue or a map here, or *something*.'

'I should love to believe it,' said Miss Trout, 'but I fear that the secret died with my ancestor. It is useless to place any reliance on finding the necklace. No,' she went on with a sigh. 'Whoever wrote those letters was right: I should be far better off if I were to leave Poldarrow.'

Angela saw Clifford Maynard shoot his aunt a warning glance.

'Which letters do you mean?' she asked.

'Oh, didn't I mention them?' said Miss Trout, shaking her head at her nephew. 'I thought I had. It's nothing really, but someone has been sending me some rather silly anonymous letters.'

CHAPTER SEVEN

ANGELA WAS INSTANTLY alert.

'What kind of anonymous letters?' she asked.

'Oh, telling me to leave the house immediately or something terrible will happen to me—the usual sort of thing, you know.'

'What do you mean, "the usual sort of thing"?' said Angela in surprise.

Miss Trout went pink with confusion.

'Oh dear!' she said. 'I just meant the kind of thing one reads about.' She lowered her voice confidentially. 'I am afraid that my tastes run rather shamefully to novels of the less literary sort.'

'I love a good detective story, myself,' said Barbara.

'Oh, Aunt,' said Clifford, 'I thought we had agreed not to mention the letters.'

'I know, dear, but Mrs. Marchmont has been so kind with her offer of help that I thought it better to tell her everything,' said Miss Trout.

'How many letters have you received?' asked Angela.

'Four so far,' said Miss Trout. 'Of course, I thought it was just a ridiculous joke when the first one came about ten days ago, so I took no notice, but then another one arrived and another, and then a fourth this morning, and I am not certain what I should do about it.'

'Might I see them?' said Mrs. Marchmont.

Miss Trout went over to an ancient-looking desk and took from a drawer a small bundle of envelopes, which she handed to Angela.

Angela examined the envelopes and looked closely at the postmarks.

'They were all posted here in Tregarrion, I see,' she said, and extracted a letter. It read thus:

'Dere Miss So-Called Trout,

You are not wanted heer. I giv you fare warning: leave Poldarrow Point at wuns or it will be the wors for you.'

'What a sneaking coward!' said Barbara indignantly. 'I should like to meet whoever wrote it and give him a jolly good piece of my mind.'

Angela held the paper up to the light, looking for a water-mark.

'I don't recognize the paper,' she said, and passed on to the next letter. It said:

*'Yur life is in grav danger if you do not leav Poldar-
row at once. Don't think yor nephew will save you.'*

'His spelling is even worse than mine!' said Barbara. She
took the other two letters and read them. The third said:

*'You hav ignored my earlier warnings to leav. This
was foolish. This warning will be yr last.'*

What a stupid thing to say!' said Barbara. 'If you're going
to make a threat you ought at least to carry it out. It's not the
final warning at all, you see, because there's another one.' She
read:

*'You have bene told. The ghost of Poldarrow Point
wil hav its revenge on thos who fale to hede its warnings. Bewar!'*

Barbara snorted.

'Rot!' she said in disgust. 'What ghost of Poldarrow Point?
Why, everyone knows that there are no such things as ghosts.
They are just trying to frighten you. It's quite absurd.'

'*Is* there a ghost of Poldarrow Point?' asked Angela of Miss
Trout.

'Oh, there are several ghosts if one believes the legends,'
said the old lady. 'In a house of this age it's only to be expected. One story in particular tells of an old man who wanders
the upper floors clad only in a nightgown, wringing his hands
and muttering to himself. Another tells of a smuggler who
tried to steal a large barrel of contraband wine for himself and

drowned in the attempt. He is said to wander the cliff top and occasionally to enter the garden. I don't believe the stories myself, however.'

'I wonder what the writer of the letters hoped to achieve by sending them,' said Angela. 'Why should anyone want you to leave the house?'

'I have no idea,' said Miss Trout.

'It must be because of the necklace!' exclaimed Barbara. 'It's the only explanation. Someone wants you out of the way so they can get in and search for it.'

'Well—' began Miss Trout doubtfully.

'When can we begin our search?' went on Barbara unheeding. 'I can come tomorrow. Or the next day. Do say yes, Miss Trout. I should love to help. I want to find the necklace before that horrid letter-writer does.'

She was not to be put off. Miss Trout laughed uncertainly and glanced at Angela, who recognized the girl's mood and saw that there was no use in interfering. It was clear that Miss Trout would have Barbara racketing around her house for the next few days whether she liked it or not.

'If Miss Trout says so, you may come again,' she said, 'but you must promise not to get in the way or make a disturbance. And you know,' she went on to the old lady half-apologetically, 'she may even find what you are looking for.'

'I should be so glad if she did,' said Miss Trout, 'although I hardly dare hope for it.'

'And Angela will investigate the anonymous letters,' said Barbara, 'won't you, Angela?'

Angela, seeing that she had no choice, agreed to look into the matter as far as she could, and then they took their leave, having agreed that Barbara should return the day after next. They took with them Preacher Dick's memoirs, since Barbara was certain that they contained some vital clue and wanted to examine them more closely. She chattered in excitement all the way back to Kittiwake Cottage, but Angela listened with only half an ear, for she was thinking about the anonymous letters. She gave very little credence to the story of the necklace and privately thought that Miss Trout and her nephew would have no choice but to leave Poldarrow Point when the lease expired, but threatening letters were quite another matter. Who could have sent them? It was most odd: after all, Miss Trout would most likely be leaving the house very soon anyway—what, then, was so urgent that the mysterious letter-writer wanted her out of the way now?

It had been a strange afternoon altogether, now she came to think about it. Miss Trout was a jolly soul with a strength of character which belied her frail appearance, but Angela was curious about her nephew, Clifford. Had he really come to live with his aunt for no other reason than pure affection for her? If his home had previously been in London, then how did he live now he was here in Cornwall? There had been no mention of a job, and Miss Trout had made their poverty quite clear. Would he stay with his aunt after they left the house, or would he return to London? If the latter, then perhaps he would take Miss Trout with him. It would be a sad end to the family's connection with Poldarrow Point, if so.

It was past six o'clock when they arrived home to find the tabby cat pressed against the French windows and Marthe studiously ignoring it. Barbara ran out to give the cat some food and Angela followed her onto the terrace, where she had left her book. As she looked over at Shearwater Cottage, she saw that Mrs. Walters had evidently wormed her way into another acquaintance, for she and Helen were sitting outside with the Dorseys, engaged in conversation.

'Oh, Mrs. Marchmont, do join us,' Mrs. Walters called as she caught sight of Angela. 'I have some people I should like you to meet.'

Angela had been intending to take a little rest and read her book, but obligingly went out through her own gate and in at the Walters', followed by Barbara, who had an insatiable curiosity for everything and was troubled by no idea of her company's ever being unwanted.

Mrs. Walters made the introductions and everyone put on their best smiles, then they sat down. Lionel and Harriet Dorsey were from London and were staying in the area for a few weeks, they said. They had just returned from a trip into Penzance, but whether they had enjoyed it was unclear, since they had a perpetual air of indifference about them that gave nothing away. Angela supposed them to be suffering from that boredom which some city people experience on being suddenly transplanted to a much quieter place, although they were politely if unenthusiastically complimentary about the beauties of Cornwall.

'Do you play tennis, Mrs. Marchmont?' asked Mrs. Walters. 'Harriet is quite the proficient, I believe. You must play with her one day. They have a very good court at the hotel, you know.'

Mrs. Dorsey disclaimed the compliment with a toss of her head, and Angela murmured a polite reply.

'What a pity there are no men to make up a doubles match together with Lionel,' went on Mrs. Walters.

'I'll quite happily take on the women,' said Mr. Dorsey. 'A two-game handicap in each set should even things out nicely.'

'Hardly,' said his wife.

'Oh yes, and then Helen could join you,' said Mrs. Walters. 'I do like to see young people enjoying themselves together.'

'We must see about that, then,' said Mr. Dorsey, and the subject dropped.

'We've just been to tea at Poldarrow Point,' said Barbara to Helen. She was still bursting with excitement about her proposed treasure-hunt and could think of nothing else.

'Of course, I had forgotten you were going,' said Mrs. Walters with a gleam in her eye. 'And how did you find Miss Trout and Mr. Maynard?'

'They were jolly good sports,' said Barbara, 'especially Miss Trout. I liked her a lot. In fact, I am going back there on Thursday. I am going to hunt for—ow!'

'Oh, I beg your pardon, Barbara,' said Angela, who had just kicked the girl hard under the table. 'I didn't realize your leg was in the way. I do hope I haven't hurt you.'

Barbara rubbed her ankle.

'Not at all,' she said through gritted teeth.

'What did you say you were going to hunt for, dear?' said Mrs. Walters.

'Birds' eggs,' said Barbara. 'They have a lot of trees in the garden and I want to see if I can get some puffin's eggs to take back to school.'

'Do puffins nest in trees?' asked Helen. 'I thought they preferred to live on cliffs.'

'Some of them do,' agreed Barbara, 'but I'm looking for the Cornish Tree Puffin in particular. It's a quite different species. They have blue beaks and sing like blackbirds, and they're extremely rare.'

'Miss Trout was telling us that she may have to leave the house soon, as her lease will be up shortly,' said Angela before Barbara could expand into further flights of fancy.

'But I thought the family had owned the house for over a hundred years,' said Mrs. Walters.

'They sold the freehold some time last century, apparently,' said Angela, 'and now they merely rent it. It would cost too much to extend the lease, so it looks as though she will have to move out on the fifth of August.'

'Poor Miss Trout,' said Helen. 'I don't know her at all, but she looks like such a cheerful old lady, and always smiles in the most friendly way whenever we pass.'

'Who owns the freehold now?' asked Harriet Dorsey, who had been listening attentively. 'Is he going to move into the house after Miss Trout leaves?'

'He is someone who lives in Penzance, I think she said,' replied Angela, 'but I have no idea what he is planning to do with the place.'

'I wonder if he'd be willing to rent it to us,' said Harriet. 'It's a lovely old place—perfect for a quiet holiday.'

'The house is rather run-down,' said Angela doubtfully. 'I think you would be more comfortable staying at the hotel.'

'Oh, but I love quaint old houses like that. We shouldn't mind a bit of discomfort, should we, darling?' she said, turning to her husband. 'Not for those views.'

Lionel Dorsey made a non-committal face and shrugged.

'Well, I shall see if I can find out who the new owner is, at any rate,' said Mrs. Dorsey.

Angela could hardly imagine a place less suited to this sophisticated, fashionable couple than Poldarrow Point, but said nothing.

'Don't expect her to leave before the fifth, though, because she won't—I shall make sure of that,' said Barbara fiercely, startling them all.

Angela judged it to be a good moment to take their leave, and reminded Barbara that they had planned an early dinner. They had done no such thing, but Barbara recollected herself and they went home, having made vague promises to meet the Dorseys at the hotel for a game of tennis in a day or two.

Barbara yawned as they entered the house.

'How tired one gets, spending all day in the fresh air,' she said, 'I shall sleep like a top tonight.' An idea came to her. 'Angela, I think all doctors ought to send their patients to Cornwall for a jolly good rest. It would do them no end of good.'

'That sounds like a delightful idea,' said Angela dryly.

CHAPTER EIGHT

THE NEXT MORNING Angela took a solitary walk into Tregarrion, leaving behind Barbara, who was determined to go down to the cove and find the tunnel that led from the beach up to Poldarrow Point. It was a fine, breezy day, the sun obscured only occasionally by the odd white cloud scudding cheerily across the sky. The square bulk of the Hotel Splendide looked bright and clean in the sunlight, and the path was dotted with holiday-makers enjoying a stroll along the cliff top. Angela glanced at the hotel terrace as she passed. A few late risers were still at breakfast, and among them she spotted the Dorseys, who were yawning glumly over their eggs. Lionel Dorsey looked up at Angela as she went by and raised his hand in salutation. He said something to his wife, who also turned to look. Her eyes narrowed for a second, then she produced a thin smile and returned to her breakfast without a word.

Tregarrion was busy that morning, its cobbled streets bustling with townsfolk and tourists alike. The quaint little fishermen's cottages that lined the harbour appeared to their best advantage in the July sunshine, as though dressed in their Sunday finery, and the salty tang in the air was bracing and refreshing. The whole scene suited Angela's mood exactly, and she wandered the streets of the little town in a pleasant day-dream, thinking of not very much except the sights and sounds before her.

On the harbour pier an artist had set up an impromptu exhibition of sea scenes and landscapes, which were supposed to represent local beauty spots. They were rather garish. Angela was gazing at one particularly gaudy painting of a Cornish lugger and wondering how it was expected to stay afloat given that it was listing alarmingly to starboard, when she became aware of a presence at her shoulder. She turned and saw George Simpson standing next to her. He was as immaculately turned-out as ever, wearing a light suit that was just the right side of elegant, and seeming altogether at ease with himself. He smiled and gave a slight bow as Angela recognized him.

'I see you are a lover of art, Mrs. Marchmont,' he said.

'I don't know quite how to reply to that,' said Angela, laughing. 'I hope you're not referring to these paintings. They are certainly intriguing, although whether one could call them art is another question altogether.'

Simpson laughed too.

'I confess I was being polite,' he said. 'One has to be very careful in matters of taste—especially other people's taste. But I am glad we seem to be in agreement on these paintings, at least. How do you like Tregarrion?'

'I like it very much,' said Angela. 'The place is undeniably beautiful and we have been most fortunate with the weather so far.'

'How long are you intending to stay?'

'I'm not sure. For another week or two at least,' she replied. 'The lady who owns Kittiwake Cottage broke her leg and so was unable to come, but sooner or later her leg will mend and she will want her house back. I shall be sorry to leave. I believe you are staying at the hotel?'

He bowed in assent and invited her to walk along the pier with him.

'In the interests of beginning our acquaintance on the right foot, I believe I must confess that I knew something of you already before we met,' he said. 'In fact, I recognized your face immediately when I saw you on the cliff top the other day.'

'Oh? I suppose you have seen me in the papers. I am rather hounded by reporters these days owing to some recent unfortunate events.'

'Yes, but not only that,' he said. 'I believe you are a friend of my colleague Inspector Jameson.'

Angela looked up, surprised.

'Your colleague? What, are you—then you must be—'

He nodded.

'Yes, I am a Scotland Yard man too, for my sins. Inspector Simpson at your service—although here I am plain *Mr.* Simpson, if you don't mind. Even representatives of the law take holidays once in a while, and for some reason the word "Inspector" inspires every Tom, Dick and Harry to bother one constantly with tales of lost dogs and dishonest waiters.'

'Of course, I entirely understand, and I shan't mention it to anybody.' said Angela. 'Of all people, you deserve a rest now and again.'

So that was why he had attracted her attention. Angela could only suppose that her recent encounters with the law had turned her into one of those people who could recognize a policeman at fifty paces.

They walked on, remarking occasionally on some aspect of the view that caught their attention and talking about things they had seen in Tregarrion and around. He seemed remarkably well-informed about the area, and told her some interesting stories of local history that she had not previously heard. The conversation then turned to their mutual acquaintances.

'Are Mrs. Walters and her daughter friends of yours?' he asked.

'No, I met them only a day or two ago,' she replied. 'They are staying in the cottage next door to mine. Mrs. Walters is an invalid who has come here for her health.'

'With Miss Walters to look after her,' he said. 'It must be a great advantage to have someone to call upon at such times, although I don't suppose it is much fun for the daughter.'

'No,' agreed Angela. 'If her mother were really sick then it would be another matter, but I can't help thinking that Mrs. Walters' indisposition is as much for her own convenience as anything else. I have noticed that she is often quite well when it suits her.'

He smiled.

'Poor Miss Walters,' he said. 'Such a shame for a young girl to be held prisoner by her own mother.'

'Yes, I suppose she is a prisoner, although I had not thought of it in quite those terms. Still, perhaps she will break free one day and surprise us all.'

'Perhaps,' he said. 'I believe you have a little girl staying with you,' he went on, by way of a partial change of subject. 'Is she your daughter?'

'No, I have no children. She is my god-daughter. She turned up unexpectedly a day or two ago when the family with whom she was supposed to be spending the holidays all caught scarlet fever.'

'She looks to be something of a handful.'

'Oh yes,' said Angela fervently. 'To tell the truth, I have no idea what to do with her or how to manage her. Fortunately she is a good child at heart and has a very independent spirit, so I think there is no harm in letting her run wild a little while she is here. She has rather foisted herself upon the people at Poldarrow Point, though, so I shall have to keep an eye on her to make sure that she doesn't bother them too much.'

'The people at Poldarrow Point?' he said. 'Do you mean Miss Trout and her nephew?'

'Yes—do you know them?'

'Not to speak to. I understood from Mrs. Walters that they are not very sociable.'

'They have been very friendly to us,' said Angela. 'We visited them at home yesterday and Miss Trout was telling us all about her ancestors, who were smugglers.'

'Her ancestors at Poldarrow Point?'

'Yes.'

'That is very interesting,' he said. Angela expected him to continue but he said nothing more and indeed seemed to have fallen into a brown study. They walked in silence until they reached the end of the pier and stopped to look at the water. The sea was choppy, alternating bright green and dark blue as the clouds passed over, and fishing-boats swept in and out of the harbour, accompanied by scattering crowds of shrieking gulls.

'I should like to go out in a boat,' said Angela impulsively. 'I wonder whether it is possible to hire one hereabouts. I should like to go up and down the coast and see the shore to full advantage.'

'I dare say one might be found,' said Simpson. 'Do you sail?'

'I did many years ago, but I am quite out of practice. And in any case, I was thinking more of hiring a boat complete with pilot. I am here on doctor's orders and I intend to take it easy,' she said, laughing.

'Have you been ill?' he said with concern.

'Oh, nothing too serious—just a bout of influenza. But I was glad to take the excuse for a holiday.'

'And you have picked the right place for it. I can't imagine anywhere healthier in England—although the breeze is a little chilly out here. Shall we go back? I should hate for you to get ill again.'

They turned and headed back towards the shore. A group of excitable young people were standing before the paintings, exclaiming in delight. They were all asking questions at once of the artist, who knew a good prospect when he saw one, and was wearing his most ingratiating smile.

'I wonder whether Barbara has found the smugglers' tunnel that leads from Poldarrow Cove to the old house,' said Angela as they strolled up through the town. 'When I left her she was determined to find it. Miss Trout told us some story of a treasure which is meant to be hidden in the house, and I think Barbara imagines that she will find it in the tunnel.'

'A treasure, indeed! That must be very exciting for a child. What kind of treasure is it?'

'A necklace that is supposed to have been made for Queen Marie Antoinette. It was brought here secretly a hundred and fifty years ago and never seen again. Whether it ever existed is uncertain—I doubt it myself—but Barbara has decided that she will find it come what may, and save Miss Trout from being evicted from her home. I fear that Miss Trout is fated to spend the next week or two discovering exactly what it is like to have a twelve-year-old girl rummaging about noisily in one's house.'

'Did Miss Trout herself tell you about the necklace?'

'Yes—she said it was a family legend that had been passed down over the years, and she showed us a journal written by Richard Warrener, the house's original owner, which hinted at its existence—albeit inconclusively, to my mind.'

'So it has never been found,' he said thoughtfully. 'Is Miss Trout to be evicted, then? I thought the house belonged to her family.'

'It is only leased, and the lease expires on the fifth of August. I think Miss Trout is hoping that "something will turn up," as Mr. Micawber said.'

'And that something is the necklace?'

'She did not say so, but I got the impression that she believed in its existence, yes. She put up a show of polite resistance, but I think she was only too glad to have someone young to help her in the search.'

'And shall you help?'

'I should rather not be drawn into a wild-goose chase,' said Angela. 'I have already agreed to look into another matter. It appears that Miss Trout is also receiving anonymous letters, which make vague threats of doom if she doesn't leave Poldarrow Point immediately.'

Simpson stopped dead.

'Anonymous letters?' he said, and looked grave. 'But that is very serious. Very serious indeed.'

'Oh? What do you mean?'

'Why,' he said, 'if I am right, it means that Miss Trout and her nephew may be in some danger.'

CHAPTER NINE

'GOOD GRACIOUS!' EXCLAIMED Mrs. Marchmont. 'Are you sure?'

'Let us say I strongly suspect it,' he said.

'But I have seen the letters, and I shouldn't have said that
they presaged any danger at all—rather, they seemed the work
of some disgruntled neighbour who wanted to make mischief.'

He gazed at her thoughtfully, as though debating something in his mind, then he nodded.

'Very well,' he said, 'I believe I shall have to "come clean,"
as they say. 'Let us go somewhere where we shall not be overheard.'

Angela's curiosity was aroused and she agreed immediately. They headed away from the town and back up towards the
cliff path. Just before the Hotel Splendide, in a sheltered spot,
was a bench. They sat.

'What did you mean, when you said Miss Trout was in danger?' asked Angela impatiently, when Simpson showed no signs of beginning the conversation.

He sighed.

'Mrs. Marchmont, I fear I have misled you slightly. I told you that I was here in a private capacity. That was not true. In fact, I have come to Tregarrion in search of a very dangerous criminal. But before I go on, you should know that I am supposed to be working under-cover, so I beg of you not to tell a soul of this.'

'Naturally I shan't say a word,' Angela assured him. 'Inspector Jameson can vouch for my discretion, if you doubt me.'

'I don't doubt you at all. I have heard him speak highly of you many times,' he said with a smile.

'Then tell me about this criminal,' she said.

'His name—as far as we know, for it may be an alias—is Edgar Valencourt, and he is notorious all over Europe as the most brazen of jewel-thieves. He first came to our notice about ten years ago with the theft of the fabulous jewelled tiara of the old Dowager Queen Dorothea von Hollenstern of Austria—a daring robbery that was only the first of many. He has a taste for the finest jewels owned by the great aristocratic and royal houses, and his method is always the same: he works himself into the confidence of wealthy dowagers and widows of grand families, posing sometimes as an art expert or director of a museum, sometimes as a well-known academic who is writing a history of the family in question—at any event winning their trust in one way or another. There is no reason to doubt him, since he impersonates real experts and comes furnished with impeccable credentials. After a short time, he is allowed to look at the jewels. He admires them and flatters their foolish owner into believing that they make her look as young and beautiful as she ever was, then makes sure they are replaced and locked safely away in the presence of witnesses. Then he disappears, and shortly afterwards it is discovered that *M. le Directeur* from the museum is in fact away at present and has never heard of the Lady So-and-So, much less visited her country *château*, and that the diadem, or the necklace, or the bracelet, which was supposed to be locked away safely in its case, is in fact made of paste and the real one has gone!'

'I see,' said Angela. 'Presumably he makes the exchange at an opportune moment while the lady's attention is elsewhere. He must make his preparations very carefully—especially if he goes to the trouble of having duplicates made of the things he intends to steal.'

'He is a most clever and audacious man,' said Simpson, 'and the police of several countries have been fooled on numerous occasions. We have come close to catching him several times but somehow he always escapes our clutches at the last minute. But I have resolved not to let it happen again—in fact, you might say that I have made it my personal mission to bring him to justice, come what may.'

'Do you believe him to be in Tregarrion at this moment?' asked Angela.

He nodded.

'Yes,' he said. 'I won't bore you with the whole story, but through a rather convoluted route we recently received a report that Valencourt was intending to come to Cornwall in pursuit of a priceless jewel. The report indicated Tregarrion as his most likely destination. Of course, this puzzled us rather, since we had no knowledge of any members of European royalty staying in the area.'

'It doesn't seem quite the sort of place a foreign dignitary would choose to spend a holiday,' agreed Angela.

'Quite. I thought it was probably all a mare's nest, but I didn't want to miss any opportunity to catch Valencourt, however unlikely, so I came down here with the intention of keeping my eyes open. I had just begun to think that there was nothing in the report after all, and had in fact almost decided to leave Tregarrion tomorrow, but what you told me just now has given me pause for thought, and renewed hope that we may have run him to earth at last.'

'Do you think Valencourt is after the necklace?' asked Angela doubtfully.

'I do not know for sure, but you must admit that it is a strange coincidence: we have reports that a notorious jewel-thief is in the area, and at the same time we discover that a jewel of untold value, with a connection to the Queen of France, is thought to be hidden in a house nearby, which is inhabited by a frail old lady who is unlikely to be much threat to any determined thief.'

'Miss Trout is a very pleasant lady,' said Angela, 'and even though she is rather frail, I shouldn't say that she would be easy pickings. She appears to have all her wits about her—

more so than many people of more tender years, as a matter of fact.'

'Is that so?' he said. 'That is a very good thing for her, given her situation.'

'But what is her situation, exactly? I must say, it sounds rather far-fetched to me. Even if, as you say, Edgar Valencourt is in Tregarrion, why do you think he is intending to steal the necklace? After all, it has not been seen for a hundred and fifty years, and we don't even know for certain whether it was ever in the house, let alone whether it is still there today. How on earth does he expect to find it?'

'That I cannot say, but I have had experience of the man, which you have not, and I can only assure you that there is seemingly no end to his cunning. If a man like Edgar Valencourt thinks it worth his while to come here in quest of a legendary jewel, then it seems almost certain that it is there for the taking. And what you tell me of the anonymous letters merely confirms my suspicion that he is here and up to no good.'

'I wonder what his plan is,' said Angela. 'Those letters were very crudely written, and hardly seemed like the kind of device a sophisticated thief would use to get his victim out of the way.'

'Perhaps not, but they may have been intended as a preliminary salvo—an attempt to remove Miss Trout with the minimum of effort on his part. I have no doubt that he has some more subtle plan up his sleeve if that one doesn't work. Did Miss Trout seem worried by the letters at all?'

'No—she seemed more bemused than anything else. They really were rather feeble, you know. I have them at home and can show them to you, if you like.'

He waved his hand.

'Yes, I shall take a look at them later, but I doubt they will tell us anything useful.'

He stroked his chin, thinking.

'What is to be done now?' asked Angela. 'Do you intend to warn Miss Trout of the danger?'

'I think not—as a matter of fact, it is probably better if she knows nothing of the affair. We should only worry her unnecessarily. He may be a bad lot, but Valencourt has never been known to use violence against his victims, so she is not in any danger of physical harm. And what is the worst that can happen if she knows nothing? Why, that Valencourt steals the necklace and she loses something that she never had in the first place! No, it is far better to keep it a secret from her.'

'I see what you mean,' conceded Angela, 'but I can't say I like the idea of his stealing the necklace and getting away with it. If it can be found then presumably either it will belong to Miss Trout, to do with as she wishes, or at the very least she will receive a large reward for finding it and will be able to stay at Poldarrow Point.'

'Oh, rest assured that I have no intention of letting Valencourt get away scot-free,' said Simpson. 'On the contrary, I plan to arrest him and have him put in prison for a very long time. But since I am working under-cover, the fewer people who know about it the better.'

'What does this Valencourt look like?' asked Angela. 'I shall keep an eye out for him myself.'

Simpson looked rather sheepish.

'I am ashamed to say it, but we have no idea. He is a master of disguise and has assumed a different appearance for each of his robberies. All we know is that he is a man of about thirty-eight or forty, who was born in England of a French father and English mother. He was apparently brought up in various countries, and so speaks many languages fluently, but beyond that we know very little. He has successfully eluded us for several years now.'

'Does he work alone, or with a gang?'

'Alone, for the most part, although he will avail himself of accomplices on occasion. He has a network of dishonest jewellery dealers all over Europe, who collude with him to sell the stolen pieces—or, if they are too easily recognizable to sell, to break them up and dispose of the stones separately.'

'I see,' said Angela. 'Very well, if you don't intend to warn Miss Trout of her danger, what are you going to do?'

Simpson smiled.

'Why, I am going to request the help of a well-known lady detective,' he said.

'I assume you mean me,' said Angela. 'Of course, you know that I am not really a detective?'

'Perhaps not, but your frequent appearance in the newspapers means that you will be forever considered as such in the mind of the English public. Confess it, though: you do not really object to the deception.'

Angela did not reply directly, but only said, 'I will certainly confess to having more than my share of natural curiosity and a desire to get to the bottom of any mystery that happens to present itself.'

'Then may I count on your help?' said Simpson.

'What is it that you wish me to do?'

'Oh, very little. I do not demand that you catch the man single-handedly—no, leave it to the police to do that. All I ask is that you keep me informed of anything that happens at Poldarrow Point. Did Miss Trout ask you to investigate the anonymous letters?'

'Yes, and I agreed to do so, although I hardly know where to start.'

'Very good. Then you will see her often and she will tell you of any developments. In addition, your god-daughter is going to search for the necklace itself. I think I hardly need tell you that if she finds it, you must keep it safe and tell me at once. It might even be better to get it out of the house immediately if you can, so Valencourt does not have the opportunity to steal it from under your noses.'

'Very well,' said Angela. 'I shall see what I can do. I should hate to see Miss Trout forced to leave her home just when the recovery of the necklace ought to make her quite safe from eviction.'

'And don't forget to keep the thing quiet,' he said. 'If Valencourt gets wind of the fact that we are on to him, then he will disappear and we shall have to start all over again. I don't mind telling you that I take his continued freedom personally. I don't like to lose a man even once, let alone several times, and Valencourt is as cunning as the devil. I shall be very glad to see him behind bars where he belongs.'

Angela promised to do as he asked, and they parted for the present, since Simpson had to report the new developments to his superiors.

'I am at the hotel if anything comes up,' he said as he was about to leave. 'You may summon me at any time and I shall come.'

Angela walked slowly back to Kittiwake Cottage, her mind full of what she had just heard. What an extraordinary story! To think that a notorious jewel-thief was here under their very noses, planning his latest crime. It almost defied belief that such a thing could happen in this peaceful spot.

'I shall have to take another look at those anonymous letters,' she said to herself. 'I can't say I took them very seriously before, but it looks as though they may be more significant than I thought.'

CHAPTER TEN

BARBARA STOOD ANKLE-deep in the shallows and watched the waves come in. Farther out, the breeze whipped the sea up into white, choppy peaks, but here in the little cove, all was calm thanks to the shelter provided by the rugged cliffs that loomed above and all around.

Helen Walters was swimming with powerful strokes up and down the little bay. She caught sight of Barbara and slowed her pace, then stopped and waved, treading water.

'Hallo,' she called. 'Are you coming in? The water is simply splendid this morning.'

'Not today,' Barbara called back. 'I don't have my bathing things.'

She kicked the water grumpily with a bare foot. She wanted the place to herself so she could look for the smugglers' tunnel, but the girl from next door was spoiling everything by taking her bathe now. Soon the tide would come in and cover the beach, and then she wouldn't be able to get anywhere near the cliffs.

'I can scout about a bit, at any rate,' she said to herself. 'Helen needn't know what I am up to.'

She walked back up the beach and pulled her shoes on over wet feet, then headed to the section of cliff that she thought was most likely to contain the entrance to the tunnel. Stopping now and again by a rock pool and poking about amongst the seaweed (might as well make it look as though she were merely hunting for interesting sea-creatures), she worked her way slowly along the cliff face, glancing up occasionally in the hope of seeing an opening that might be the entrance.

At last she came to a little rocky outcrop that looked as though it might be just the thing: just after it, the cliff appeared to fold in on itself and form a kind of recess. Barbara's eyes gleamed in excitement. Surely this was it! She glanced up to see where Helen had got to, and saw that she had come out of the water and was wrapping herself in a towel while proceeding slowly across the sand back towards the cliff path that led back to her cottage. Barbara waited a minute or two until Helen was out of sight then turned back to look more closely at the cliff face. As far as she could judge, the recess was almost directly below Poldarrow Point itself. This was promising. She skirted round a large seaweedy pool and rounded the rock, then almost jumped out of her skin as she came face to face with a man who was crouching in the recess in a most suspicious manner.

'Oh!' she exclaimed. The man straightened up in a hurry. He was clearly as surprised as she was. He went pink in the face.

'I am very sorry,' he said. 'I do not wish to frighten you.'

'That's all right,' said Barbara. 'I just got a shock, that's all. I didn't know anyone was here, you see.'

She looked more closely at the man. He was obviously foreign, and was dressed in a rather odd pair of knee breeches and a hat with a feather. Despite his luxuriant moustache, he was younger than she had first thought. On the ground next to him was a knapsack, attached to which were one or two glass jars and a number of digging implements. He saw her curiosity and waved a hand towards the equipment.

'I am Pierre Donati, from Switzerland,' he said. 'I am a scientist.'

'Oh!' said Barbara. 'How fascinating. Are you studying something here?'

He went pink again.

'Yes,' he said. 'I look for the hore.'

'The what?' said Barbara.

'The hore. Metal, yes? Cornwall is rich in hore. Tin, copper. Also other things, such as wolfram, or tungsten as it is also known.'

'Oh, *ore*—yes, of course,' said Barbara. 'I did know that. We learned about it at school, but I'm afraid I wasn't listening very carefully.'

'It can be a little dry for a young mind,' he agreed, 'but it is very important, for if metal can be found in the soil, it may be worth many thousands of pounds.'

'I say!' said Barbara. 'That sounds more like it. Perhaps I shall pay more attention in future. You can't carry much in those jars, though.'

'No, no,' he said. 'I do not dig up the hore itself. I merely take little samples of the soil here and there, which I will test later.'

'But there's no soil in here, only sand.'

'Ah, yes,' said Mr. Donati. 'I come here for a little break from my work. The view is most beautiful.'

'What, from behind this rock?'

He looked confused, and coughed.

'No, I was on the beach, then I happened to see this little— what do you call it?—cave, and I was very curious, so I came to take a closer look.'

'Oh, so it *is* a cave,' said Barbara in excitement. 'Might I see?'

He stepped out of the way to allow her to enter the recess. Sure enough, there was a narrow fissure in the cliff face that was quite screened from the view of anyone who might be looking from the beach. It appeared to be the entrance to a passage.

'Have you been inside?' she said to Donati.

'No, I have not the torch,' he replied.

'I have a torch,' she said. 'Would you like to come in with me?' She spoke out of politeness since he had, after all, found the cave first, but was relieved when he shook his head.

'No, I thank you,' he said. 'I must return to work now. Goodbye. Perhaps we shall meet again soon.'

'Oh yes, goodbye,' said Barbara, then turned her attention back to the cave and promptly forgot about the strange man, who had picked up his knapsack and was already heading back towards the path, clanking as he went.

77

She ducked in through the low entrance and followed the passage which, after six or seven feet, took a sharp turn to the right. Beyond that point it was too dark to see, so she took out her electric torch and switched it on. By the dim light she saw that a few yards ahead the little tunnel opened out into a larger space. She hurried forward, then stopped and looked about her, waving the torch around as she turned her head this way and that. She was in a cave of perhaps thirty feet square which had presumably been hollowed out by the tides of many millions of years. Water dripped from the ceiling, and the walls glistened and oozed with festoons of clinging seaweed. Underfoot, rippled paths of wet sand wound in and out among dark rock pools. The air was damp and chill.

Sure that she had found the right place, Barbara started forward into the cave and began to explore it carefully. She walked slowly around it, shining her torch on any recess that might be the entrance to the tunnel, or any large patch of seaweed that might possibly conceal an opening. After three circuits of the place, however, by which time she had in desperation begun pulling aside smaller and smaller patches of seaweed that could not possibly hide anything, she was forced to concede that there was no tunnel here. The thought rather cheered her, since it meant that the discovery was still all her very own to make without any interference from Swiss scientists, and she emerged into the sunshine undaunted and as determined as ever.

She proceeded along the bottom of the cliff, examining the face carefully but finding nothing—although she noted that the tide had advanced surprisingly far while she had been inside the cave. She had now reached the very furthest extremity of the Poldarrow Point headland without finding the smugglers' tunnel, and there seemed to be nowhere else to look: any farther on and she would be past the headland and into the other side of Tregarn Bay proper.

'Where on earth can it be?' she said to herself. 'I've searched every inch of this cove, it seems, but I haven't found anything. Could that cave be the entrance after all? Perhaps the tunnel has been blocked by a rock-fall, or something. Or perhaps it's back there, where the path comes out onto the beach.'

She clambered up to sit on a large, flat outcrop at the base of the cliff and gazed back in the direction she had come, searching for any signs she might have missed, but saw nothing that looked a likely prospect. She sighed and began to spin around idly on her seat, debating whether or not to leave the search for today and come back tomorrow, as the tide was approaching rapidly now. It would be lunch-time soon, too, and Barbara realized that she was hungry. Then she remembered that Cook had promised to bake some more scones, and that decided it. She was going back.

She spun herself round one more time—too violently, for she lost her balance and before she could regain it, fell off the rock and landed six feet below on the far side of it.

'Oof!' she said, and then, 'Ow!'

She lay there for a moment or two to get her breath back, then sat up gingerly and rubbed her elbow. Nothing seemed to be broken. She was about to utter a word that would certainly be forbidden at school, when her eyes widened and her mouth dropped open, for there it was—the entrance to the

79

smugglers' tunnel, as plain as the eye could see, right there before her. No wonder she had missed it: the slab of rock hid it completely from the beach, and except at very low tide, it was totally inaccessible. It was a low, wide opening in the rock which a quick inspection showed opened out into a little cave. Without bothering to stand up (it was too low to walk under in any case), Barbara scrambled inside and saw that she had at last found what she was looking for. She got to her feet. The ceiling of this cave was lower than the other one, and the floor made mostly of rock, but this one too was dripping and strewn with wet seaweed. Barbara glanced out through the entrance into the sunshine and saw that the sea was not twenty yards away. She briefly considered leaving her expedition until the next low tide, but then the gleam of the torch happened to fall on the tunnel entrance itself at the back of the cave, and her decision was made.

She crossed the slippery floor carefully and entered the passage, looking about her. Her heart beat in her chest as the tunnel dipped down steeply and then began to wind upwards, and she gripped her torch more firmly, thankful that she had remembered to bring it. After a hundred yards or so the damp passage emerged into a sort of chamber that was much drier. Barbara had a vague recollection of having once read a book about Cornish smugglers, and supposed that in the olden days, when customs men might turn up at any time or the tide take them by surprise, the men must have brought the smuggled booty to this place first of all. Afterwards, once it had all been brought ashore safely, they would carry it up to the cellars of Poldarrow Point at their leisure.

The chamber was rather cold. Barbara could feel a draught of air on her skin, which was welcome after the stuffiness of the tunnel, and a faint light came from somewhere—or at least, the darkness was less impenetrable here. Barbara's eyes gleamed as she spotted two old wooden barrels standing against the wall, and she went across to examine them. The first one was empty and the wood quite rotten: it fell to pieces when she touched it, and she started as a large spider ran out and attempted to climb up her arm. She brushed it off hurriedly and pointed the torch at what remained of the barrel. It was quite empty. The second cask was made of stronger stuff, being bound with metal rather than wooden hoops. It was impossible to get into, so Barbara ended by tipping it up and rattling it about in order to find out whether it contained anything, but it, too, was empty. She did not really expect to find a priceless necklace inside an old wine cask, but told herself that a true detective should leave no stone unturned.

There was nothing else to see in the chamber, so Barbara continued on through the tunnel. The path had become much steeper now, and she panted as she pressed on eagerly. Surely she must be close to the house by now. At last she came to a fork. One branch led straight on, while the other doubled back and curved sharply out of sight a short distance ahead. Supposing that the first path led to the house, Barbara decided to see where the second one went, but was brought up short after about thirty yards by a rock-fall that blocked her way. She returned the way she had come and, shortly afterwards, arrived at the bottom of the shaft that led up to the trap-door into the cellar of Poldarrow Point. She recognized the metal rungs down which she had climbed herself only the day before.

'Well,' she said, 'I have found the tunnel, at any rate, although there's no sign of any necklace. I suppose Preacher Dick must have taken it into the house—of course, he must have, since all his men knew about this tunnel and it wouldn't have been safe to hide it here.'

At that moment it occurred to her that she had spent rather a long time wandering around in the dark, and that the tide was coming in rapidly. She turned and hurried back down the passage as fast as she could. The light from her torch had been growing weaker for some time, but she judged that it would last until she got outside. She passed rapidly through the barrel-chamber, as she called it in her mind, and into the bottom section of the tunnel. Then she stopped short and a chill ran through her. Ahead of her, the path dipped slightly and rose again, and into that depression a thin stream of water was flowing. She ran forward and through the pool that had formed, then gave a whimper of dismay. The path sloped steeply downwards from here to the cave, and it was completely flooded and impassable. As she stood there, she felt a little rush of water that threatened to knock her off her feet and she retreated hurriedly. She had obviously been gone much longer than she thought, and the tide had come in and blocked her way out of the tunnel.

At that moment her torch gave out.

'Bother,' said Barbara.

CHAPTER ELEVEN

MRS. MARCHMONT SAT on the terrace at Kitti-wake Cottage, reading the anonymous letters and frowning to herself. At last she gave a sigh and threw them down upon the table.

'It's no use,' she said to Marthe, who was picking up Barbara's things from where she had strewn them all over the garden. 'I am not Sherlock Holmes and never shall be.'

'*Pardon, madame*? Who?'

'Sherlock Holmes. He is a great detective in a book. If he were here, he would take these letters and at once tell us who sent them, whether he is left- or right-handed, what he does for a living, and probably even what he had for supper last night.'

'Pfft! That is easy,' said Marthe in disdain, and picked up a letter. 'One can see immediately that this was sent by a woman, and that she was left-handed.'

'Really?' said Angela in surprise. 'How can you tell?'

Marthe shrugged.

'Look at those loops. Only a woman would write so. A man would place the letters closer together.' She lifted the paper to her nose and sniffed delicately. 'Ah! *Shalimar*. I knew it!'

Even more astonished, Angela took the letter and sniffed at it herself. She detected the faintest of scents.

'I can smell perfume,' she said, 'but I couldn't possibly have identified it. But how can you tell she is left-handed?'

'Here, you see,' said Marthe. She indicated one or two places where the ink was smeared. 'Her hand went through the wet ink when it passed over what she had already written. She was probably writing with a pen to which she was not accustomed, otherwise she would not have made such a mistake.'

'But whoever sent the letters was not accustomed to writing at all, to judge by the spelling, which is quite illiterate.' Angela stopped and frowned. 'But that can't be right either. What would such a person be doing wearing expensive perfume?'

She looked at the letters again.

'How silly of me not to notice,' she said. 'Of course, the writer is only pretending to be uneducated. Look—it's all wrong. She spells "here" and "give" incorrectly, and yet she is perfectly capable of getting "nephew" and "earlier" right. And she spells "once" wrongly in one letter, and right in another. So, then, the letters were written by a left-handed woman with a certain level of education and income, who was pretending to be illiterate, presumably in order to disguise her identity. Thank you, Marthe. I shall certainly come to you in future if I require any more deductions of this sort.'

Marthe preened.

'But you haven't told me what she had for supper last night,' went on Angela slyly.

'*Madame,*' said Marthe, in the manner of one stating the obvious, 'a woman who wears *Shalimar* does not eat supper.'

'Ah, of course,' said Angela.

Marthe went inside, leaving Angela smiling and shaking her head.

'I wonder if Sherlock Holmes had a lady's maid,' she said to herself.

A few minutes later Marthe came back out and informed her that lunch was served.

'Where is Barbara?' asked Angela. 'It's not like her not to turn up to lunch. And I thought Cook was making scones today. Most odd.'

She sat down to her meal, expecting Barbara to come rushing in at any moment and throw herself down at the table with a perfunctory apology for her lateness, but to her surprise no Barbara appeared. Angela, forgetting about the tides, supposed that she had found the tunnel and was happily exploring it, in hopes of finding the necklace.

The thought of the necklace reminded Angela of her conversation with George Simpson that morning, and she wondered whether she perhaps ought to accompany Barbara to Miss Trout's the next day. She did not relish the thought of spending another afternoon in that musty old house, but she had promised Simpson that she would keep an eye on things, and she could hardly do that from a distance.

'What if Barbara finds the necklace?' she said to herself. 'Can the three of them between them be trusted to have the sense to put it somewhere absolutely safe? A bank would be the best place, naturally—at least until we can hand it over to the police. Perhaps I ought to go too, so I can persuade them if necessary.'

Having made this resolution, Angela decided to go out for a little while to walk off her lunch, which had been a hearty one (the sea air certainly gave one a healthy appetite). She had one or two things she needed to buy, and so she headed back into Tregarrion, where a number of general stores supplying all kinds of goods had sprung up in recent years, in response to the arrival of the tourists.

She completed her purchases and emerged into the street, where she immediately bumped into a man who had not been looking where he was going. It was Clifford Maynard. He began to apologize profusely, and then saw who she was.

'Oh, it's you, Mrs. Marchmont,' he said. 'Do forgive me. I was wandering along in a day-dream. I am quite prone to it, I'm afraid, and Aunt Emily often laughs at me for my inattention. I do hope you're not hurt?'

Angela reassured him that there was no harm done, and asked after his aunt.

'Oh, she is well, very well,' he replied. 'She is very much looking forward to seeing young Barbara tomorrow. Old people are very fond of the company of the young, I find. It reminds them of their own childish days. You won't let her forget, now, will you?'

'I'm sure Barbara is looking forward to it very much,' said Angela. 'As a matter of fact, I was wondering whether your aunt would mind if I came with her. I have never taken part in a treasure-hunt, and I must confess that it sounds rather entertaining. And you know, many hands are supposed to make light work.'

'Why, we should both be delighted to see you again,' said Mr. Maynard jovially. His manner suddenly changed, and became confidential. 'By the way, Mrs. Marchmont,' he said in a low voice, 'there was something I wanted to speak to you about.'

'Oh?'

'Yes. Let us go over here.' He took hold of Angela's elbow in a proprietary manner and led her out of the way of the crowds. Angela raised her eyebrows slightly but allowed herself to be conducted across the street without fuss. He stopped next to the window of a shop which appeared to specialize in selling waterproof clothing. It was closed, and a hand-written sign hanging on the door read, 'Back Next Week.'

'I feel I ought to apologize for yesterday,' began Mr. Maynard without further ado. 'I fear that my aunt has imposed upon you, rather.'

'Because of the necklace?' said Angela. 'Please, don't give it a moment's thought. Barbara is terribly excited to be allowed to join a real treasure-hunt, and I confess it pleases me that she has something to occupy her time. It must be dull for her here, with no other children to play with.'

'I didn't mean that, exactly,' he said. He lowered his voice still further. 'My aunt is very old, Mrs. Marchmont, and I fear that she may be getting—how can I put it?—a little bit vague in her mind.'

'I see,' said Angela. 'Do you mean she is losing her memory?'

'Partly,' he said. 'But it's not only that. Much as it pains me to say it, I am afraid her imagination has also begun to run away with her, although she denies it, of course.'

'I don't quite understand. What do you mean, exactly?'

'I mean that she has begun to tell some rather tall stories. They are not lies as such, because I am fairly sure that she believes them implicitly herself, but I have caught her out on several occasions recently. For example, only a week or so ago, while we were wondering what to do about this problem with the lease, the conversation turned to our family history, as you might expect. I was saying what a pity it was that the Trouts had been so poor as to need to sell the freehold of Poldarrow Point, and she said something like, "Ah, yes, but of course, throughout history the illegitimate descendants of royalty have always been treated unfairly." Naturally, I had no idea what she was talking about, and when I asked her what she meant, she said, "Don't be silly, Clifford—of course you know that Preacher Dick was the illegitimate son of the Duke of Gloucester, who was the brother of George the Third." This was quite a surprise to me, and I asked her if she was quite certain of it, and she said, "But I thought everybody knew. The Duke had a secret mistress here in Cornwall, who lived here in Tregarrion and gave birth to a son, Richard—our ancestor. But the Duke did not do right by the poor woman, and denied that the child was his. She eventually married a man named Warrener and the boy took his name."'

'It is certainly an extraordinary story,' said Angela. 'Are you sure it is not true?'

'Of course it's not true,' said Mr. Maynard impatiently. 'Why, our family history is perfectly well documented locally, and there is no record of the Duke of Gloucester's ever having even visited Tregarrion, much less taken a mistress here. It was all in her imagination—a fact proved a day or two later when I mentioned the story again and she denied ever having said such a thing—seemed astonished, in fact, and accused me of making up silly stories.'

'Dear me,' said Angela.

'Indeed, I was most dismayed,' he said, 'but that is merely the most striking example of what I have been saying. There have been other, minor incidents which are not worth relating, but which all seem to point to one inescapable conclusion: that Aunt Emily is no longer as sound in her mind as she used to be. Most of the time she is as sane and sensible as she ever was, but I fear these episodes will become increasingly frequent as she gets older.'

'Poor Miss Trout,' said Angela. 'Do you believe, then, that she invented the story of the necklace?'

'Oh, no, no,' he said. 'That's true enough—or at least, the legend certainly exists. Whether there is a necklace, and whether it is in the house, I cannot presume to say. And everything she has said about Preacher Dick and his smuggling activities is also true. No, I was referring to this story of hers about the anonymous letters. I am afraid it is all nonsense.'

Angela remembered Mr. Maynard's admonishment to his aunt when she had embarked upon her tale.

'Do you think she made it up?' she said. 'Then who wrote the letters? Are you suggesting that she wrote them herself?'

He looked distressed.

'That's just it, I don't know,' he said. 'But I can't think of any reason why someone should want her to leave Poldarrow Point. Why, our family have lived here for generations. There's simply no sense to it. And since I have caught her out on other occasions—well, you may imagine how difficult it is for me to say such things about my own dear Aunt Emily, who is almost the only relation I have, but I hardly know what to think, except that old people do, sadly, sometimes become a little confused.'

Angela did not reply for a second. Clifford Maynard was, of course, unaware that the police believed the letters came from a dangerous criminal, but were the police right? Marthe was certain that they had been written by a woman, and Angela had great faith in Marthe's intelligence and perspicacity. Perhaps Edgar Valencourt had a female accomplice—Inspector Simpson had mentioned that he had been known to work with other people. Perhaps he was even married. Or, as Clifford had said, perhaps the letters had been written by a confused and lonely old lady who would resort to any stratagem in order to ensure that her visitors kept coming back.

'What do you want me to do?' she asked at last.

Mr. Maynard looked relieved.

'Why, whatever you think best,' he said. 'I had to tell you of this, as I should hate you to waste your time in investigating something that I am certain is the product of her lively imagination, but I will leave the course of action to you—although

I am sure you will be kind enough not to let my aunt know that you suspect her of anything.'

'Of course,' said Angela. 'Perhaps I shall make a show of looking into it, for her sake.'

'That is very good of you,' he said with a smile, 'and now I'm afraid I must rush off, as I only came out to get Aunt her medicine. We shall see you later.'

He nodded briskly then went away, and Angela walked slowly home. Barbara had not returned, and Angela was puzzled. She went down to the garden gate and looked right and left, but there was no sign of the girl.

'Hallo, Mrs. Marchmont,' said Helen Walters, who was just then coming out of her own gate. 'Are you looking for someone?'

'Yes,' said Angela. 'I seem to have lost Barbara. I don't suppose you've seen her today? She did not come home for lunch, and that is most unusual, as I am sure you can imagine.'

'I saw her this morning, down on the beach,' said Helen, 'but I left before she did. She was poking about among the rocks. I thought she was looking for crabs, or something. But the tide is quite high now, so she must have left the beach some time ago.'

Angela frowned. She had warned Barbara against the tides herself, so there was no excuse for her staying down there too long. She could only suppose that the girl had gone off somewhere else—perhaps into Tregarrion—for reasons of her own. She was bound to be back in time for tea, though.

Angela called for Marthe to bring her some coffee and sat down with her book, but did not read. Instead, she watched the seagulls as they made patterns in the air above her, finding a sort of music in their harsh cries. The wind was still strong, but here in the garden it was sheltered and warm. Evidently she was not the only one to find the situation agreeable: after a few minutes, the cat came and jumped onto her lap, and she scratched its chin absently. It purred and kneaded her skirt, then settled down for a nap. Angela sipped her coffee and leaned back more comfortably in her chair, taking care not to disturb her guest. Jewel-thieves and unruly children notwithstanding, she was having a most pleasant time of it.

CHAPTER TWELVE

BARBARA STOOD IN the pitch darkness for a moment or two, listening to the sloshing, whooshing sounds of the water as it advanced inexorably into the tunnel. Now that the light had gone, the noise seemed almost deafening, and she wondered how on earth she had failed to notice it before. She felt another wave rush over her foot and decided to make good her retreat. Stretching her hand out to the side, she felt the tunnel wall cold and hard under her fingers. She pressed herself against it and groped her way slowly and carefully back up the slope towards the barrel-chamber, fearful all the while that the encroaching sea would catch up with her stealthily and overcome her before she could reach safety.

After what seemed an age she felt a slight gust of air and began to make out faint shapes in the darkness, which told her that she had arrived in the chamber. Now she knew she was safe—from the sea at least, since the presence of the barrels indicated that the tide did not advance this far.

But what to do now? Barbara judged that it must be about one o'clock. Low tide had been at ten, as far as she could remember, which meant that high tide would not come until four and she would be trapped here for at least four hours after that, until the water had receded enough to allow her to leave through the cave. Her stomach gave a loud rumble and she thought wistfully of Cook's scones. The idea of staying here in the dark until the evening hardly appealed; besides, Angela would surely wonder where she was. Perhaps she was even now scouring the area anxiously, calling Barbara's name and wringing her hands.

This idea pleased Barbara so much that she dwelt on it for several minutes, embellishing the picture to her satisfaction. She saw the whole town of Tregarrion throwing down their tools and rising up as one in order to hunt high and low for her. Burly fishermen and farm-hands would form search-parties with dogs, while the womenfolk huddled in corners worriedly and told each other that she had been such a delightful child. After hours and hours they would find her, and a great cheer would go up, and they would take her back to Kittiwake Cottage, bearing her on their shoulders triumphally, and Angela would weep with joy and Marthe would smile for once and let her have as many scones as she liked.

Then she returned to reality.

'Silly girl,' she said to herself. 'Even if they did come looking for me, they wouldn't find me anyway, until the tide goes out—and by that time I will be able to get out quite easily by myself.'

There was nothing else for it: she would have to go back up to the trap-door that led into the cellars of Poldarrow Point. She crossed the floor to where she could just make out a darker shadow against the back wall, which must be the start of the next section of the passage, and groped her way in carefully. Once again, the darkness was complete and Barbara wished she had not wasted her time exploring the first cave, for then her torch might have lasted longer.

At last she came up against the metal rungs that led up to the trap-door and began to climb them laboriously, feeling for each one and being careful not to lose her balance. She panted as she climbed. How much more difficult everything was in the dark! Now here was the trap-door, and she hoped against hope that nobody had been down into the cellar since they had all left it yesterday. Barbara never did a thing without doing it thoroughly and, having some vague, romantic idea that she might soon need to spirit the Queen's necklace away from a band of marauding jewel-thieves, had taken good care to leave the trap-door unbolted yesterday when she was supposed to be fastening it. She gripped the top rung with her left hand and pushed hard on the door with her right. It was heavier than she remembered but was not bolted, at which she gave a sigh of relief. She pushed again—too hard this time, because she lost her hold on it and it fell open with a loud clap onto the cellar floor.

Barbara pulled herself cautiously out of the hole and listened for sounds of movement upstairs. She had no wish to attract the attention of Miss Trout and her nephew, judging—

probably quite correctly—that they would not be too pleased at her having left the trap-door open, thus allowing anyone who happened to discover it to come through the tunnel and into the house. After a minute or two, she decided that all was safe. She shut the trap-door and felt her way to where she thought the stairs must be. For a minute or two she stumbled about fruitlessly, but then her eyes gradually distinguished a horizontal slit of light above her head, which must surely be coming in under the door into the hall. Her heart leapt and she scrambled up the stairs as fast as she could. She listened carefully at the door and then turned the handle. It was locked. Barbara could have cried with frustration. What on earth was she to do now?

She sat down on the top step and rested her chin glumly in her hands for a minute or two, then turned and placed her cheek to the floor in order to peer under the door. The gap was a large one and she could see quite clearly the entrance-hall beyond. How provoking to be so close to freedom and yet not quite able to attain it! She remembered the little key that Miss Trout had turned yesterday when they went into the cellar, and wondered if it was still in the lock. No light came in through the keyhole so she supposed it must be. If only she could find some way to turn it from this side of the door!

She poked a finger experimentally into the hole, but it was too big to go in very far. Then she had a thought, and reached up to remove a hair-pin from her hair. It fitted into the hole perfectly. Holding her breath, Barbara prodded and poked carefully and, after what seemed an age, felt something give. A second later, the key fell out of the lock and clinked onto the floor on the other side of the door. Barbara's hand just fitted under the crack. With a hiss of triumph, she put her fingers on the key and slid it carefully towards her. It turned easily in the lock and she emerged into the hall, congratulating herself on her own cleverness.

But there was no time to waste: Miss Trout or Mr. Maynard might turn up at any moment and want to know what she was doing skulking about in their hall, and there was no telling whether they would be sympathetic or not. On the whole, Barbara preferred not to risk finding out. The place was silent and there seemed to be no-one at home. Perhaps they had gone out.

She slipped quietly across towards the front door, then froze. What was that sound? She listened carefully, but heard nothing. She reached out a hand to the door. There it was again! What was it? It sounded like somebody moaning softly upstairs. Who could it be? Was Miss Trout ill? Why was her nephew not here to look after her?

Barbara's curiosity overcame her and she decided to investigate. She tiptoed up the creaky old stairs as silently as she could and peeped through the banister at the top of the first flight. Up here all was dim and dingy: the doors were closed and very little light came in. A musty smell hung in the air. There was the moaning sound again. It seemed to be coming from above. Did Miss Trout sleep at the top of the house? That was odd. Barbara crept up the next flight of stairs. Up here the banisters were less ornate and the carpet was ragged and threadbare. She advanced her head cautiously around the newel. These must be the old servants' quarters. A narrow passage stretched into the distance, with a number of low doors set into it.

It was freezing cold up here, and Barbara shivered. Her feet were soaking wet and uncomfortable, and she longed to get back outside into the sunshine, but she could not bring herself to leave without first finding out the source of the noise. The moaning was louder now. It seemed to be coming from the end of the passage. Barbara turned her head and her eyes widened in astonishment as she saw a ghostly figure in white drift into view. It was moaning and whimpering and rubbing its hands together.

'No, no, no,' said the figure tragically, and broke into great, heaving, gasping sobs.

It was too much for Barbara, who had already had a trying morning. She turned and dashed down the stairs as fast as she could, heedless of the noise she was making. She reached the hall, wrenched the front door open and ran outside, slamming the door behind her. She felt the sun on her face and gave a great whoop of relief, then ran as fast as she could all the way back to Kittiwake Cottage.

CHAPTER THIRTEEN

OH, THERE YOU are,' said Angela, looking up calmly from her book as Barbara burst onto the terrace. 'You have missed lunch. And whatever have you been doing to make yourself look like such a scarecrow?'

Barbara was indeed looking very bedraggled after her adventure in the tunnel, with damp clothes and shoes, and grubby hands and knees.

'I found the tunnel,' she said, 'but I made a bit of a mistake and got trapped in there by the tide.'

'I did warn you,' said Angela. 'Would you like something to eat?'

'Yes please!' said Barbara. She paused. 'I did rather think you might be desperately worried and combing the area with a pack of bloodhounds,' she said.

'Don't be silly,' said Angela. 'Cook is still here, I believe. I'm sure she'll be able to rustle something up.' She returned to her book, and Barbara gave it up and went inside.

She returned some time later looking rather cleaner (Marthe had taken one horrified look at her and marched her off to wash) and with a stomach pleasantly full of cold meat and warm scones. Angela looked up and put down her book.

'That's better,' she said. 'You looked as though you had been ploughing a field with your face, or something.'

'Why must Marthe *scrub* so?' complained Barbara. 'I'm sure she took off four inches of skin.'

'One must suffer for beauty, apparently.'

'Then I shall be ugly and happy,' said Barbara. She sat down and pulled the cat off Angela's lap and onto her own. It protested briefly then settled down to resume its nap.

'How did you get out of the tunnel, by the way?' asked Angela. 'It's still high tide.'

'I came through the trap-door into the house.'

'Really? I'm surprised they could hear you knocking from upstairs.'

Barbara nodded and attempted to change the subject.

'Did you have a nice time in Tregarrion this morning?' she asked brightly, but Angela was not to be fooled. Her eyes narrowed.

'Barbara,' she said, 'what did Miss Trout and Mr. Maynard say when they found you in the tunnel?'

'Oh, very well,' said Barbara, 'I admit it. They didn't know anything about it because I left the trap-door unlocked yesterday when we went for tea, and I sneaked out without anybody seeing me.'

'But why did you leave it open?'

Barbara looked sulky.

'I just thought I might need to get through it urgently one day. And I did, didn't I?'

'Still, though, you oughtn't to have done it—especially not when you particularly led them to believe you'd bolted it.'

'Sorry, Angela,' said Barbara, doing her best to look ashamed and carefully omitting to mention that she had done exactly the same thing again today.

'I should think so. Now, tell me about the tunnel.'

Barbara related her adventures of the morning and Angela forgot to look disapproving as she listened with interest.

'It sounds as though it is exactly what it purports to be, then,' she said, 'and that is, a means of getting from the cove to the house. From what you say, it doesn't seem as though anything is hidden down there, unless there is something in one of those barrels.'

Barbara shook her head.

'That's no go,' she said. 'One of them fell to pieces when I touched it, and I rattled the other one ever so hard but it made no sound. And lots of people knew about the tunnel in the olden days, so it wouldn't be the best place to hide something valuable. No, I think the necklace is somewhere in the house, and I mean to find it.'

'Perhaps I shall come with you tomorrow.'

'Will you?' asked Barbara eagerly. 'That would be splendid. Not that I'm scared, of course, but I should like to have you there to help.'

'Why should you be scared?'

'I told you—I'm not. And even if there *are* ghosts I'm sure they don't mean any harm.'

'What on earth are you talking about? Which ghosts?'

'Don't you remember? Miss Trout said the house was supposed to be haunted by an old man who wanders around upstairs in his nightgown.'

'But you said you didn't believe in ghosts.'

'Of course I don't!' said Barbara stoutly. 'Why, the very idea is absurd.'

'Then why did you say there might be ghosts?'

'I didn't.'

'Yes you did, just now.'

'I didn't mean it. But I shall be glad to have you there all the same.'

'Well, then, that's settled,' said Angela, with a vague feeling that she had missed something. 'I shall come with you tomorrow and we shall spend the day looking for this necklace which may or may not exist.'

'Of course it exists!' said Barbara, on safer ground now. 'It must be there somewhere, and I think there must be a clue in Preacher Dick's journal as to its hiding-place. I'll go and get it.'

She ran into the house and returned with the battered old book.

'It's awfully difficult to read,' she said as she peered at the crabbed writing.

'Let me see,' said Angela. She turned the leaves carefully, running her finger down each page as she did so. 'Most of it appears to be lists of goods taken ashore and sold,' she said at last. 'Preacher Dick may have led an exciting life but I fear he lacked the gift of narrative. The most interesting part seems to be the story of the package, but the page is torn out there.'

'I wonder what happened to it,' said Barbara. Her eyes lit up. 'I say!' she said. 'Do you think it had a map of the hiding place on it? If so, perhaps it was taken deliberately. Perhaps it was even stolen by the same person who wrote the anonymous letters.'

'That doesn't seem very likely,' said Angela.

'Let me see,' said Barbara, and took the book back. 'Look,' she said. 'I believe the page has been torn out recently.'

'Really?' said Angela. She craned her neck to look. Sure enough, she saw that the torn edge of the paper that remained looked almost new and was a lighter colour than the rest of the leaves. 'I believe you are right,' she said in surprise. 'That's odd. But perhaps Miss Trout or Mr. Maynard did it themselves accidentally.'

'Then why didn't they mention it at the time?' said Barbara. 'They didn't seem to know anything about it.'

'That's true,' conceded Angela.

'I knew it!' said Barbara excitedly. 'Someone else is after the necklace. Miss Trout must have shown the memoirs to someone and mentioned the family legend, and whoever it was decided to look for the treasure and keep it for himself. So he wrote those anonymous letters in order to frighten Miss Trout out of the house and allow him to get in and search it in his own time. I do hope he hasn't already been into the house and found it.'

'No, I don't think he has,' said Angela.

'Why not?'

'Because the last letter arrived only yesterday, remember? Presumably that means the thief hasn't got his hands on it yet.'

'Oh yes, I see,' said Barbara. 'Well, then, now that we know someone else is after the necklace, we must search all the harder for it and be sure to get there first.'

Angela was about to say that they did not know for certain whether or not someone else was looking for the necklace, but thought better of it. It seemed useless to deny that Barbara was most likely right. Naturally, the girl knew nothing of Edgar Valencourt and his exploits, or that Scotland Yard was already on the case, but her reasoning was logical.

'I wonder where it is,' she said instead.

'I have been thinking about that,' said Barbara eagerly. 'It can't be locked in a cupboard or a drawer or anything like that, because someone would surely have found it by now if it's been in the house for more than a hundred years. No, I think there is probably a secret panel somewhere, perhaps with a safe behind it.'

'Yes, that's certainly possible,' said Angela. 'I suppose we shall have to go and tap on all the walls.'

'Perhaps there is another secret passage in the house,' said Barbara.

'Don't you think one is enough?'

'I like secret passages.'

'What, even after getting trapped in one this morning?'

'It was an adventure,' said Barbara. 'Things are so deadly dull most of the time. I am glad I came here, Angela,' she said suddenly. 'I'm having *such* fun. You're not dull, like the El-lises. You don't get all cross and bothered if I turn up late for lunch, or if I get into a scrape. I thought they'd never let me out of my room again at Easter after I ran their car into a tree. It was only the tiniest little dent—hardly noticeable at all, but you'd have thought I'd run over Great-Aunt Cicely and squashed her flat, the way they went on. Besides, if you don't want people taking your motor-car without permission you should lock it away.'

Angela's eyes had opened wide, but before she could speak, she heard a male voice calling her name from the bottom of the garden, and she looked up to see George Simpson, who was just then passing behind the cottage. He stopped for a moment or two and was introduced to Barbara, who said:

'It's no use trying to get down to the beach now—the tide's too high.'

'Yes,' replied Simpson, 'I was halfway down the path before I realized that I had left my walk too late.'

'Or too early,' said Barbara. 'You can always try again this evening. There should be a bit of a beach by six o'clock, I think.'

He smiled.

'Tides and other forces of nature are always something of a difficulty for town-dwellers such as myself, who are used to being able to arrange matters to their own convenience in their daily lives,' he said. 'I have been here for almost two weeks now, and I still forget that I can't go where I please, when I please. Mother Nature is not to be trifled with.'

'That's true enough,' agreed Barbara. 'I got into a bit of trouble only this morning because of it.'

'Oh? I understand that you have been searching for a secret tunnel. Did you find it?'

'Yes,' said Barbara shortly. She glanced at Angela, uncertain as to whether she ought to tell him about it. For her part,

Angela was unsure as to whether she was permitted to tell Barbara that Mr. Simpson could be trusted, and why, and she hesitated. Simpson came to their rescue.

'You don't have to tell me about it if you don't want to,' he said to Barbara. 'I shall understand. A secret is no longer a secret if you tell other people about it.'

'Oh yes,' said Barbara. 'Then I shall keep it to myself if you don't mind too dreadfully.'

'Not at all,' he said, then took his leave and walked slowly back up the path.

'I say,' said Barbara, as she watched him retreat. 'He's rather jolly, isn't he? Is he a friend of yours?'

'Just an acquaintance,' said Angela, who was also watching him. 'I met him the other day. He is staying at the hotel.'

'I believe you like him,' said Barbara suddenly.

'What?'

'You do, don't you? You like him.'

'Of course I like him,' said Angela, slightly flustered. 'He's very nice. You saw for yourself.'

'That's not what I meant.'

'I have no idea what you're talking about. And by the way,' said Angela, deflecting attention from herself by going on the attack, 'what *exactly* were you doing to crash the Ellises' car into a tree?'

Barbara saw she had been caught.

'Oh, it was just an accident,' she said airily. 'Honestly, Angela, it could have happened to anyone. I mean, they should have cut that tree down years ago—Gerald said so himself. It was nothing, truly.'

'I see,' said Angela, and was about to press further, but Barbara forestalled her by escaping into the house. Angela followed her shortly afterwards, and they sat in separate rooms for the rest of the afternoon to avoid any conversation that might prove mutually awkward.

CHAPTER FOURTEEN

'HERE WE ARE!' announced Barbara brightly when Clifford Maynard opened the door to them the next morning. 'We've come to look for the treasure—and we mean to find it, too!'

Miss Trout greeted them with a beaming smile as they entered the drawing-room.

'Oh, I'm so glad you have come,' she said to Angela. 'The more help we have, the better—especially now that time is so short. Although, of course, I'm sure that Barbara would have done a fine job of searching the place by herself. Did you find the other end of the tunnel, yesterday, my dear?'

'Yes,' said Barbara, 'and I followed it all the way to the end, but there was nowhere to hide anything that I could see.' She and Angela had agreed that it would be better not to mention the small fact of Barbara's having escaped from the tunnel through the house.

'I have never been inside the tunnel myself,' said Miss Trout, 'as naturally I am too old for that kind of thing, but Clifford has explored it several times and never found the necklace either. I think, therefore, we must assume that it is not in the tunnel at all, and concentrate our searches on the house itself.'

'We thought it might be behind a secret panel somewhere,' said Barbara. 'This looks just the sort of house to have secret panels.'

'Yes, it does, doesn't it? I shouldn't be a bit surprised if there were one.'

'Don't you know of any for certain?' said Angela. 'I should have thought you of all people would have known of any concealed hiding-places that existed at Poldarrow Point.'

'I'm afraid not,' said Miss Trout. 'I have heard rumours, but never seen one myself.'

'Where shall we begin?' said Barbara, looking about her. 'Miss Trout, we thought we might start here in the drawing-room.'

'That sounds like an excellent plan,' said Clifford Maynard. 'Aunt Emily, we will search while you sit and rest.'

'But I should like to help,' said Miss Trout.

'Nonsense—I won't have you exerting yourself beyond your strength.'

'Oh, do let her help, Mr. Maynard,' said Barbara. 'Miss Trout won't do anything to tire herself out, will you, Miss Trout? After all, it's her necklace, and she has more of an interest in it than any of us, since it will allow her to stay here if we find it. Of course she ought to be in on it.'

Clifford relented.

'Very well,' he said, 'but I insist on your sitting down often, Aunt.'

'Naturally, Clifford,' said Miss Trout. 'I have no wish to exhaust myself.'

Barbara was already examining the chimney-breast for signs of a hidden cavity. Angela supposed she ought to make herself useful too, and began rapping on the walls. Clifford took the hint and pulled up the corner of the rug, looking for trap-doors. For some time nothing could be heard but the sound of knocking, tapping and banging as they listened for a tell-tale hollow sound that would indicate a void where something might be hidden. After an hour or so Barbara, who had been trying to pry off a section of skirting-board by the window, suddenly let out an exclamation of pain and sat back on her heels.

'Ouch!' she said. 'I've got a splinter in my finger.' She examined the offending extremity and squeezed at it. 'I can't get it out. Be a darling and do it for me, will you, Angela?'

Angela looked up from a rickety old writing-desk, where she had been searching for a secret drawer or compartment, and came over to oblige. Barbara wrinkled up her forehead in pain but made no sound as Angela poked the splinter out using a pin.

'Thanks,' she said, sucking her finger. 'Nothing in that desk, then?'

'It doesn't look like it,' said Angela. 'It's a pity—it looks like the perfect place to hide something.'

'I don't believe it's in here at all,' said Barbara. 'We've looked everywhere. You can stay here if you like, but I am going to try the dining-room.'

She was as good as her word. Five minutes later, Angela followed the sound of tapping and found Barbara knocking on the scroll-work of an antique mahogany dining-table. There was no doubting her dedication. Angela set to work herself. She began by looking behind all the pictures that hung around the walls. Several of them were large and heavy and she had to fetch Clifford to help her. They had just replaced the largest painting—a large Cornish landscape which hung over the fireplace and was dingy with soot and age—when something caught Angela's eye. She climbed down from the chair on which she had been standing and peered more closely at it, then tapped the wall. It sounded hollow.

'Have you found something?' said Barbara.

'I'm not sure,' said Angela. 'What do you think?' She pointed at a part of the wall just above the mantelpiece.

Barbara came forward and stared, but saw nothing except the dark wooden panelling.

'I can't see anything.'

'Run your hand over it,' said Angela. Barbara did so.

'Oh!' she said in surprise. 'This section is slightly loose.'

'Yes,' said Angela.

'So it is,' said Clifford, at their shoulder. 'Let me see.' He put his hand to the wall and felt around carefully, then held his hands out to indicate a rectangular shape of about eighteen inches by fifteen just above and to the right of the fireplace.

'That would be the perfect size for a secret panel or a safe,' said Barbara, thrilled.

'I wonder how it opens,' said Angela.

'Don't do anything yet,' said Barbara. 'I'm going to fetch Miss Trout.'

She ran out of the room and returned with the old lady, who looked as excited as anyone and said she did not want to miss anything.

'Allow me,' said Clifford commandingly. Angela made no comment but stood back to let him work. He poked at the panel for several minutes, then stood back and stared at it thoughtfully, chin in hand. He then repeated the performance, achieving exactly the same result.

'It won't open,' he said. He tried to grasp the edges of the panel with his finger-nails and pull it out, to no avail.

'I don't think that will work,' said Angela, 'but perhaps there is some kind of mechanism or spring that will open it.'

She moved forward and began examining the rest of the panelling above the mantelpiece, running her hands over it every so often.

'Hmm,' she said. She turned her attention to the wall to the right of the fireplace and below the panel, then stopped and prodded experimentally at something. There was a cracking sound. She prodded again, and the cracking sound was repeated as the rusty old mechanism strained to work after decades of inactivity.

'I think it may need a little help,' said Angela.

Her heart was beating loudly as she put her hand to the panel and pushed gently. Everyone gasped as, with some small persuasion, it turned inwards to reveal a dark recess. They all crowded forward to look.

'Let me see! Let me see!' said Barbara, pushing her way to the front. 'Is the necklace inside?'

She reached into the hole and felt around. Her face fell almost comically.

'Why, there's only an old key,' she said. She brought it out and held it up for them all to see. It was indeed a large, old key of the barrel type.

'Is there nothing else inside?' asked Miss Trout. Her nephew shook his head and she looked crestfallen.

'What a shame,' said Barbara, 'and just when we thought we'd found it, too.'

'I wonder what the key is for,' said Angela.

'Perhaps it fits the box with the necklace,' said Barbara, whose spirits were never dampened for long.

'I doubt it,' said Angela. 'It looks to me like the key to a door.'

'Give it to me,' said Barbara, 'and I'll go and try all the doors with it.'

'None of the doors in the house is missing a key,' said Miss Trout hurriedly.

Angela, taking pity on their hosts and the fate of their personal belongings if Barbara were to go rampaging unchecked around the house, shook her head and put the key in her pocket.

'No,' she said. 'Let's keep searching. We have already found one secret panel, so I shouldn't be a bit surprised if we were to find another.'

They all began tapping at the panelling but without success. There were no more hiding-places in the chimney-breast.

'I suppose it was too much to hope that there would be *two* secret panels in one wall,' said Barbara.

'No, but there may be another somewhere else,' said Angela.

'I'm going to look in the kitchen,' said Barbara.

'Wait a moment,' said Angela, seeing Barbara about to run off. 'There's no use in searching places at random. Preacher Dick lived here with his wife and presumably his servants. Would he have hidden an article of such great value in the kitchen, where anybody might have found it, do you think?'

'I suppose not,' conceded Barbara. 'Where would he have put it, then?'

'What about his bed-chamber?' suggested Clifford. 'That's where I should keep something of value that I didn't want anybody to find.'

'Yes, that's certainly possible,' said Angela. 'Who sleeps in that room now?'

'Nobody,' said Miss Trout. 'It's too big and draughty. Not comfortable at all, in fact.'

'Why don't we go and have a look?'

This was agreed to and they all trudged up the stairs, Barbara glancing fearfully about her and sticking close to Angela.

Clifford led them along the landing and stopped outside a door.

'This is the one,' he said and stepped back to allow them to pass.

They were in a large, old-fashioned bed-chamber in the centre of which stood an enormous four-posted bed. Barbara went to it and tested it.

'I should love to sleep in a bed like this!' she said.

'I'm afraid this one is very damp,' said Miss Trout. 'As you can see, some of the panes have come out of the window and the rain does tend to drive in, rather. Clifford and I prefer to sleep at the back of the house, away from the sea side, where it is less picturesque but much more sheltered.'

'This room must be above the drawing-room,' observed Angela.

'Yes, it is.'

'I should have expected it to be larger, since the next door is along at the other end of the landing.'

'These crooked old houses can be rather deceptive,' agreed Miss Trout. 'Shall we begin?'

They set to work. After a few minutes Clifford insisted that his aunt return downstairs and sit down, which she did without too much fuss. Angela suspected that the search was tiring her more than she would own. They were all absorbed silently in their task when there was a loud banging that made them all start, Barbara especially.

'Is that the shutter?' said Angela. 'It must have worked loose again.'

'Yes,' said Clifford, who was already making towards the door. 'I shall go and fix it.'

'Well,' said Angela, when he had gone, 'I am starting to think that this necklace is lost forever. It certainly doesn't seem to be in here.'

'Oh, don't say that!' said Barbara. 'It must be here somewhere, it must.'

But it looked as though Angela were right. Following a fruitless search of Preacher Dick's bed-chamber they were invited to stop for lunch, after which they returned to their quest, but by five o'clock, after they had searched the study, the day-room, and one or two of the unused rooms at the front of the house, they were forced to admit temporary defeat.

'We haven't searched the cellars or the attics yet,' said Angela. 'We shall have to come back another day.'

They left Poldarrow Point with many mutual commiserations at their lack of success and hopes that another day would bring better luck, and walked back to Kittiwake Cottage along the cliff top. It was very refreshing to be out in the open air after a day spent indoors and they laughed as the strong breeze blew them about and pushed them towards home.

'What a shame we didn't find the treasure,' said Barbara as they arrived at their own front door. 'I was so certain it would be behind that secret panel.'

'Yes, I was rather excited myself,' said Angela, 'but all we found was that old key. I wonder where it is from.'

'May I see it?' said Barbara. Angela reached into her pocket and handed it to Barbara.

'A hot bath is required, I think, after all that dust and dirt,' said Angela as they entered the house, 'and then I believe I shall have an early night.'

She stopped to pick up a pile of letters from a little table by the door and opened the first.

'Mrs. Uppingham has written in reply to my letter thanking her for the use of her house,' she said. 'She mentions Miss Trout.'

'What does she say?' asked Barbara, who was examining the key closely for clues.

'Oh, just that she is interested to hear that we have made her acquaintance, since she is reputed to be something of a recluse and Mrs. Uppingham herself has been curious to meet her. I wonder—oh!'

She broke off as she saw the next letter.

'What is it?' said Barbara, looking up.

'Look,' said Angela. She held out the envelope to Barbara, whose eyes widened at the sight.

'Why, it's another anonymous letter!' she said.

CHAPTER FIFTEEN

THEY STARED AT the envelope for a moment.

'Go on, open it,' said Barbara.

Angela did so. It contained a single sheet of paper, and they read it together. It said:

'*Dere Mrs. Marchmont,*

Stay away from Poldarrow Point if you value yor life. Ther is nuthing for you there.'

'Is that the best they can do?' said Barbara in disgust. 'I must say, if I were to take to writing threatening letters I should jolly well make a much better fist of it than that.'

'All the same,' said Angela, 'it is not pleasant to think that somebody wishes one harm. Perhaps that is the purpose of the letters: to unsettle rather than to frighten. After all, one does not like to have one's holiday spoilt. Perhaps whoever sent it counted on my leaving in disgust rather than fear.'

'Yes, but that theory doesn't work in the case of Miss Trout, who has nowhere to go even if she did want to leave.'

'True,' said Angela. 'Well, then, I don't know the answer. Marthe,' she called.

Marthe emerged from the sitting-room, an inquiring look on her face.

'Yes, *madame*?' she said.

'Here is another one of those letters, this time sent to me,' said Angela. 'What do you think?'

Marthe took the letter.

'Yes, it is the same person,' she said. 'The same writing, you see, and the same scent. What does she mean by it?'

'She?' said Barbara. 'Were they sent by a woman?'

'It appears so,' said Angela.

'Then who could it have been?'

'Well, we can draw at least one conclusion from it: that it must have been sent by somebody who knows of our connection with Miss Trout.'

'Someone we know, then?'

'Not necessarily,' said Angela. 'Tregarrion is a small place, and anybody might have overheard me talking about it to Mrs. Walters, for example, or even have seen me walking from Kittiwake Cottage to Poldarrow Point. The cliff path is very exposed to view. Thank you, Marthe.'

'Hmph,' said Barbara. 'There would be no need for whoever it was to eavesdrop on your conversation, at any rate. Mrs. Walters is a frightful old gossip and will cheerfully broadcast any secret one might care to tell her to everyone in Tregarrion—probably within the hour, in fact. She's bound to have told at least twenty people that we were going to tea with Miss Trout.'

'That is true,' admitted Angela. 'Well, then, that probably doesn't help us to narrow down our search much.'

'I shall pump her when I see her,' said Barbara. 'I'll find out who knew.'

'You'd better not,' said Angela. 'You'll give the game away and everybody will know our business. Let me do it. I don't suppose it will come to much, though.'

Barbara ran to look out of the window.

'There they are, in the back garden,' she said. 'Do let's have them round now. We can all have cocktails.'

'*We* can have cocktails,' said Angela severely. '*You* may have a glass of lemonade if you like.'

Barbara made a face and Angela went outside to speak to the Walters' over the fence and ask them round for drinks. Mrs. Walters was only too happy to oblige.

'They are coming round in ten minutes,' said Angela. 'Now, listen: I am going to tell them about my anonymous note, but I shan't mention the other ones, and you must keep quiet about them too. We don't want everybody finding out about them.'

'All right,' said Barbara. A thought struck her. 'I say,' she said. 'I wonder if Mrs. Walters sent them herself.'

'Why should she do that? What could she have to gain?'

'I don't know,' said Barbara. 'But she seems the type—you know, an old woman with nothing to do but stir things up among her neighbours. Perhaps I shall ask her.'

'You shall do no such thing,' said Angela in alarm.

'Of course I was joking,' said Barbara. 'What do you take me for? No—don't answer that.'

'Just be on your best behaviour,' said Angela.

Their visitors duly arrived, Mrs. Walters as garrulous and Helen as subdued in her mother's presence as ever. A sea fret had begun to descend and the air was growing chilly, so they decided to stay indoors.

'What will you have?' said Barbara brightly. 'A martini or a fizz? Or just with tonic? We always have *gallons* of gin at home, because you know Angela simply can't bear to be without it morning, noon and night—as a matter of fact, she even keeps a glass of it by her bedside in case she wakes up in the middle of the night with a raging thirst. Her grandmother was Irish, you know, and used to swear by it.'

'Go and get the glasses, Barbara,' said Angela in flinty tones.

'Such a queer sense of humour the young people have these days, don't they?' said Mrs. Walters. 'I confess that I can't keep up with half of what they say.'

Helen looked as though she were trying not to smile as she sat down gingerly on the most uncomfortable seat in the room. Barbara flashed her a wicked grin as she returned with the glasses and politely announced that Marthe would bring the drinks shortly.

'Oh,' she said as she happened to glance out of the window. 'It's that funny Swiss man. He must have been prospecting again.'

Everyone looked up. Mr. Donati was walking past the house, carrying his odd assortment of baggage and equipment as usual. He turned his head and saw them all watching, and bowed politely before passing on his way.

'He is certainly dedicated to his task,' said Mrs. Walters.

'Oh yes,' said Barbara. 'I met him down on the beach yesterday and he said he was looking for metal ore. What was it now? Copper, tin and something else, he said.'

'Tungsten?' suggested Angela.

'Something like that,' said Barbara. 'There are lots of mines in Cornwall, aren't there? He said that any metal he found might be worth many thousands of pounds. Of course, he didn't expect to find it on the beach. He was just taking a breather, he said. Didn't you see him yesterday, Helen? He was there at the same time as you.'

'No,' said Helen, 'I didn't. I must have been too absorbed in my bathe.'

Marthe brought in the drinks and poured them out. Barbara gave a *moue* of disgust at her lemonade. Mrs. Walters took a doubtful sip of her martini.

'I rarely take cocktails,' she said, 'but one must be open to new experiences, mustn't one? Especially in such a gay place as this.'

'Mother has even been dancing,' said Helen.

'Indeed?' said Angela, trying unsuccessfully to picture the staid Mrs. Walters doing the Charleston or the Foxtrot.

Mrs. Walters laughed archly.

'Oh yes,' she said. 'We were at the hotel yesterday evening, and Mr. Dorsey was so kind as to ask me to dance—and then, if you'll believe it, Mr. Simpson did too! I was quite fluttered.

Such handsome young men! I have not done such a thing for many years. Helen, of course, never dances.'

Helen looked as though she would have liked to dance, but said nothing.

'As a matter of fact, I'm surprised that Mr. Dorsey has enough energy to dance, he stays up so late,' went on Mrs. Walters, 'but of course the young can do anything without suffering for it later. Don't drink too much of that, dear,' she said to her daughter. 'You know it will give you a headache and I shall almost certainly need you tonight. I feel one of my turns beginning.'

'Perhaps you should stop drinking too, then,' said Barbara. Mrs. Walters pretended not to hear.

'How do you know that Mr. Dorsey stays up late?' said Angela.

'Not just Mr. Dorsey, his wife too,' said Mrs. Walters. 'They are quite the pair of night-owls. I have seen them returning to the hotel at four or five o'clock in the morning. I sleep badly, you know, and so often get up in the night. Who knows what they find to do in the early hours? I dare say they frequent night-clubs and suchlike. Are you an *habituée* yourself?'

'Of night-clubs?' said Angela. 'Not at present. I am under doctor's orders and this last week have been going to bed at nine prompt. The sea air is very health-giving, but spending the day outside does tire one out.'

'Have you been getting out and about?' said Mrs. Walters. 'Mr. Simpson said he met you in the village yesterday.'

'Yes,' said Angela. 'He found me looking at some of the paintings down by the harbour.'

'Oh yes! Aren't they simply delightful? I have bought two already and I shouldn't be surprised if I were tempted to buy another before we return home. Such a mastery of light and shade! The blues and the reds! I have never seen anything quite like it.'

Angela, who had been about to comment disparagingly on the glaring over-abundance of primary colours, closed her mouth with a snap and merely nodded politely.

'And how was Miss Trout when you saw her today?' went on Mrs. Walters.

'Very well,' replied Angela, 'but I had rather a disturbing experience when I arrived home.'

'Oh?' said Mrs. Walters, sensing that she was about to be thrown a choice tidbit of gossip.

'Yes. I received an anonymous letter.'

'What? An anonymous letter? From whom?'

'Well, that's just it—I don't know,' said Angela.

'Of course, how silly of me. But what did it say?'

'Have a look for yourself,' said Angela. She brought out the letter and handed it to Mrs. Walters, who applied her glasses to the end of her nose and peered at it eagerly. Helen came and read it over her mother's shoulder. They both looked up at the same time with equally blank expressions.

'But what does it mean?' said Helen. 'Who wants you to keep away from Poldarrow Point, and why?'

'Does Miss Trout know about this?' asked Mrs. Walters.

'Not yet,' said Angela. 'I only received the letter a few minutes ago, when I got home.'

'But you must report it to the police. Whoever wrote it has made a threat against your life.'

'Oh, do you think so?' said Helen. 'I didn't read it like that. I thought it was a warning.'

'Of course it's a warning, you silly girl,' said her mother. 'The writer is saying that if Mrs. Marchmont persists in visiting Poldarrow Point, then he will kill her.'

Helen went pink.

'Helen is right,' said Angela, taking pity on the girl. 'It might mean one of several things. As you say, it might be a direct threat by the writer to cause me harm, or it could be a genuine warning from a well-wisher to tell me that my life is in danger for some unknown reason.'

'But that's just silly,' said Barbara, who was not the most tactful of people. 'Nobody could possibly imagine that Miss Trout or Mr. Maynard were capable of causing harm to anyone. Why, it's perfectly obvious that the letter is a threat, not a warning.'

'You must find out who sent it,' said Mrs. Walters. 'Go to the police. They will investigate.'

'It may be possible to solve the mystery without bringing in the police,' said Angela, 'but for that I will need your help.'

'*My* help?' said Mrs. Walters, surprised.

'Yes. Whoever sent the letter knew that I have visited Poldarrow Point. Now, I am a visitor to this place and therefore a relative stranger, and yet *somebody* knew of my acquaintance with Miss Trout. You, for example.'

'I? Are you suggesting that *I* sent the letter?' said Mrs. Walters, preparing to be outraged.

'Of course not,' said Angela hurriedly. 'You misunderstand me. I merely meant that as you have a large number of friends in Tregarrion, it is possible that you may have mentioned it in passing to someone. I have no friends in the area myself, but you know everyone here, and they all come to you as they know that you are always the first to hear any news of importance.'

Mrs. Walters looked slightly mollified and Angela went on artfully, 'Naturally, your elevated position in society here also means that people are more likely to tell you things. It is possible, therefore, that you hold in your hands the clue to the identity of the sender of this letter—perhaps even without realizing it.'

'I assure you, nobody has confessed any such thing to me,' said Mrs. Walters.

'No, I didn't mean that, exactly. I merely meant that someone may have unwittingly given himself away. Let us say, for example, that you happen to mention in passing to Mr. A that your neighbour, Mrs. Marchmont, has become friendly with Miss Trout and Mr. Maynard of Poldarrow Point. If Mr. A is interested in this fact for secret purposes of his own, then you might be struck by the undue interest he seems to be taking in what you are telling him.'

'Ah, I see what you mean,' said Mrs. Walters, pleased at Angela's subtle flattery. 'Now, let me think. Whom have I been talking to lately? I know I mentioned it to Mr. Simpson, as he was talking about having first seen you on the cliff path near Poldarrow Point. And Mrs. Adams knows, because she was there at the time. And the Dorseys, of course. Did I speak about it to Colonel Renton? I know he recognized you from the newspapers and was asking me about you, so I may well have done. And—'

She stopped with a look of confusion, and Angela guessed that she had just realized and was embarrassed by the number of people she had told.

'In a small place such as this, everybody knows everybody else's business,' she said with a smile.

'Yes, indeed!' said Mrs. Walters. 'It's quite unavoidable. But of the people I have spoken to recently, none of them that I can remember showed any out-of-the-ordinary interest in your doings. And anyway, surely you don't suspect any of our friends? I should have thought that the culprit was far more likely to be someone local.'

'Perhaps,' said Angela.

'What do you intend to do about it?'

'Nothing, at present. I shall wait and see if I receive any more before I decide which course of action to take.'

'Mark my words, the letter was sent by some local tradesman who has some complaint against Miss Trout and wants to do her a bad turn,' said Mrs. Walters.

'I dare say you are right,' said Angela. 'I shall put it out of my mind for now. But you will tell me, won't you, if you remember something that might give a clue?'

'Of course I shall,' said Mrs. Walters.

Marthe came in just then with more drinks and the conversation turned to other matters.

'Well,' said Barbara after their guests had left, 'what do you think? I still say she could have done it herself.'

'I don't think so,' said Angela. 'They both looked puzzled enough when they saw the letter.'

'She's obviously told everyone in Tregarrion about you, so that doesn't help narrow it down.'

'Yes.'

'And now she's going to tell everyone in Tregarrion about your anonymous letter,' said Barbara. 'We should have thought of that before.'

'I did think of it,' said Angela, 'but decided on reflection that there was no harm in it. Perhaps it might even help.'

'How?'

'I don't know, but it might spur the letter-writer into some sort of action.'

Barbara looked doubtful.

'Well, I hope we haven't frightened whoever it is into doing anything dangerous,' she said. 'We don't want anyone to get hurt.'

'Don't be silly,' said Angela. 'Nobody is going to get hurt.'

CHAPTER SIXTEEN

B Y THE NEXT morning, the sea fret had turned into a settled drizzle, to the disappointment of Barbara, who wanted to bathe, and for the first time they were forced to take breakfast indoors. They were just finishing when a note arrived for Angela. She glanced at the envelope, and saw that it was addressed in an unfamiliar hand. She tore it open.

'Is it another anonymous letter?' said Barbara.

'No, it's from Miss Trout,' said Angela. 'Good gracious!' she said, as she read it.

'What is it?' said Barbara, bouncing up and down with impatience.

'Mr. Maynard has been attacked!' said Angela.

'Attacked?'

'Yes—in the night, it seems.'

'Who did it?'

'They don't know. Miss Trout just mentions a "mysterious assailant". She wants us to go there at once.'

'Didn't I tell you?' said Barbara. 'You see what's happened? Mrs. Walters has gone away and told all her friends about the letter and one of them has taken fright and attacked Mr. Maynard.'

'Nonsense,' said Angela. 'Why, if the attack was anything to do with the letter then surely the target would have been me, not Mr. Maynard. What has he to do with the matter? I don't believe there's any connection at all.'

'Oh, but there must be,' said Barbara. 'It's far too much of a coincidence for there not to be.'

Fifteen minutes later they were walking along the cliff path towards Poldarrow Point.

'Is Mr. Maynard all right, do you think?' asked Barbara.

'I don't know,' said Angela.

'I wonder whether he was stabbed or shot? Is he dead, do you think? Or perhaps he has been beaten to a bloody pulp and will have to take his food from a spoon, and Miss Trout will have to nurse him until he fades gently away.'

'Barbara, please,' said Angela.

Barbara closed her mouth, but continued the bloodthirsty speculation happily in her head until they arrived at Poldarrow Point.

They found Clifford Maynard in the drawing-room, reclining on a divan, with Miss Trout sitting by him and patting his hand sympathetically.

'Oh, Mrs. Marchmont, I am so glad you have come!' the old lady exclaimed. 'Poor Clifford has had quite an awful time of it.'

Clifford moaned feebly. He certainly looked in a bad way. He had a black eye and a graze on one cheek, and wore a bandage round his head. He dabbed occasionally at his face with a cold compress.

'Don't you need a doctor, Mr. Maynard?' asked Angela. 'Barbara can fetch one if you like.'

'No, no, don't worry about me,' said Clifford with a martyred air. 'I shall be quite all right. Just a few bruises here and there. There's no need for a doctor.'

'Are you quite certain?' said Angela.

'I've tried to persuade him, but he won't hear of it,' said Miss Trout.

'An old groom of ours was kicked in the head by a horse once,' said Barbara, 'and his injuries looked just like yours. He said there was nothing wrong with him and refused to see a doctor, and went back to work quite cheerfully that afternoon.'

'You see?' said Clifford to his aunt. 'What did I—'

'A week later he dropped down dead,' went on Barbara.

'There!' said Miss Trout to Clifford in triumph. 'One ought always to see a doctor for a head injury. You don't want to meet the same fate as Barbara's groom, now, do you?'

'Of course, it might not have been the horse that did it,' said Barbara reflectively. 'He was ninety-three, after all, and they *said* it was a heart attack that carried him off.'

'What exactly happened to you, Mr. Maynard?' asked Angela.

Clifford put on an indignant expression and struggled to sit up.

'I have been brutally assaulted, Mrs. Marchmont,' he said. 'And in my own home, too!'

On further questioning, it emerged that early that morning, at about four o'clock, Clifford had suddenly woken up, sure he had heard a noise downstairs, and had decided to investigate. On creeping down the stairs and into the hall he had heard the noise again, coming from the drawing-room. Picking up his walking-stick as a weapon, he opened the door carefully—but unfortunately for him, he had forgotten that the hinges needed oiling, and it squeaked loudly. Whoever was in the room went silent.

'Who goes there?' called Clifford, plucking up all his courage, but almost before he had finished the sentence, a shadowy figure had hurled itself on top of him and thrown him violently to the floor. Clifford had struggled mightily and put up a valiant fight, but his assailant had caught him by surprise and thus had the advantage. The thief had belaboured him soundly about the head and then jumped up and escaped.

'How did he get out?' asked Angela.

'Through the window,' said Clifford, waving a hand weakly in that direction. 'I imagine that is how he got in, too. He must have left it open in order to give himself a quick means of escape.'

'It was very brave of you to tackle him alone,' said Miss Trout. 'You ought to have come and fetched me first.'

Clifford did not look as though he appreciated this doubtful compliment. He raised the compress to his eye and did not reply.

'Have you called the police?' said Barbara. 'What did they say?'

'No, we have not,' said Miss Trout, 'and we have no intention of doing so.'

'Yokels!' said Clifford, sitting up suddenly. 'I want nothing to do with them.'

He fell back again against the sofa cushions and dabbed gingerly at his wounds.

'Clifford had a rather unfortunate experience a few weeks ago with some young men who had come down from Oxford for the holidays,' said Miss Trout. 'They had just finished their exams and were—in somewhat high spirits, let us say.'

'Delinquents!' said Clifford. 'Criminals, in fact.'

'What happened?' asked Barbara.

'They stole my hat from my very head while I was taking my morning walk into Tregarrion, and placed it on the statue of Queen Victoria that stands in the market square,' said Clifford.

'I say!' said Barbara in delight.

'It was not funny,' said Clifford with dignity. 'They knocked me to the ground in order to remove it. I might have been seriously hurt.'

Barbara attempted a solemn expression and almost succeeded.

'The police, I am afraid to say, were inclined to take a lenient view of the affair,' said Miss Trout.

'They laughed when I said I wanted to press charges,' said Clifford. 'There was one in particular—a red-headed sergeant, who was most disrespectful. If *that* is how the law is enforced in this area, then I shall do without the help of the police, thank you.'

'But what was the man doing in the house?' asked Angela. 'Was he searching for the necklace, do you think?'

'I think he must have been,' said Miss Trout.

'Did you hear the altercation yourself?'

'No,' said Miss Trout. 'Or perhaps I did, but did not notice it. I often hear noises in the house at night—especially recently, but I always assumed that they were due to the wind blowing in a particular direction at this time of year. I'm afraid, therefore, that poor Clifford had to face the thief all on his own.'

'Oh, Angela,' said Barbara, 'we *must* find the necklace soon. Someone else is after it and we can't let them get it first, we simply can't. Angela has had an anonymous letter too, you know,' she went on to Miss Trout.

'What?' said Clifford and Miss Trout at the same time. Barbara nodded.

'Yes,' she said. 'It said that she would be killed if she came to Poldarrow Point again.'

'That's not *quite* what it said,' said Angela.

'Was it the same as the other letters?' asked Clifford. He looked almost cross.

'Yes,' said Angela. 'It was certainly from the same person, and said much the same thing as before.'

'I see,' said Clifford, and relapsed into a moody silence.

'There must be a connection between the letters and the attack on Mr. Maynard,' said Barbara, 'and even if there isn't, I think we ought to have another look for the necklace.'

'I think you might be right,' said Angela. She was thinking hard. Who was the mysterious attacker? Could it be Edgar Valencourt, making an attempt to find Marie Antoinette's necklace in the dead of night? If so, had he been here before? Miss Trout said she often heard noises in the night. Perhaps he had been here already, searching the house carefully night after night until finally his luck ran out and he was caught in the act by Clifford.

'I'm going to search the kitchen,' said Barbara. 'Are you coming, Angela?'

'I shall come too,' said Miss Trout. 'We shall have to do without Clifford today, I fear.'

'Oh yes,' said Clifford. 'My head aches and I can hardly think. Shall you be able to manage alone, Aunt Emily?'

'I think so, dear,' said Miss Trout. 'I shall call you if any difficulties arise.'

'She won't be alone,' said Barbara. 'She will have us.'

They went out, leaving Clifford lying in a dramatic attitude on the divan and groaning with great feeling.

CHAPTER SEVENTEEN

I F THE NECKLACE isn't in the house, then where can it be?' said Barbara the next day. Their second search had proved just as unsuccessful as the first and she was very grumpy about it, feeling somehow as though the necklace were defying her by remaining firmly hidden despite their efforts.

'I don't know,' said Angela, frowning abstractedly over her post. She had received a letter from Marguerite Harrison, expressing her best wishes for Angela's quick recovery while at the same time berating her for cancelling her trip to Kent.

'What are you doing today?' said Barbara.

'Apparently I promised to play tennis with the Dorseys this afternoon,' said Angela. 'Or, at least, that is what Mrs. Walters tells me.'

Barbara wrinkled her nose.

'That sounds awfully dull,' she said. 'I don't think I'll join you.'

Since nobody had invited her anyway, Angela made no objection, and a short while later Barbara went out on mysterious errands of her own. Angela was glad of this, as she wanted to speak to Inspector Simpson in private. Accordingly, she walked down to the Hotel Splendide to find him. He was not on the terrace, but when she asked at the desk he was swiftly located and came out to meet her. He greeted her as an old friend, and invited her to take a stroll along the lower promenade.

The sun had re-emerged after the rain of the day before, and the day promised to be a warm one. As they walked down the steep steps, Angela related to him the results of their search of Poldarrow Point, and he nodded.

'It was only to be expected,' he said. 'Something that has been hidden for so long is unlikely to be found so easily. Do you intend to keep trying?'

'I suppose so,' said Angela. 'It's hardly how I expected to be spending my holiday, but Miss Trout is so kind that it is very difficult to refuse her—especially since she is clearly so reluctant to ask.'

Simpson laughed at her rueful face.

'The dangers of an active conscience!' he said.

'Yes,' said Angela. 'But it's not just that. Barbara is still keen, too, and someone needs to keep an eye on her or she will carry all before her. She is my responsibility, I suppose, and believe me when I say that nobody deserves to have Barbara inflicted upon them when she is in the full flow of one of her enthusiasms.'

Where is Miss Barbara this morning, by the way?' he said.

'I have no idea,' said Angela, 'but I shouldn't be surprised if she has gone to look for more secret passages. She has an insatiable appetite for mischief.'

Simpson laughed.

'And she looks a sharp one, too,' he said. 'When I saw her in the garden the other day as I was passing I dared not ask to see the anonymous letters—which, of course, were the real purpose of my visit.'

'Yes, I guessed as much,' said Angela. 'That is why I brought them with me today.'

When they reached the promenade at the bottom of the steps they sat down on a seat and she took the small sheaf of papers from her pocket and handed them to him. He read them through carefully, then handed them back to her.

'Interesting,' he said. 'What did you make of them?'

'Not much, myself,' said Angela. 'I'm afraid all the credit must go to my maid, Marthe, who knew immediately by the style of the writing and the scent of the paper that they were written by a woman.'

'A woman, eh?' he said. 'Yes, I suppose the handwriting is more feminine than masculine.'

'Then they could not have been written by Edgar Valencourt,' said Angela. 'Unless, of course, he has a female accomplice. His wife, perhaps, or a sister.'

'He is not married,' said Simpson.

'But do you know that for certain? Pardon me, but you seem to know very little about him, and people do tend to marry as a rule.'

Simpson considered the point.

'He was said to have had a wife once, but she died,' he said. 'We have always assumed that he did not remarry, but of course he might well have done. I am not married myself, so I dare say I look at life from the bachelor's point of view and therefore assume that Valencourt is working alone. There you have the advantage over me, Mrs. Marchmont, since you can see things from the wife's side.'

'You couldn't be more wrong,' said Angela, before she could stop herself. There was an under-current of bitterness in her tone and he looked up sharply.

'I beg your pardon,' he said. 'I didn't mean to offend you. I had no idea you were a widow.'

'You didn't offend me,' she said, 'and I'm not a widow.'

'Then—' he hesitated.

'My husband and I parted company some time ago,' she said. There was an uncomfortable pause. Then she smiled. 'But this is all quite beside the point,' she said. 'I have not yet told you about the latest letter.'

She brought out the anonymous note that had been sent to herself and handed it to him. He read it with concern.

'So you have received one too,' he said. 'This is a rather worrying development.'

Angela nodded.

'I must confess I was not convinced initially by your view that the writer of these letters was dangerous,' she said, 'but subsequent events have given me pause for thought.'

'What do you mean?'

Angela told him about the attack on Clifford Maynard and his frown deepened.

'Was he badly hurt?' he asked.

'Not as badly as he wanted us to think,' said Angela. 'I believe he was rather enjoying the attention, and so perhaps exaggerated his injuries somewhat. He refused to have a doctor.'

'I see. And what are the police doing to find the attacker?'

'Nothing,' said Angela. 'Mr. Maynard would not have them called.'

'Why not?'

'It appears that there was some disagreement with the local constabulary a few weeks ago in the matter of a stolen hat,' she said.

His eyes twinkled.

'Perhaps that is for the best,' he said. 'Things are already complicated enough as it is.'

'Well, I have told *you* now,' said Angela, 'so at least the police do know about it.'

'Yes we do,' he said, 'and I shall add it to my notes this evening.'

'Have you had any more luck in finding Valencourt?'

'None at all, I'm afraid,' he said. 'We are very much hamstrung by the fact that we have no accurate description of him. Up to now his victims have only seen him in disguise, and he has disappeared from the scene before anybody has been able to unmask him. He could be tall or short, fat or thin, bearded or clean-shaven—we simply don't know.'

'That is certainly a disadvantage,' agreed Angela. She seemed to be thinking about something, and it caught his attention.

'Do you have any suspicions yourself?' he asked, with a sharp glance at her.

'Not exactly,' said Angela slowly, 'but it did occur to me to wonder why the Dorseys have been staying out all night recently.'

'Now, that is interesting,' said Simpson. 'Who told you that?'

'Mrs. Walters. She has seen them on several occasions returning to the hotel at about four or five o'clock in the morning. She assumed they had been out dancing, but Tregarrion is still a small town and I don't believe it has any night-clubs.'

'No, it doesn't. Perhaps they have been going into Penzance.'

'Perhaps,' said Angela. 'What do you know about the Dorseys, Mr. Simpson?'

'Only what I have learned from themselves since I arrived,' he said. 'They are from London and are here on holiday. I don't know what Dorsey does, but they seem to live comfortably. They have not exactly put themselves out to make friends, and such as they do have appear to have been procured for them by the indefatigable Mrs. Walters, who insists on knowing everyone's business and forcing people to be sociable.'

'That's true enough,' said Angela, laughing. 'She can be rather tiresome.'

'But through her I have met you, so she can't be all bad,' he said gallantly.

'I am supposed to play tennis with the Dorseys and Helen Walters this afternoon,' said Angela, shaking her head at the compliment. 'Mrs. Walters has arranged it all for us. I shall have to see what I can discover.'

'Three women and one man?'

'Yes. It's not ideal, but Mr. Dorsey has promised to give the opposing side a two-game head start in each set. Is Valencourt a dab at tennis, do you happen to know?'

'I have no idea,' said Simpson with a laugh. 'So that's your little theory, is it? Dorsey as the fugitive from justice? I suppose it's always possible that Valencourt is now disguising himself as a respectable married man. Perhaps I shall come down and watch you this afternoon, in that case.'

'Do,' said Angela, 'and you shall see exactly what happens when a middle-aged woman who is completely out of practice tries to remember how to return a back-hand. I only hope the hotel has plenty of spare balls.'

He laughed and offered her his arm, and they strolled off amicably.

CHAPTER EIGHTEEN

AFTER LUNCH, MRS. Marchmont picked up her tennis racquet and set off to the hotel as agreed to meet the Dorseys, stopping to call for the Walters' on the way. Somewhat to her surprise, only Mrs. Walters accompanied her, since Helen was feeling unwell and had asked to remain at home.

'So inconvenient when I need her to hand,' said Mrs. Walters. 'What if I am taken ill myself? Who is to look after *me*?'

'Oh, but you have been so well lately,' said Angela encouragingly. 'You told me yourself that the sea air had made you feel much better. I am sure you won't need any assistance.'

'Let us hope not,' said Mrs. Walters. 'I should be quite lost without my daughter, Mrs. Marchmont. She is all the world to me. Such a pity that *you* have no-one of your own to look after you when you reach the age of infirmity—although perhaps your god-daughter might be persuaded.'

Angela suppressed a smile as she tried to imagine Barbara as the patient and constant companion of a demanding old woman.

'I think that if it ever comes to that, I shall hire myself a nurse,' she said. 'I don't think Barbara would take too kindly to the idea of spending half her life attending to the whims of a tiresome invalid. And I should certainly never ask it of her. What—demand that she give up her youth—all fun, and dancing, and laughter, and love—to attend to an old woman who can afford to pay for help? Why, I shouldn't dream of it!'

Mrs. Walters had no reply to make and Angela, who felt sorry for Helen, hoped the shot had gone home.

They reached the hotel and found the Dorseys standing by the tennis court, talking to George Simpson.

'My dears,' exclaimed Mrs. Walters, 'I'm afraid we are one short this afternoon. Helen finds herself very unwell today and unable to get up. She asks to be excused.'

'Oh, what a shame, poor darling,' said Harriet Dorsey in her usual uninterested tones.

'It looks as though the doubles match is off, then,' said Lionel Dorsey, 'unless you'd both care to take me on at once.'

Mrs. Walters had a better idea.

'Do you play, Mr. Simpson?' she said.

Simpson looked surprised.

'Sometimes,' he said. 'When the occasion presents itself.'

'Well, now's your chance,' said Lionel Dorsey.

Simpson took little persuading and went off to change into his whites. He returned a few minutes later, and Angela was surprised at the transformation in him. She had not supposed him to be particularly athletic, but he looked completely at home in his tennis gear, displaying a suppleness and energy that she had not noticed in him before. He took a few practice swipes with his racquet and declared himself ready to be beaten, and they all went off to the court.

Angela found herself paired with Lionel Dorsey and play began. As she had suspected, the Dorseys were excellent players and she had to concentrate very hard to keep up with their pace. The real revelation, however, was George Simpson, who astonished everyone with his prowess, serving ace after ace and returning volley after volley. He seemed to be everywhere at once, diving for shots that Harriet had missed and slamming the ball over the net faster than the eye could blink. The result was a foregone conclusion and the game was over in two sets.

'You never said you could play tennis,' said Lionel Dorsey accusingly, as he shook hands somewhat reluctantly with Simpson. 'I believe you kept it quiet on purpose.'

'I did play a little at Cambridge,' admitted Simpson apologetically, 'but it was a long time ago, and I don't play anywhere near as much these days. I certainly didn't mean to show off.'

'Of course you weren't showing off,' said Mrs. Walters, who had been watching the play with interest, 'but what a talent! Why, I have never seen anything like it! You ought to play in competitions. Helen will be so sorry to have missed it.'

They stopped for a rest, then resumed play. This time Simpson was paired with Angela, who felt herself to be the weakest player of them all and was glad of the support. Now the opposing sides were much more evenly matched—so much so that Angela began to suspect that Simpson was deliberately lowering his game, either in deference to her or in order to avoid irritating Lionel Dorsey, who had not taken kindly to being beaten by the older man and appeared to be harbouring a grudge. Angela concentrated on keeping her end up—not an easy task when playing against Harriet, who had a tricky left-handed serve—and was pleased when she managed to return several difficult shots and win two games in a row.

'Good work!' said Simpson admiringly. 'That'll settle them.'

Despite his words, this time the match went to three sets and Angela and Simpson were just edged out by the Dorseys, thanks to a stunning back-hand shot from Harriet, which whizzed past them and ended the game.

'What a beautiful shot, Harriet!' cried Mrs. Walters from her seat. Harriet looked almost pleased for once, and shook hands good-naturedly with her opponents. Lionel was cock-a-hoop at having made up the lost ground, and was all for a best-of-three, but the ladies demurred, so they all went and had cold drinks on the hotel terrace, complimenting each other on their play. Mrs. Walters was particularly fulsome in her praise, although it was clear from her remarks that she knew little of the game. It was evident to all, however, which of them was the best player. Mr. Simpson disclaimed all extraordinary compliments and insisted that his partners had done at least as much work. Angela was by now pretty certain that he had thrown the last match, but said nothing. She wanted to remain on good terms with the Dorseys, as she was anxious to find out more about them.

'You shall all have to play again very soon,' said Mrs. Walters, 'and next time perhaps Helen will be well enough to join in.'

Harriet Dorsey had relapsed into her usual indifference and merely nodded as she leaned forward to allow her husband to light a cigarette for her. She drew in a mouthful of smoke and Angela noticed that she held the cigarette in her left hand, between fingertips that ended in red-painted nails.

'Oh yes,' said Angela, 'we must do it again. How long are you staying at the hotel, Mrs. Dorsey?'

Harriet shrugged.

'I don't know,' she said. 'Perhaps another week or two. Lionel's business is slow in summer so we can please ourselves.'

'Oh? What is your business, Mr. Dorsey?'

'Imports and exports,' said Lionel shortly. He seemed to realize that he had sounded unduly blunt, and went on, 'I deal mostly with the Italians and the Greeks, and they all take the summer off.'

'And so you can too,' said Mrs. Walters, with a little trill of laughter. 'It must be such a relief for you to take a well-earned rest once a year,' she went on. 'I always find that by the time May comes round, one feels the need for a holiday growing ever stronger, and when the time finally arrives, it is so delightful to breathe in the sea air and let one's cares slip from one's shoulders.'

Angela glanced at the plump and well cared-for Mrs. Walters and wondered uncharitably what cares the woman could possibly have. She turned her head and saw Mr. Simpson looking at her with an amused expression, and had the oddest feeling that he knew what she was thinking. He nodded almost imperceptibly, and she took her cue.

'Yes, I was hoping for a nice rest, myself,' she said brightly, 'but this affair of the letters has quite ruined any hopes I might have had of a quiet holiday.'

Mrs. Walters nodded sympathetically and the Dorseys looked up—warily, Angela thought.

'What's that?' said Mr. Dorsey. 'What letters?'

'Oh, didn't Mrs. Walters tell you?' said Angela. 'I received an anonymous letter a day or two ago, which warned me not to go to Poldarrow Point again or my life would be in danger.'

'How extraordinary,' said Harriet. 'Why should anybody send you a letter like that? And who was it?'

'I have no idea,' replied Angela, 'but I imagine it was the same person who has sent several similar letters to Miss Trout herself.'

'Really?' said Mrs. Walters in surprise. 'You never mentioned that before.'

'I wasn't sure whether I ought to make it public,' said Angela, 'but now I have reached the conclusion that the more people who know about it, the better. Some of the letters were quite threatening, you see, and I thought it might be a good idea to get the matter out into the open, so to speak. I am thinking of the safety of poor Miss Trout, who has been threatened with all kinds of dire things if she doesn't leave her home immediately. Think of that! Who could possibly write such terrible things to such a kind old lady? Why, I never should have thought it possible.'

'It was probably someone local,' said Lionel Dorsey. 'Someone with a grudge against her, perhaps.'

'Perhaps. But who could have a grudge against *me*? I haven't been here long enough to make any enemies,' said Angela.

'What does Miss Trout say about the letters?' asked Mrs. Dorsey, with a sudden show of interest. 'Is she frightened, do you think?'

Angela saw Mr. Simpson observing Harriet covertly, and replied, 'Not at all, I should say. She is certainly mystified, but I shouldn't say she was the type to be easily frightened.'

'That's exactly what I should have said,' said Lionel Dorsey, as though that settled a long-standing argument. His wife pouted but said nothing.

'I don't think there's any reason for Miss Trout to be frightened for her own safety,' said Simpson. 'I have always understood that the sort of people who write anonymous letters are generally not the sort of people to take direct action themselves. That is, they write the letters *instead* of taking action, in the hope that the letters will be enough in themselves to achieve the aim they have in mind.'

'Until yesterday I should have agreed with you,' said Angela, 'but recent events have contradicted that view.'

'What do you mean?' said Mrs. Walters.

'Why, that yesterday, Miss Trout's nephew, Clifford Maynard, was attacked by an intruder in the middle of the night.'

The others all gave exclamations of surprise and concern, and Angela related the events of the day before.

'Was he badly hurt?' asked Mrs. Walters.

Angela thought she saw a disbelieving look pass briefly over Harriet's face, but it was replaced immediately by her customary mask of detachment.

'I don't think so,' said Angela. 'He has some bruising to the face and is in a certain amount of discomfort, but there is no danger to his life. Nonetheless, it was a serious incident.'

'Do you think there is a connection between this attack and the anonymous letters?' prompted Simpson.

'It would be a great coincidence if there weren't, don't you think?' said Angela.

'Rot,' said Lionel Dorsey rudely. 'Why, I'll bet there's no connection at all. In fact, I'll bet there wasn't even an intruder. Maynard was probably sneaking downstairs in the middle of the night to help himself to the contents of the drinks cabinet and tripped over his own feet. He was too embarrassed to confess it, so had to invent a story about a burglar to explain his injuries without looking like an idiot.'

His wife giggled.

'It is possible, I suppose,' said Angela politely.

'Mark my words, that's what happened,' said Lionel. 'The silly old fool.'

Shortly afterwards the Dorseys stood up and prepared to leave. They were going out that evening, they said. Angela wondered whether they were going to make another late night of it. As they were going, Harriet Dorsey brushed past Angela, leaving a strong gust of scent behind her.

'I like your perfume,' said Angela boldly. '*Shalimar*, isn't it?'

'That's right,' said Harriet. 'It's my favourite.'

They separated and Mr. Simpson accompanied Mrs. Walters and Mrs. Marchmont back along the cliff path. He deposited Mrs. Walters with great ceremony at her door, then walked the few yards to Kittiwake Cottage with Angela.

'What did you think?' said Angela as they stood together at the gate.

Mr. Simpson raised his eyebrows significantly.

'About the Dorseys? Yes, I do think they bear further investigation,' he said.

'Harriet is left-handed,' said Angela, 'and Marthe says the letters were written by a left-handed woman. And she wears *Shalimar*.' Simpson glanced at her questioningly and she said with a smile, 'I rely on Marthe more than I can possibly say. If she says that a sheet of note-paper smells of *Shalimar*, then she is almost certainly right.'

'I was interested to observe the Dorseys' reaction to the story of the assault on Clifford Maynard,' he said ruminatively.

'Yes, that was odd, wasn't it? They didn't seem to give it any credence at all,' said Angela. 'But if it is true that Lionel Dorsey is Edgar Valencourt, then he must have carried out the attack himself, while he was searching Poldarrow Point for the necklace in the dead of night. At the very least one would have expected him to show pretended concern for Mr. Maynard, but instead he insisted that the story must have been entirely fabricated.'

'Perhaps Dorsey wasn't the intruder, then.'

'What, you mean that someone quite different was responsible for the attack? That doesn't seem likely, does it? If we accept the theory that Harriet Dorsey has been writing the anonymous letters, then surely that means her husband is the man we are after. There can't be *two* lots of people searching Poldarrow Point for Marie Antoinette's necklace, can there?'

'Three, if you count ourselves,' said Simpson. 'No, it hardly makes sense, does it?'

He bade her goodbye and went off. Angela watched him go then turned to open the garden gate. She started when she saw Barbara, who had been lurking behind a tall shrub and had evidently heard the whole conversation.

Barbara glared accusingly at her.

'Who is Edgar Valencourt?' she said loudly.

CHAPTER NINETEEN

'SHH!' HISSED ANGELA. She grabbed Barbara's arm and hurried the girl into the house.

'What on earth are you doing? Have you gone mad?' said Barbara as Angela pushed her inside and shut the door.

'They'll hear you next door if you're not careful,' said Angela, 'and then it will be all over the village by tomorrow.'

'Oh, I see, it's a secret, is it?' said Barbara. 'Come on, spill the beans. What were you and the divine Mr. Simpson talking about just then? Who is this Edgar Valencourt of whom you speak?'

'I'm not supposed to say,' said Angela.

Barbara gave her a look of pure mischief, then threw open the French windows and ran back into the garden.

'Edgar Valencourt!' she yelled. 'Edgar Va—'

'All right! I'll tell you,' said Angela hurriedly, 'but come back inside and for goodness' sake stop shouting!'

'That's better,' said Barbara in her normal voice. She stepped back into the house and shut the door. 'Spit it out.'

Angela sighed.

'Mind, you are not to tell a soul of this,' she warned.

'Of course I shan't,' said Barbara. 'Who is he?'

'Edgar Valencourt is a well-known jewel-thief, and the man whom we suspect of being after the treasure at Poldarrow Point.'

'"We" suspect? And who are "we", exactly?'

'Mr. Simpson and I.'

'That's all very cosy,' said Barbara, regarding Angela with narrowed eyes. 'What has he to do with it?'

'He is a Scotland Yard detective, and he is here under-cover in the hope of catching Valencourt once and for all.'

Barbara cast her suspicions aside. Her eyes widened and she gave a gasp of excitement.

'Oh!' she said. 'A real detective! How thrilling! So you are working together, you and he? I wondered why you had got so friendly with him. Is that why you came to Cornwall, to look for this Valencourt fellow?'

'No, not at all,' Angela assured her. 'I really did come here for a holiday, but mysteries seem to be following me about lately, and I have somehow found myself caught up in this one now. Mr. Simpson knew who I was and asked me to keep an eye on things up at the old house, that's all.'

'I wish you'd told me before,' said Barbara.

'Mr. Simpson particularly asked me not to tell *anyone*,' said Angela. 'I don't know what he'll say when he finds out I've told you.'

'Don't worry, you can trust me not to say anything to any-one else,' said Barbara. 'Miss Trout knows, of course.'

'Nobody knows,' said Angela. 'Not even Miss Trout. Mr. Simpson didn't want to worry her, and I think he is quite right.'

'But you said Mr. Dorsey was Edgar Valencourt, I heard you. Why doesn't Mr. Simpson just arrest him? Then we can all get on with searching for the necklace without any silly interruptions from jewel-thieves and suchlike.'

'We don't know for certain that Mr. Dorsey is Valencourt. All we know is that his wife may possibly have been respon-sible for sending the anonymous letters, but we can't say for sure what her motive was since we have no other evidence.'

'Then we must find some!' said Barbara. There was a gleam in her eye that spoke of trouble.

'There is no need for us to do anything,' said Angela firmly. 'Mr. Simpson is taking care of all that side of things. All that is required of us is to keep looking for the necklace. Even if there were no-one else searching for it, we should still only have until the fifth of August to find it, since that is when the lease on Poldarrow Point runs out.'

'Oh yes,' said Barbara, 'I'd almost forgotten that. If only there were something we could do to allow Miss Trout to stay in the house until it is found.'

'Yes,' said Angela, 'I wonder, now—' she paused in thought.

'Was it Mr. Dorsey who attacked Mr. Maynard?' asked Bar-bara suddenly. 'Is that where the Dorseys have been going ev-ery night? Have they been getting into the house to search?'

'Perhaps,' said Angela, her mind elsewhere.

'Don't you think it's unfair not to warn Miss Trout?' said Barbara. 'After all, Mr. Dorsey might come back and do it again.'

'I don't think so,' said Angela. 'From what I have seen of Mr. Maynard, I don't think he will risk getting out of bed again if he hears another noise in the night. Don't worry—I don't think they are in any danger.'

Barbara said nothing, but her sense of fair play was offended. She had promised not to tell anybody about Simpson and Valencourt, but she resolved that she should not sit by and do nothing while her friends were in danger. There was nothing for it: if Angela would not act, then she would have to spy on the Dorseys herself. The idea of playing at detective appealed to Barbara, and she spent a few minutes indulging in pleasant day-dreams in which she caught Mr. Dorsey and his wife red-handed as they tried to escape through the window at Poldarrow Point with the necklace. Perhaps they would give her an award of some kind and her photograph would appear in all the newspapers. Then when she was old enough she should join the police and become the first woman Chief of Scotland Yard, and her portrait would hang in the National Portrait Gallery after she died.

She emerged from her day-dream to see the cat in the garden, stalking a mouse. The tiny creature was cowering, terrified, under the table, as the cat stared at it intently.

'Poor thing,' thought Barbara, and went out to rescue it. 'Shoo!' she said to the cat, which ignored her and went on staring at its prey. She bent over and scooped the mouse up carefully in both hands. It was frozen with terror but did not appear to be badly hurt. She took it to the bottom of the garden and released it gently onto the cliff path.

'Off you go,' she said. The mouse twitched once or twice then scurried off as fast as it could. Barbara went back into the garden.

'Don't look at me like that,' she said to the cat, which was glaring at her reproachfully. 'You shouldn't pick on things that are smaller than you—it's cowardly. Go and find another cat to fight with.'

'That was kind of you,' said a voice from over the fence. It was Helen Walters.

'Was it?' said Barbara, as Angela came out into the garden.

'Oh, hallo, Helen,' said Angela. 'I hope you are feeling better now.'

'Yes, much better, thank you,' said Helen colourlessly. 'I think I must have had a bad oyster or something. For an hour or two I felt certain I was going to die, and it was all I could do to get into bed. It's passed now though, thank goodness!'

'Oh dear,' said Angela. 'How unfortunate. It's a shame you missed the tennis. It was rather good fun.'

'Yes, so Mother said. I understand that Mr. Simpson stepped in and turned out to be an excellent player.'

'Yes—apparently he used to play at Cambridge. You must come along next time.'

'I'd love to,' said Helen. Just then, her mother called from inside the cottage, and Helen smiled apologetically and returned indoors.

Angela turned away to find Barbara making a variety of expressive faces and gestures, pointing at Helen's back and then holding her hands up.

'What are you doing?' asked Angela.

Barbara put a finger over her lips and drew Angela away from the fence.

'Don't believe a word of it,' she said in a stage whisper.

'Don't believe a word of what?'

'What *she* says. She wasn't in bed this afternoon.'

'Oh?'

'No,' said Barbara. 'I saw her myself walking along the path towards Poldarrow Point earlier. I don't believe she was ill at all.'

'Are you sure?'

'Of course I'm sure. She didn't see me but I saw her all right.'

'What was she doing?'

'Nothing in particular—just walking along the cliff top by herself. I wasn't following her or anything, so I didn't pay much attention. If she hadn't just told you that she spent the afternoon in bed I dare say I shouldn't even have remembered it.'

'How odd. I wonder why she lied about being ill.'

'I'd lie if I had a mother like that, just to get a bit of time off,' said Barbara, 'but if you ask me, she was going to meet someone.'

'Really?' said Angela in surprise. 'Why do you say that?'

'Because she was all dressed up in her best frock and gloves, with lipstick on and everything,' said Barbara. 'I almost didn't recognize her. She's rather pretty when she makes the effort. She must have come back and scrubbed her face in a hurry to get all the muck off before her mother got home and then hopped into bed and started groaning. She's a dark one, for all her "poor me" ways.'

Angela had not considered Helen in this light, having always taken her situation at face value. Whom could she have been meeting? Angela said nothing, but resolved to watch Helen when they next met.

CHAPTER TWENTY

THEY HAD AN early dinner at Kittiwake Cottage and spent the evening quietly. At half-past nine Angela yawned and said she was going to bed.

'Don't stay up too late,' she said as she left the room.

'I shall be going to bed shortly myself,' said Barbara. This was perfectly true, although she did not think it necessary to add that she was intending to get up again soon afterwards, as she had plans for that night. As good as her word, she followed Angela upstairs a few minutes later and went into the room she shared with Marthe. She got into bed fully dressed and pulled the covers up over her head. After a little while, the maid came in. Barbara heard the rustle of clothing as she undressed, followed by a creak of springs and a sigh as she got into bed. She waited, and after half an hour or so heard the sound of rhythmic breathing which told her that Marthe had fallen asleep. She listened for a few minutes to make quite certain that all was safe, then rose cautiously and crept out of the room, shutting the door quietly behind her.

There was no light under Angela's door, so Barbara judged that she must be asleep too. She tiptoed down the stairs, being careful to avoid the creaky step halfway down, then let herself out through the front door and ran down the path and out through the gate. It was dark now, the last few streaks of mid-blue having disappeared from the sky and been replaced by a deep indigo studded with glimmering white. The moon was almost full, and Barbara found she had no need of her torch as she set off briskly in the direction of the Hotel Splendide, whose windows and terraces glowed brightly, rendering it visible from miles around. As she drew nearer, the sound of drifting music grew louder, and she began to distinguish the sound of voices chattering and laughing, and the clatter of china. She stood in the shadows at the edge of the hotel terrace, and saw that all the doors had been thrown wide open on this warm evening. Waiters and waitresses bustled about the restaurant, clearing away the plates of the last few stray diners, while farther along she could just get a glimpse through the outer doors of the ball-room, from where the music was emanating. Barbara crept closer, keeping out of the light, and watched as couple after couple whirled past, some in time with the music, others less so. The noise was very loud now and she watched attentively, wondering whether she had perhaps left it too late and whether her informant had misled her.

Although Angela did not know it, Barbara had spent much of that day at the hotel, doing a little investigating on her own account. She had long ago decided that the writer of the anonymous letters was after the necklace, and had seen no evidence since then to prove her wrong. Barbara intended to find out who it was. She started from the assumption that the culprit did not belong to Tregarrion—not an unreasonable deduction, in her view, since the necklace had been in the house for one hundred and fifty years and yet the letters had begun arriving only recently. Someone, therefore, had got wind of the treasure and had come to Tregarrion in the hope of finding it—and where should they stay if not the hotel?

Her first step had been to find out more about the Dorseys, who she had decided were the chief suspects, since: 1) they knew about Angela's visits to Poldarrow, and 2) they were known to wander about late at night and might easily therefore have been responsible for the attack on Clifford Maynard. Accordingly, she had spent the morning hanging around the restaurant until she spotted a likely new ally: the boy who collected the glasses was an observant young fellow of fourteen with too much time on his hands, who was only too happy to pass a few minutes showing off his superior knowledge to his new friend. He told her that the Dorseys were well known in the hotel for taking all they could get and being mean with their tips. They were among the latest at breakfast every day, and the last to leave the ball-room at night. After that, they usually went out—he couldn't say where—and goodness knows it wasn't as though there were many places to go around here, but he had seen them several times leaving the hotel at eleven or twelve o'clock, and who could say at what time they returned?

Barbara intended to discover if she could where the Dorseys went on these mysterious night jaunts of theirs, and
planned to follow them when—if—they left the hotel that
evening. First, however, she had to find out where they were.
Keeping to the shadows, lest someone see her and send her
back home to bed, she crept closer to the open door of the
ball-room. A low wall ran around the edge of the terrace and
she crouched down behind it and peered over the top. From
her position she had a good view of the comings and goings
inside the great hall. She could just see the orchestra as they
puffed and plucked and hammered at their instruments, faces
shining and brows wrinkled in concentration. The crowd was
gradually thinning, as guests left the room in twos and threes,
and headed for their rooms giggling or yawning, and there
were a number of empty tables, which made it a little easier
to distinguish faces.

Barbara gazed intently through the door, but could not see
the Dorseys anywhere, either on the dance floor or sitting at a
table. Of course, it was always possible that they were seated
against the near wall, in which case she would not be able to
see them even if they were there. Throwing caution to the
winds, she scrambled to her feet and sidled up to the door.
Nobody paid her any attention as she craned her neck round
the door-post and scanned that part of the hall which could
not be seen from the terrace. Close to, the music was deafening and the atmosphere sweltering, but it was all lost on
Barbara, who had attention only for her quarry.

'If you're looking for the Dorseys, you won't find them in
there,' said a voice in her ear, making her jump almost out of

her skin. She whirled round to find her friend of that morning, the pot-boy, standing at her shoulder, a cigarette dangling out of the corner of his mouth.

'Oh, hallo, Ginger,' she said. 'Have you seen them, then?'

He darted a shrewd look at her. 'What you got against them?'

'Nothing,' she said.

'Come on, out with it,' he said. 'Nothing, indeed! Why, for all I know you're one of them juvenile thieves I'm always hearing about, come to fleece the guests. What's to stop me going up to them right now and telling them there's a girl hanging around spying on them?'

'Oh, please don't!' said Barbara, thinking quickly. 'You'll spoil everything. You've no idea how long it's taken me to find them. I couldn't bear it if you gave me away and I lost them again!'

'What are you talking about?'

She gazed at him with sad eyes.

'It's really none of your business,' she said, 'but if you must know, they—they are my real parents.'

'What?'

Barbara nodded.

'Yes. I was brought up as an orphan, and only recently found out that my mother and father were still alive. I was stolen as a baby, you see, by a jealous aunt, who had no children and longed for a daughter of her own. She took me home, but treated me with terrible cruelty—almost like a servant. She beat me, and kept me in a cold attic, and starved me half to death.'

She stopped, wondering whether she had gone too far, but Ginger was enthralled.

'Coo!' he said sympathetically.

'It was only quite by chance that I discovered my parents were still alive,' said Barbara, warming to her theme, 'and that they were staying in this very place! I've been watching them for days now, but I can't just go up to them and tell them I'm their long-lost daughter, now, can I? Why, they'd die of shock! I'm trying to think of the best way to approach them, and I'm keeping an eye on them as best I can, but I have to do it in secret, or my aunt will find out, and I daren't think what she might do to me if she knows I am out tonight! Please don't tell anybody.'

She gazed at him pleadingly. He was touched by her plight.

"Course I won't tell anybody,' he said. 'You carry on and watch them all you want. I'd be the same in your position. They're in the lounge now—leastways, that's where they were ten minutes ago when I did my rounds. Just don't tell the head waiter I saw you, or he'll have me out on my ear.'

'Thanks, Ginger. I won't forget this,' said Barbara, clasping her hands together in gratitude. She flashed him a grin and ran off round the other side of the building, to where she remembered the hotel lounge to be. She was very nearly too late, for after watching the front entrance for a minute or so she happened to turn her head and saw the Dorseys walking rapidly away along the cliff path in the direction of Poldarrow Point, having evidently left the hotel through another door.

Barbara bolted after them until she had almost caught them up, then slowed down to follow them at a discreet distance of twenty yards or so. The Dorseys walked briskly, neither looking about them nor, it seemed, talking to each other. Away from the bustle and noise of the hotel the night was still and quiet, with only the sound of the waves to be heard far below as Barbara followed along silently behind her quarry. The moon was bright now, and lit their way forward. It glinted off Harriet Dorsey's golden hair, making it easy for Barbara to keep them both in sight with no need for a torch.

The little procession carried on for several minutes until they passed Shearwater and Kittiwake Cottages and arrived at the place, a little farther on, at which Poldarrow Point came into full view from the cliff path. Here the Dorseys stopped so sharply that Barbara, whose attention had wandered, came within a few yards of them before she realized and hastily beat a silent retreat. She crouched down behind a gorse bush and watched. For about ten minutes they stood in the same spot, watching the old house intently without saying a word. They seemed to be waiting for something.

'What on earth are they doing?' Barbara muttered to herself.

She had not given much thought to the question of how the Dorseys had been getting into the house each night—if indeed they had been getting in—but had vaguely supposed that there was a window with a loose catch somewhere, and that they had been entering that way. What was all this, then?

Lionel Dorsey looked at his watch and shifted impatiently from one foot to another. He muttered something to his wife that Barbara could not hear, and Harriet appeared to nod in agreement. At that moment Barbara saw what they had been waiting for, when a light flashed three times in quick succession from one of the downstairs windows of Poldarrow Point.

The Dorseys froze for a split second, watching, then set forth again unhesitatingly towards the house. Barbara waited for a second, then scrambled out of her hiding place and followed them. What could it mean? Who was signalling out of the window? Did they have an accomplice who had entered the house earlier and had been waiting for them to arrive? Was this mysterious figure the person who had attacked Clifford Maynard the other night?

The gate had been left open, and the Dorseys went through it and up the path, treading softly so as not to be heard. Barbara stood by the gate-post and watched as they walked up to the front door. A dim light could now be seen approaching through the stained glass above it. Harriet gave a low knock, and immediately the door opened to reveal a figure holding a torch, who admitted them quickly and shut the door behind them. Just for a second the light from the torch fell on the face of the person carrying it, and Barbara gasped as she saw who it was. It was Clifford Maynard.

CHAPTER TWENTY-ONE

BARBARA REMAINED ROOTED to the spot for several minutes, indignant thoughts tumbling one after another through her mind. Mr. Maynard was in league with the Dorseys! He had been letting them into the house every night to allow them to search for the necklace. They must be planning to find it and steal Miss Trout's rightful property from under her very nose! Barbara's mouth fell open as she marvelled at the audacity of it, and she spent a good few minutes applying unrepeatable epithets to Clifford in her mind. Of all the low-down, contemptible tricks to play on a sweet old lady! What kind of despicable rotter would steal his own aunt's birthright and turn her out of her family home and onto the streets?

Barbara stood there in astonished rage, desperate to act. First, she contemplated marching into Tregarrion that instant and reporting Clifford to the police, but quickly realized that by the time she got there, made her report and returned, the

Dorseys would most likely be gone. And what exactly could she say to the police? 'I want you to arrest a man on suspicion of allowing a respectable couple to enter his own house to search for Marie Antoinette's necklace'? Even Barbara had to admit that it sounded pretty ridiculous. They would just laugh at her and take her home—or worse, give her a ticking-off for wasting their time. But she couldn't just do nothing. She had to stop them searching for the treasure before they had a chance to find it—but how? Several ideas came into her head and were immediately abandoned as being impractical or downright dangerous. For one mad second she even considered setting fire to the house, criminals and all—but of course, that would never do since firstly, Miss Trout was in there and might not get out in time, and secondly, she might, in destroying the house, destroy the necklace too.

After a minute or two, however, Barbara calmed down and began to think more rationally. There was no need to panic. The necklace had defied both her own searches and those of the intruders up to now, and there was no reason to suppose that it would be found that night. Surely, therefore, the first thing to do was to try and see what the Dorseys were up to, and to make sure that they were in fact doing what she suspected them of doing. After all, she thought fairly, perhaps they were merely friends of Clifford's who happened to have dropped in that night to pay him a social visit. She rejected that thought immediately, however. What, at almost midnight? And why all the hole-and-corner business with the flashing light signals, when the house was in darkness? Where was Miss Trout? Presumably in bed, or all the sneaking around would not be necessary. Had it been a simple friendly visit then they would have walked up to the front door quite openly and knocked. No: clearly they were up to no good, and Barbara was determined to prove it.

Having reached this decision, she approached the house cautiously and prowled around the outside. The place seemed to be in darkness—but of course they would not have switched any lights on if they wanted to search without being seen. Where were they likely to be? Not the drawing-room or the dining-room, she thought, since she and Angela had searched those rooms themselves. And not the study or the kitchen either, for the same reasons. Down in the cellars, perhaps, or up on the top floor. Barbara remembered the white figure she had seen floating down the passage the other day, and shivered. There was safety in numbers, however, and perhaps the ghost was reluctant to manifest itself before a group of several people: she had always heard that they preferred to appear to one person at a time. The thought arrested her for a moment, and she looked around warily. Hadn't Miss Trout mentioned something about the ghost of a drowned smuggler who haunted the garden? She had already seen one ghost, so perhaps that meant she was susceptible to that kind of thing. What did the clairvoyants call it? Sympathetic, or some such word.

Apparently there were no departed souls wandering about the grounds that night. Barbara shook herself and proceeded on her way. She had made almost a full circuit of the house without seeing anything when she suddenly spotted a flash of light at the next window along. As far as she could judge, it was the study, and she was puzzled: why hadn't Clifford told them that the study had already been searched? A large and ancient rose-bush stood guard by the window, preventing her from getting a good view through it, but she found a place where the branches were a little thinner and less thorny, and wriggled carefully past it and up to the window. She had only a partial view of the study from where she was standing, but it would have to do. The first thing she saw was the dim outline of Harriet Dorsey, carrying a torch and clearly absorbed in the task of rummaging through everything in the study. She was taking out the contents of a large cupboard one shelf at a time, then replacing them with meticulous care. Despite her indignation, Barbara approved of the woman's methodical approach, which was presumably designed to avoid raising Miss Trout's suspicions by making sure that everything stayed in the same place.

She watched Harriet for a few minutes, then ducked in a panic as a light flashed past the window, barely an inch from her eyes. It must have lit up her whole face. Had they seen her? She held her breath for what seemed like ten minutes, but heard no exclamations or sounds of running feet. She exhaled slowly. Whoever it was had obviously not spotted her. It must have been Clifford or Mr. Dorsey, she supposed.

After a few minutes she plucked up her courage and peeped cautiously through the window again. This time she saw Lionel Dorsey, engaged in pulling out all the contents of a writing-desk and examining its drawers closely. Barbara wondered at this activity—first, because while conducting their own searches the other day, they had all agreed that there was not much sense in looking in drawers or cupboards, given that the furniture had been in use for many decades and thus presumably anything hidden in it would have turned up by now. More importantly, however, Barbara recognized the writing-desk as a newish one that Miss Trout had mentioned as having belonged to her brother. Yes—she was sure of it: she remembered it distinctly. The old lady had said something about the desk being one of the few things that had not been in the house for centuries. Why, then, was Clifford standing by and saying nothing as Lionel Dorsey searched through it? Perhaps he was unaware that it belonged to his aunt—but no, that wasn't true either: he had been there when Miss Trout talked of it; had even made some remark about it.

Barbara shrugged. She supposed that Clifford had forgotten about it, or that he had not noticed that Mr. Dorsey was wasting his efforts in looking for an eighteenth-century treasure in a modern writing-desk. She peeped through the window again and watched as Dorsey pulled out the drawers and shone his torch into the cavities, as though searching for signs of a secret hiding-place. His quest was evidently unsuccessful, for she saw him give a grimace and turn his attention to a bookshelf nearby. He began to remove the books one by one and examine them. Barbara grinned. She had done exactly the same thing herself only the other day.

'You won't find anything there,' she murmured to herself. 'There are no priceless treasures hidden inside dusty old Bibles on *that* shelf, I can tell you that!'

Mr. Dorsey must have come to the same conclusion very quickly, for she saw him shove a book back onto the shelf crossly and then turn around and say something to his wife. She came to join him and picked a book up, then put it back and said something, gesturing at the shelf. Lionel Dorsey at once began trying to pull it away from the wall.

'That's going to make the most frightful racket,' Barbara said to herself, and sure enough she heard a loud scraping sound as the heavy wooden bookshelf moved along the floor. Mr. Dorsey stopped tugging immediately and leapt back, looking almost comically aghast. Barbara watched in amusement the little silent pantomime as Harriet Dorsey upbraided her husband for his carelessness and he replied sullenly. There was now enough of a gap between the shelf and the wall to allow the searchers to see behind it, and Harriet began moving her torch up and down, presumably looking for a secret hiding-place in the small space.

Barbara suddenly wondered where Clifford was. She had been so absorbed in watching the Dorseys that she had quite forgotten him, and she craned her neck, thinking that perhaps he was rooting about in some invisible corner. But no sooner had she noted that he was nowhere to be seen than she was given almost the fright of her life and very nearly shrieked when the light of a torch flashed not two feet from her, and Mr. Maynard's voice called out peremptorily, 'Who goes there?'

Thankful for the presence of the rose-bush, which formed a screen between her and Clifford, she shrank back as quietly as she could into the dark shadows and against the house wall, hoping that he would go away. He must have seen her face after all, when he flashed the torch past the window, but it sounded as though he had not recognized her. That was something, at least. She crouched, quiet as a mouse, hardly daring to breathe, while he moved the torch slowly over the rose-bush. To her relief, the beam of light passed by without falling on her and Clifford moved away slowly. Just at that moment Barbara, to her dismay, felt a sneeze begin to threaten. She pinched her treacherous nose and blew out her cheeks, shook her head and nodded violently—anything to stave it off—but it was no good: the sneeze would out, by hook or by crook. In a last attempt to keep it quiet, at least, Barbara jammed her fist into her mouth and two fingers up her nose just as the explosion happened.

'Ah—*choo!*' went the sneeze. Even muffled, it was a fine, loud one. Barbara cringed, eyes watering, as the sound of retreating footsteps came to a sudden halt and the beam of the torch was directed immediately back towards the bush. There was a second of silence, then the footsteps began to move back towards her. Any moment now, she would be discovered. What would Clifford do to her? Would he kill her, to silence her? Or would he let her live but keep her prisoner in an attic and torture her cruelly to find out what she knew?

She was on the point of jumping out of her hiding-place and throwing herself on his mercy with some hastily-concocted story, when Clifford faltered and suddenly swung his torch away from the rose-bush. He retreated a little farther into the garden.

'Who goes there?' he said again. Barbara could not bear the suspense. She risked a peek and saw that he seemed to be listening for something. Just then, she heard it herself: a stealthy rustling somewhere nearby. It sounded like an animal of some kind—a fox, perhaps, or a cat. Evidently, Clifford was thinking the same thing, for after listening for a little while he made a disgusted noise and said, 'Stupid thing,' and kicked at a nearby shrub. He then returned the way he had come. Barbara suspected that his courage was not especially high, out there in the dark, shadowy garden, and that it was diminishing rapidly the longer he stayed out. She waited until he had disappeared from sight, and was just about to allow herself a sigh of relief when she heard another sound. Her head whipped round, and to her astonishment she saw that a nearby rhododendron appeared to be coming to life. She stared, open-mouthed, as a man extricated himself carefully from the middle of the bush and tiptoed away into the night. She had no difficulty in recognizing who it was: there was no mistaking Mr. Donati's moustache and quaint clothing.

With no room in her head to wonder about this latest oddity, Barbara emerged from behind her rose-bush and, keeping low, scurried as fast as she could around the side of the house and out through the front gate. From there she ran as fast as she could until she had put a safe distance between herself and Poldarrow Point. She reached Kittiwake Cottage without further incident and let herself in quietly. Marthe was still sleeping soundly when she crept into their room, and Barbara did no more than remove her shoes and frock before falling into bed and into a deep sleep.

CHAPTER TWENTY-TWO

B UT WHAT ON earth were you doing creeping around the garden in the middle of the night?' said Angela, her cup of tea suspended halfway to her lips.

'Well, *someone* had to keep an eye on the Dorseys, and you hardly seemed eager to do the hard work,' said Barbara scathingly, in between mouthfuls of porridge.

'There are other ways of getting things done than scurrying about, hiding behind rose-bushes, you know,' said Angela. 'Besides, I never promised to chase criminals—I merely said I would keep my ear to the ground and pass on any information I received that would allow others to do the chasing.'

'It's a good thing you have me, then,' said Barbara. 'Otherwise we might never have found out about Mr. Maynard.'

She pushed away her empty dish and yawned. She would have preferred to stay in bed, but her adventures of the night before were too good to keep to herself, and Angela's astonishment when she told of her midnight quest had been quite as great as she had hoped.

'Yes, Mr. Maynard,' said Angela thoughtfully.

'You don't seem very surprised,' said Barbara.

'No,' replied Angela, 'I'm not. Somehow I was never particularly convinced by his devoted nephew act. It seemed a little overdone. After all, Miss Trout said she had not seen him since he was a child. Why, then, should he come all the way down here from London, to dedicate himself to an aunt whom he barely knew? At first I wondered whether he had an eye out for a future inheritance, but of course Miss Trout has no money. However, a priceless necklace would certainly be a fine return on the small investment of time and effort required to ingratiate himself with his aunt.'

'He's a beastly rotter,' said Barbara, 'but if he is really looking for the treasure with the Dorseys, then who attacked him? Not Lionel Dorsey, surely. Otherwise they would not be on speaking terms now.'

'I wonder now whether Mr. Dorsey mightn't have been right when he said that Clifford did it himself,' said Angela. 'Perhaps he thought his aunt was getting suspicious of his motives, and decided to do something to throw her off the scent.'

'What, you mean he punched himself in the face?' said Barbara disbelievingly.

'No,' said Angela, 'but don't you remember what he told us? He was an actor in London before he came down to Cornwall. He could easily have made himself up to look as though he had been assaulted.'

'Oh yes, of course,' said Barbara. 'I'd quite forgotten that. That would explain why he didn't want to see a doctor.'

'Yes, a doctor would spot immediately that the injuries were faked. And he wouldn't be too keen to bring in the police, either. He didn't want to draw attention to himself, given what he was planning.' Angela suddenly remembered something. 'He tried to throw me off the scent too, the other day.'

'Did he? How?'

'He tried to convince me that Miss Trout had written the anonymous letters herself.'

'Why on earth should she do that?'

'He implied—or rather, he said outright that she was old and losing her mind.'

Barbara snorted impressively.

'Ridiculous!' she said. 'Why, Miss Trout is as sharp as you or I—and I'd bet half a crown that she's sharper than Clifford.'

'It wasn't a particularly convincing story,' agreed Angela. 'He said she had told him that the Warreners were descended from royalty, and then later denied having said any such thing. And there were other little incidents too, he said. But I agree with you—I have never seen any sign that Miss Trout is failing in her mind at all.'

'Of course she isn't. Why do you think he wanted to make you believe she was?'

'Do you remember when we first heard about the letters? Maynard seemed dismayed that Miss Trout had decided to tell us about them—which, if the Dorseys wrote them, is entirely understandable. He certainly wouldn't want strangers knowing of his friends' attempts to frighten his aunt out of her house.'

Barbara laughed.

'He must have been pretty sick that *you* of all people were one of the strangers in question,' she said. 'His nice little plot to drive her out of the house, ruined at a stroke by a famous detective!'

'I do wish you wouldn't keep calling me that,' said Angela. 'You know I'm not a real detective, don't you?'

'Yes, but *he* doesn't!' said Barbara triumphantly. 'And what does it matter? Your presence was still enough to put the wind up him. No wonder he wanted to convince you that the letters were all a mare's nest. He could have invented a better story, though.'

'Perhaps it was the best he could think of on the spur of the moment,' said Angela.

'So,' said Barbara, who liked to get things straight, 'Let's see. This is what must have happened: Clifford Maynard is living in London, in need of money, when he hears that the lease on Poldarrow Point is about to expire and his aunt is going to be thrown out of her house. He knows the family legend about the Queen's necklace, and decides that it's now or never: he's going to find the thing, steal it from under his aunt's nose, then sell it and keep the proceeds for himself. So he goes down to Cornwall and butters her up until she asks him to stay. That gives him plenty of opportunity to search for the necklace when she's asleep in bed.' She stopped, thinking. 'Why did he ask the Dorseys to help him, though? He'd be far better off doing it himself and keeping the money. Now he'll have to split it.'

'Perhaps they are going to sell it for him,' said Angela. 'After all, it can't be that easy to get rid of a treasure like that. You can't just go into a jeweller's and offer to sell them a famous necklace that was made for a Queen and caused a national scandal. Questions are bound to be asked.' She suddenly remembered something. 'Lionel Dorsey said his business was imports and exports,' she said. 'I wonder if he deals with antiques and suchlike. Perhaps he runs a legitimate business but is not above engaging in illicit activities now and again if he thinks it is worth his while. It would be easy for him to smuggle the necklace abroad with a shipment of other goods. He most likely has accomplices on the Continent who can get rid of anything "hot" for him privately.'

'Do you think he's a fence, then?' said Barbara. 'I thought he was supposed to be the notorious villain Edgar Valencourt, famous all over Europe for his exploits, not just some common little man who sells stolen goods.'

'Yes, the two things don't quite square with each other, do they?' said Angela, frowning.

'So,' went on Barbara, 'the Dorseys join in the search, but they quickly get tired of having to do it at night, so Harriet has the bright idea of sending Miss Trout some threatening letters, in the hope that she will leave the house in a fright and let them search whenever they like. Of course, nobody with half a brain could possibly be frightened by such a feeble attempt, so Harriet tries the trick on you instead.'

'Thank you,' said Angela dryly.

'I can see why they wanted to get rid of you. The three of them must have been awfully miffed when we stuck our noses in and offered to help find the treasure for Miss Trout,' said Barbara.

'When *you* offered,' corrected Angela. 'I seem to remember I was given no choice in the matter.'

'Treasure-hunting is jolly good fun,' said Barbara. 'You ought to be grateful to have been given the chance. Why, just think, if it weren't for me, you would have spent your holiday lounging in a deck-chair and dozing half the day.'

'Yes,' said Angela sadly.

'There! You see, I have saved you from unspeakable dullness,' said Barbara. 'Now, where was I? Oh yes—they continue hunting without success, but now they have competition, so they have to search all the harder. That's what they were doing last night. I don't know why they were looking in the study, though, when we've already searched that.'

'Perhaps they thought there was something we had missed,' suggested Angela.

'But why were they searching through Jeremiah Trout's things? They could hardly expect the necklace to be in among his old bills and cheque-books.'

'I suppose not. Perhaps they were just being thorough.'

'I wonder if they've searched the top floor yet,' said Barbara. 'It must be difficult to search properly at night without waking Miss Trout—they made a dreadful racket just by moving a bookshelf a couple of inches.'

'I begin to wonder if there is anything to be found at all,' said Angela.

'Oh, but there must be!' said Barbara. 'Why else do half the people in Tregarrion seem to be interested in Poldarrow Point?'

'That is a very good question,' said Angela. 'The place certainly does seem to hold a queer fascination for a number of people. I wonder what Mr. Donati was doing there.'

'I don't know, but it can't have been anything above-board, or he wouldn't have been hiding in the rhododendrons. I wonder if he's got wind of the treasure too. We shall have to watch him.'

'We seem to have a lot of people to watch,' said Angela. 'Are we the only people in Cornwall who are not out to steal this necklace, do you suppose?'

Barbara stood up.

'Where's my hat?' she said.

'Are you going out?'

'Of course I am,' said Barbara. 'And you are too. We are going to Poldarrow Point to tell Miss Trout what Clifford has been up to.'

Angela shook her head.

'We had better not do that just yet,' she said.

'But of course we must!' said Barbara. 'We can't let her go on trusting him when all the while he is intending to double-cross her and run off with her money.'

'What money? The treasure has not been found yet.'

'But they could find it at any moment,' said Barbara. 'We must do something, and fast.'

'Yes, I agree we must do something,' said Angela, 'but if we tell Miss Trout now we may ruin everything.'

'What do you mean?'

'Why, if she knows that her nephew is trying to cheat her, she will no doubt confront him with the fact, and that will give him—and the Dorseys—a chance to escape.'

'But the police can catch them later. The important thing is that the necklace will be safe.'

'I don't believe Scotland Yard would agree,' said Angela. 'They have been hunting for Edgar Valencourt for a long time now, and I don't think they would look upon us at all kindly if we were to let him slip through their grasp by giving him an early warning that we are on to him.'

'But what do you propose to do? How can we protect Miss Trout?' Barbara was becoming increasingly indignant.

'Don't worry,' said Angela, 'we shall tell her very soon, but first of all we must tell Mr. Simpson about all this. He is in charge of the investigation into Valencourt and he will need to know what has been going on. He can then decide on the best thing to do.'

'But what if Mr. Maynard decides to put his aunt out of the way once and for all?'

'I don't really think Miss Trout is in any danger from Clifford. I am sure that he is more interested in making some easy pickings than in committing violence.'

'But—'

'And anyway,' went on Angela, 'before we start throwing accusations at people, we have to make certain that we will be believed. What do you think Miss Trout would say if we marched up there now and told her that her nephew was planning to cheat her?'

'Why, I—' Barbara hesitated.

'Exactly,' said Angela. 'She would just laugh at us, and thus all we would achieve by the exercise would be to warn Clifford of our suspicions while leaving Miss Trout none the wiser.'

'But how can we convince her?'

'I don't know yet,' said Angela. 'It may be that the only thing to do is to catch him in the act. Perhaps Mr. Simpson will be able to think of a plan.'

'Then you must tell him about it immediately—today.'

'That is what I intend to do,' said Angela.

'Are you going to see him at the hotel?'

'No,' said Angela. 'He is taking me out for a picnic.'

CHAPTER TWENTY-THREE

'A RE YOU SURE it's safe?' said Mrs. Marchmont, regarding the *Miss Louise* doubtfully as it bobbed up and down in the water several feet below. The battered old fishing lugger had peeling paint and several visible repairs, and looked as though its better days were far behind it.

"Course she's safe,' said Mr. Gibbs from the stern of the boat. 'She's been out every day of her life 'cepting Sundays since eighteen eighty-seven. Forty years of rough winters she's lived through. Isn't that right, Bill?'

His son, a hardy-looking lad of fifteen, nodded in agreement.

'That is what concerns me,' said Angela. 'This boat is older than I am.'

'And she'll live through forty more,' went on Gibbs, 'as long as she's treated right. Anyway, you can swim, can't you?'

Angela ignored this last remark.

'But you said you didn't go out on Sundays,' she said.

'Not for the fish, I don't,' said Gibbs. 'The fish'll still be there tomorrow. But for a nice lady and gentleman what takes a fancy to going on a picnic—well, I was young myself, once. The sunshine might be gone by Tuesday and then what will you do?'

'Mr. Gibbs comes highly recommended,' said Simpson, who was down in the boat, having stowed the picnic-basket, and was now examining the engine in the typical manner of the male of the species. 'The head waiter at the hotel sang his praises in the most effusive terms.'

'I dare say he did, but I must confess I had been thinking on the lines of a pleasure-cruiser, rather than a Cornish lugger,' said Angela.

Simpson assumed an expression of mock horror.

'A pleasure-cruiser? What, mingle with a hundred screeching and perspiring day-visitors, all fighting for the best seats and dropping their sandwiches everywhere, when we can have this quaint and traditional old fishing-craft to ourselves and enjoy the sea breeze in our faces in peace?'

'Nothing like it,' agreed Gibbs.

'Very well, I shall take you on trust, Mr. Gibbs,' said Angela, 'but if you wish for a tip, you had better get us back alive. And preferably dry,' she added as an afterthought.

Gibbs grinned and watched as she climbed nimbly down the iron rungs that were set into the pier. Simpson held out a hand and she jumped lightly into the boat.

'Down the coast, then, was it?' said the old fisherman.

'Yes,' said Simpson. 'We'd like to see the western end of Tregarn Bay, which I understand is a fine sight.'

'Ah,' said Bill, nodding.

'That it is,' agreed Gibbs. He brought out two rather grubby cushions and threw them to his guests. 'The accommodations here aren't what you might call Buckin'am Palace, but you'll be comfortable enough if you don't expect too much.'

'Shall I cast off, then, Dad?' said Bill.

'Right you are,' said Mr. Gibbs, firing up the motor.

Bill untied the rope and the engine roared and smoked as the *Miss Louise* drew slowly away from the dock. The boat turned, describing a large semi-circle, then headed out towards the harbour mouth. Angela gazed back the way they had come, and there was Tregarrion, glowing colourfully in the strong midday light, its brightly-painted houses looking more than ever like a child's building-blocks, stacked higgledy-piggledy one on top of another. They passed the small light-house at the end of the pier, with its line of fishermen sitting and day-dreaming by their rods, and then they were in open sea. The *Miss Louise* turned to the North-West and chugged along the coast, rocking gently with the waves, for it was a calm day. They passed Kittiwake Cottage and Poldarrow Cove, and came to the headland on which Poldarrow Point stood. The old house looked even more gloomy and ramshackle from the sea, if that were possible, and they could see where parts of the garden had begun to collapse over the edge of the cliff. Angela wondered whether Miss Trout would ever be able to afford the repairs that were so clearly necessary. Perhaps, after all, it would make more sense for her to leave the place, rather than have the worry of it for the rest of her life.

The sun was warm, and Angela pulled off her hat to let the breeze cool her head. She turned and found George Simpson staring thoughtfully at the house as they passed. He saw her looking at him and smiled.

'It's a fine old place, isn't it?' he said. 'If I were rich enough, perhaps I should buy it myself and spend my time in restoring it to its former glory.'

Angela looked back at the house and, for the first time, saw it as it must once have been a hundred or more years ago: a comfortable old manor house, home to a family of some local importance. The Warreners must have been responsible in great measure for relieving poverty in this area thanks to their smuggling activities, which had all been possible thanks to the secret tunnel to the house. A great many local people must have had cause to thank Preacher Dick for their livelihoods—however illicit. As was the way of all things, however, the Warreners' fortunes had declined in the end. Smuggling had all but died out and with it, the family's main source of income. Now only Miss Trout, a frail, elderly lady, remained to preserve the Warreners' legacy (Angela disregarded Clifford Maynard, who did not appear to have the necessary strength of character).

'Do you think the place could be made comfortable again?' she asked. 'You might not be able to live in it for long, as it seems to be falling into the sea at a rather rapid rate.'

'Think of the romance of it all, though,' he said eagerly. 'I can think of nothing better than to spend my days living in this remote place, among such beautiful, rugged scenery.'

'It's all very well in the middle of July, when the sun is shining and the day is clear,' said Angela practically, 'but you wouldn't say that if you had to live here through a cold and stormy November, with the wind howling through every crack and cranny of the house, chilling your very bones and making you wish for the warm fires of London.'

'Oh but I should,' he said. 'Remember, I intend to repair the place. Once it had been restored to all its former comfort I should sit by the fire in my library, reading improving books and listening to the sound of the rain battering at the windows, while feeling unspeakably satisfied with myself and my achievements.'

'I don't believe I've ever read an improving book,' said Angela, 'but I understand they are meant to be good for the soul, if a little on the dull side. They will give you something to do during the long winter, though, when the social calls begin to peter out.'

He laughed.

'Yes, perhaps it would become tedious after a while. Perhaps I shall keep Poldarrow as a holiday home, then, and come here only in fair weather.'

'Now that I do approve of,' said Angela, and turned to give the house one last look as it receded into the distance.

They had now come into Tregarn Bay proper, and they fell silent for a few minutes, admiring the beauty of the rugged Cornish coast-line. The boat kept a good way out to sea for a while, then turned in and hugged the shore, to allow them to see it more closely. Angela, lost in her own thoughts, shielded her eyes from the sun to look at a stone cross that stood on a distant hill. She wondered who had built it, and why. She turned to point it out to Simpson and found him looking at her intently. Resisting the urge to smooth her hair, she smiled and said:

'I suppose we ought to compare notes on the case.'

'Don't let's just yet,' he said. 'This is all so pleasant that I don't want to spoil it with work. Let's have our picnic first.'

'Where are we going to have it?'

'Just there,' said Simpson, pointing.

Angela looked in the direction of his finger and saw that they were heading for a narrow inlet that formed a sort of natural harbour. The *Miss Louise* nosed her way in through the entrance, which widened into a pretty little cove, surrounded by low cliffs and clumps of trees. The lugger chugged slowly shoreward, and Mr. Gibbs brought it with great care alongside a rocky promontory, which was evidently used as an occasional landing-stage, for a mooring-post had been fixed to one of the larger, flatter rocks. Almost before the boat had stopped Bill sprang out with great agility and tied it up. His father handed him the picnic-basket and he carried it to the beach, leaping from rock to rock at a breakneck pace without once missing his step. Simpson and Angela followed more slowly. Bill set the basket down without saying a word, then immediately went back to the boat, presumably for his own lunch.

'What a delightful spot,' said Angela, looking about her. The place was deserted apart from themselves, and nothing could be heard except the splashing of the waves and the gentle swish of the trees around them.

'It is, isn't it?' agreed Simpson. 'I had thought about lunch in Penzance, but Gibbs insisted that this was the better choice, and I must say I agree with him.'

Since the sun was high and rather hot, they sat down in a shady spot at the edge of the beach, under a tree, and Angela began unpacking the basket. There was a lot of food.

'I think Cook must have misunderstood my instructions, and somehow thought that she had been asked to feed an army,' said Angela as she regarded the spread of freshly-baked bread, cold ham, eggs and tomatoes, as well as an entire fruit cake, that was laid out before them. 'Either that or she must have thought that Barbara was coming.'

Simpson laughed and helped Angela to a sandwich.

'Where is Barbara today?' he said.

'She said she was going to walk to Land's End,' said Angela. 'I *think* she was joking, but one can never be entirely sure with Barbara. She is a law unto herself.'

'She has no parents, I think you said?'

'Yes, and she spends most of the year at school—although I sometimes wonder what they are teaching her. She certainly doesn't seem to be learning any discipline.'

'Perhaps not, but she seems to have her head screwed on all right,' said Simpson.

'That is my comfort,' agreed Angela. 'She is old beyond her years, and has a decent amount of common sense, so I am *almost* sure she won't end up in prison.'

They laughed and set to demolishing the picnic. It was very pleasant to feel the soft sand under the rug and the warm sun on one's skin, and to lose oneself in the beauty of the day. Angela gazed out at the distant promontory, watching the *Miss Louise* bobbing gently on the waves. She could see Mr. Gibbs and Bill busying themselves on deck, and admired their activity without feeling any inclination to imitate them. On the contrary, she rather felt as though she would like a nap. She roused herself with an effort and looked at the remains of the food. There was less than she had expected.

'Perhaps Cook was right after all,' she said. 'I must have been hungrier than I thought.'

'Yes, we have eaten rather a lot, haven't we?' said Simpson, who was lounging idly against a tree trunk. 'Your cook evidently has lots of experience in catering for boat parties. There is something about the sea air that seems to give one a tremendous appetite.'

'There is still plenty of the cake left,' said Angela. 'Barbara will be pleased. She has the schoolgirl's love of all things sweet. Perhaps Mr. Gibbs and Bill would like a slice each too.'

'I should like another slice myself,' said Mr. Simpson regretfully, 'but I'm afraid I simply haven't room for it.' He sat up. 'I feel I am about to fall asleep, which would be dreadfully rude. You must talk to me, Mrs. Marchmont, and keep me awake.'

Angela laughed.

'As a matter of fact, I do have one or two things I should like to discuss with you. Barbara insisted most particularly that I speak to you today about them.'

'Oh yes?'

'Yes. She had rather an adventure last night.'

Angela related Barbara's story and he pursed his lips in a whistle.

'So the nephew and the Dorseys are in league together? Is that the story?' He paused for a few moments, thinking. 'That certainly puts an interesting aspect on the case,' he said.

'It does indeed,' said Angela, 'and it has also caused me to wonder about the real identity of Edgar Valencourt.'

Simpson was instantly alert.

'Oh? Why is that?' he said.

'Something that Barbara said,' she replied. 'We were wondering why Clifford had asked the Dorseys to help him in his search, and had come to the conclusion that Mr. Dorsey's import and export business would make the ideal cover for the sale of stolen goods.'

'So it would,' said Simpson. 'We shall have to look into that.'

'Yes, but I had been viewing Lionel Dorsey as a possible Edgar Valencourt, not just a "common little man who sells stolen goods", as Barbara put it.'

'Don't you think he could be both?'

'Perhaps. But all the knowledge I have of Valencourt I have got from you, and the impression you gave me doesn't quite square with what I have seen of Mr. Dorsey up to now.'

'In what way?'

Angela hesitated.

'I should say that Mr. Dorsey is a rather small-minded man, not too bright, who might just have the wits to run a shady business but nothing more. I certainly can't see him as the master-mind behind a series of audacious and clever-ly-planned thefts all across Europe. From what you say, Valencourt is a man who delights in taking risks—why, he thinks nothing of going directly into the lion's den and achieving his object by sheer force of personality. Think of all the rich women he has fooled into handing over their most valuable possessions! I can't see Lionel Dorsey playing such a part. He simply hasn't the charm.'

'But you forget that Valencourt is a brilliant actor,' said Simpson. 'Perhaps he is now playing the part of Lionel Dorsey.'

'Perhaps he is,' said Angela, 'but I have someone else in mind.'

'Oh? Who?'

'Clifford Maynard.'

CHAPTER TWENTY-FOUR

AFTER ANGELA HAD gone out to meet Mr. Simpson, Barbara sat down in the garden with the cat on her lap and thought very hard about their earlier conversation. She was not convinced, as Angela seemed to be, that Miss Trout was in no danger from Clifford. In fact, it seemed to her that he had every motive to try and get his aunt out of the way. It was nearly the end of July, and on the fifth of August they would have to leave Poldarrow Point whether or not the necklace had turned up. Time was running short, and he must surely be getting desperate by now. Miss Trout had stubbornly withstood the Dorseys' clumsy attempts to persuade her to leave, and she was now the only thing standing between the three of them and the treasure. It stood to reason that Clifford would now make some other, more determined attempt to get rid of her—perhaps even resorting to violence.

Barbara vowed that she would not let him succeed, even if it meant keeping an eye on him day and night for the next week or more. Somebody had to protect Miss Trout from her designing nephew—and she decided that that person should be herself.

She pushed the cat off her knees and wandered into the kitchen, where she begged a picnic lunch from Cook, who had taken a liking to Barbara and was only too happy to oblige. Then she hunted about for the things she thought she might need on her expedition and began packing them into the picnic-bag with the food. She was going up through the tunnel again, so a torch would be necessary—no, two torches, given what had happened the other day. A pair of field-glasses went in, then some string and a pen-knife, just to be on the safe side. At the last minute, she remembered how chilly it had been in the tunnel, and threw in an old jersey. She checked her hair to make certain she had not forgotten her hair-pin, then left the house through the French windows and started off down the lower cliff path to the beach.

The tide was very low and Barbara glanced out to sea, half-expecting to see Helen Walters taking her daily bathe, but the place was quite deserted as far as she could tell. She took off her shoes and set off across the sand towards the Poldarrow headland. As she was walking, however, she happened to turn her head, and to her surprise, saw Helen walking quickly along the bottom of the cliff towards the path. She did not appear to have seen Barbara. Where had she been? She had come from the direction of the cave that Barbara had found the other day when searching for the secret passage. Had she been hiding inside it? Whatever for?

A sudden suspicion darting into her head, Barbara changed direction and headed for the rocky outcrop which hid the cave entrance. She had almost reached it when a man emerged from the little recess. He wore a hat with a feather and was carrying a knapsack that clanked. He started when he saw Barbara.

'A-*ha!*' thought Barbara triumphantly. 'Hallo, Mr. Donati!' she said out loud. 'Are you exploring the cave again?'

'Yes,' said Donati, looking slightly pink in the face. 'They are very interesting, your English rock formations.'

Barbara smiled angelically.

'I see Miss Walters finds them very interesting too,' she said. 'Wasn't that her I saw just now, walking up the path?'

Mr. Donati went pinker, and coughed.

'Ah, yes,' he said. 'I was very surprised to find her here.'

'Oh, but she comes down here every day to bathe,' said Barbara. 'I thought everybody knew that.'

A sophisticated reply was evidently beyond Donati's English vocabulary, and he hesitated as he cast around for words, but Barbara was not paying attention. An idea had just flashed into her mind—an idea so obvious, so brilliant, that she wondered why she had never thought of it before.

'Anyway,' she said impulsively, 'never mind that. I know why you're really here, *Mr. Valencourt.*'

The effect was immediate. Donati started and shot a penetrating glance at her. He straightened up and took a step towards her. The eccentric and slightly comic scientist had been replaced by something altogether more intimidating. Barbara stepped back.

'What do you know about Valencourt?' he demanded. There was a touch of menace in his voice that contrasted oddly with his appearance.

'I know he's here, trying to steal the Queen's necklace,' said Barbara boldly. She glanced about her. They were on a beach that could be seen from a mile around, and she judged—or hoped—that she was in no danger. 'But he's not going to get it. Even if he gets into the house he'll have *me* to deal with. There's no use in your denying it, you know,' she went on. 'I saw you last night, hiding in the bushes in the garden at Poldarrow Point.'

'Oh, you did, did you? And what were you doing there to see me?'

'I was watching the house,' she said. 'There are people out to harm Miss Trout and steal her property—you, among others—and I want to make sure she doesn't lose what is rightfully hers.'

'And you think I am Valencourt because I was there last night?' he said.

'Of course. Who else would be lurking about outside the house in the middle of the night?'

He regarded her with his head on one side. He seemed to be thinking quickly. Then he nodded.

'Very well, Miss Barbara,' he said. 'First of all, be assured that I will do you no harm, provided that you go back to Kittiwake Cottage and stop meddling in matters that do not concern you.'

'But—'

'Listen to me,' he said, and she noticed that his English had become much more fluent and that he now spoke with only the smallest trace of a foreign accent. 'You do not know what you are talking about. You are dealing with desperate people who will stop at nothing to obtain what they are looking for. They will certainly not let a little girl stand in their way.'

'I'm not a little girl,' said Barbara, stung. 'I'm thirteen in September.'

Donati's lips twitched beneath his moustache.

'A big girl, then,' he said. He sighed, and suddenly looked more like his former self. 'You are very brave and loyal, Miss Barbara, but you must beware, for things are not always what they seem.'

Barbara had no idea what he was talking about, but supposed he was another of those who liked to speak in that roundabout way of which grown-ups seemed so fond.

'Does Helen know who you really are?' she said curiously.

He flushed pink again.

'Yes,' he replied. 'I have told her all.'

'But doesn't she mind?' said Barbara. This was almost beyond comprehension.

'I do not believe so,' he said, giving her an odd sort of look. He patted her on the shoulder. 'This is not the right moment, or I should explain it to you, but remember what I said: do not intrude yourself into things that do not concern you.'

'But it does concern me,' said Barbara. 'I made a promise, and I intend to keep it.'

'Be careful,' was all he said, and hurried away.

She stared after him in puzzlement. She was still convinced that she had discovered Valencourt's identity, but for a notorious thief his manner was odd. Indeed, he seemed almost solicitous for her safety. Presumably he saw her as a distraction and wanted to get rid of her, and the easiest way to do that was to pretend to be concerned about her. She stood there for a second, chewing a finger-nail. She hated to admit it, but Donati had planted a seed of doubt in her mind as to whether she was doing the right thing. Perhaps he was right: perhaps she should not interfere. After all, what could she do? Then she thought of poor Miss Trout, with no-one to help her while her very family plotted against her, and set off resolutely towards the flat-topped rock that concealed the entrance to the tunnel.

She had intended to start off immediately, but her rumbling stomach forestalled her and she thought longingly of her picnic lunch. The tide was still very low, so she judged that she had plenty of time to eat—and besides, it wouldn't do to attempt serious work on an empty stomach. She climbed up onto the flat rock, and sat there munching her sandwiches and thinking hard. It had suddenly occurred to her that she did not have a plan. It was all very well rushing off to spy on Clifford and his cronies, but how exactly was she going to do it? It was going to be difficult to creep about the house without being spotted. Barbara thought about it all the way through lunch without reaching a conclusion, but finally decided that the best thing would be to see how the land lay when she got there. Perhaps she could find a suitable hiding-place that would allow her to keep an eye on what was happening in the house.

She finished her picnic and packed up her things, then climbed down from the rock and put on her shoes. The opening was there just as she remembered it, and she ducked under the low arch and ran to the back of the cave. Switching on her torch, she took a deep breath and entered the tunnel, touching one hand against the wall as she walked, as though for reassurance. It seemed to take an age before she reached the barrel-chamber—much longer than she remembered, but at last she felt a cool draught of air and began to distinguish shapes in the darkness, which told her that she had arrived. She did not stop, but hurried on to the next section of the tunnel, where the path became much steeper. She toiled upwards, passing the fork in the passage where it branched off, and finally came to the end of the tunnel and the iron rungs that led up to the trap-door into the cellar.

Barbara threw her knapsack over her shoulders, tucked her torch into her sleeve and scrambled up the ladder. To her relief, the trap-door was still unbolted; it was clear that nobody came down into the cellar very often, otherwise someone would surely have spotted that it had been left open by now. This time she succeeded in opening it quietly, and she climbed out through the hole, taking good care to make no noise.

She closed the trap-door again, then went into the next cellar-room and across to the stairs. At the top she placed her ear against the door and paused to listen. There was no sound, so she pulled out her hair-pin and set to work at the keyhole. After a few minutes the key gave in to her ministrations and clinked to the floor, allowing Barbara to slide her hand under the door and pull it towards her.

Emerging into the deserted hall with great caution, she stopped and tried to decide what to do next. She could hear nothing to indicate that Miss Trout or her nephew were at home. Perhaps they had gone out for a walk. They were bound to return soon, however. She decided that the best plan was to hide herself somewhere in the hall itself, from where she could see them when they came back, and watch all the comings and goings in the house during the day. Then, when night fell and everyone was in bed—or supposed to be, at least—she would be free to roam the house at will. But where to hide? Barbara looked about, and her gaze immediately fell on the only thing that could possibly provide a suitable hiding-place: a large and ornate cupboard in dark, carved oak, which stood against the wall between the doors to the drawing-room and the dining-room. She darted across to it and pulled it open. As she had expected, it was full of coats and boots, but she judged that there was just enough room in it for her too, if she made herself as small as possible.

Moving an umbrella out of the way, she wriggled herself in carefully and pulled the door to, leaving it open just a crack so she could see out into the hall. Then she settled down to wait. After a few minutes, she decided to sit down—after all, she might be here for hours and she did not relish the thought of standing for all that time. There was an old cushion squashed under a pile of shoes, and she edged it out as quietly as possible and sat down on it. Leaning back against an old Burberry, she yawned. It was warm and cosy in the cupboard and she was feeling drowsy after her picnic lunch—no wonder, she thought, after having spent half the night chasing the Dorseys. Being a detective was tiring work, she was discovering.

'I mustn't fall asleep,' she thought, and promptly did so.

CHAPTER TWENTY-FIVE

MR. SIMPSON RAISED his eyebrows.
'Clifford Maynard?' he said sceptically.

'Yes. Don't you think he fits the part much better?' said Angela. 'I should say he was cleverer than Dorsey, and he used to be an actor—as a matter of fact, Barbara and I have seen him at work.'

She explained their theory that Clifford had invented the story of the nocturnal assault. Simpson was surprised, and stroked his chin as he considered this new information.

'Yes, that sort of play-acting certainly seems more in keeping with Valencourt's character,' he said, 'if indeed he was play-acting. I take it you have no proof?'

'No, only a strong suspicion. But my hunch is that if we were to look through his things, we should find a case full of actors' make-up.'

'But what about Miss Trout? If what you say is true, then she must be shielding her nephew from the law.'

'Ah,' said Angela, 'but can we be entirely certain he *is* her nephew? When we first met them, Miss Trout told us that she had not seen Clifford since he was a child, and that he had turned up at her door unexpectedly only a month or two ago. But people change beyond all recognition over the years. How can Miss Trout be so sure that he is who he says he is? What if, in fact, the person who arrived at Poldarrow Point claiming to be her nephew is not Clifford at all, but Edgar Valencourt? Think about it,' she said, warming to her theme. 'It would be the perfect way for a thief with designs on the family treasure to get close to it. By staying with Miss Trout in the guise of her nephew, he can search the house with his accomplices every night while she is asleep, and then disappear with it as soon as it is found. If Miss Trout raises a hue and cry, the police will hunt down the real Clifford Maynard, who of course will easily be able to prove that he has been nowhere near Poldarrow Point, and then the game will be up—but by that time, of course, Valencourt and the Dorseys will be long gone.'

Simpson nodded.

'Yes,' he said, 'that certainly sounds more like Valencourt's method of working. There is something in what you say, Mrs. Marchmont. I shall have to look carefully into Maynard's story—and that of the Dorseys, too.' He took a notebook and pencil from his pocket and scribbled something down. 'I shall telephone the Yard as soon as we get back and put some men onto the case. If they can find the real Clifford Maynard, then there is nothing to prevent me from arresting the fake one on suspicion of being Edgar Valencourt.'

'Poor Miss Trout,' said Angela. 'She will be most shocked if it turns out that her nephew is an impostor. However, better uncover the secret now than let it continue until Valencourt finds the necklace and spirits it away.' A thought struck her. 'That still doesn't solve the problem of the lease, however,' she said.

'Does Miss Trout plan to sell the necklace if it is found, in order to buy back the freehold of the house?' said Simpson.

'I think so,' said Angela, 'although even then it may be too late. I don't know how long these things take, but I imagine a few weeks at least. Perhaps the re-appearance of the necklace will grant her a stay of execution, however—always assuming that the owner of the freehold is willing to sell it back to her.'

'A lot seems to depend on the recovery of this diamond necklace,' observed Simpson.

'It does, doesn't it? And yet we still can't be sure that the thing even exists. The only evidence for it was written on a page which has been torn out of an old book—' she stopped suddenly, and he looked up.

'Do you think the missing page may contain a clue as to where it is hidden?' he asked.

'Why was the page torn out?' said Angela suddenly. 'It was done recently. Who did it, and why?'

'I suppose whoever took it wanted to study it for clues as to the hiding-place,' said Simpson. 'Or perhaps they wanted to make sure nobody else could find it. Presumably at the very least the page contains confirmation that the necklace is actually in the house.'

Angela stared at him, as though turning over a new idea in her head.

'Now that is very interesting,' she said.

'What is very interesting?'

Angela seemed not to hear. She had turned her head and was gazing, unseeing, out to sea. After a minute she came to, looked about her, and said:

'We had better think about getting back. Shall we clear all these things up?'

They returned to the boat, Simpson carrying the picnic -basket, which was now much lighter than it had been on the journey out. Gibbs nodded a greeting as they stepped back on board.

'Where now?' he said.

'Back to Tregarrion,' said Simpson.

'Right you are,' said Gibbs. He fired up the engine and guid-ed the *Miss Louise* carefully out through the mouth of the in-let and into the open sea. A stiff breeze had got up and the water was much choppier now.

'May we have the sail up?' said Angela, then turned and saw that Bill had got there before her and was already hauling on the ropes.

'Don't want to waste a good wind like this one,' said Gibbs, taking out his pipe and settling down to enjoy himself.

The sail flapped like a gigantic sea-bird as it went up, then billowed out and drove the boat onward at a rapid pace. This time they headed farther out to sea, and Angela had to remove her hat again—this time to stop it blowing off altogether. The wind plucked at her clothes and whipped her hair about, and she felt altogether exhilarated. The noise was too loud to allow much conversation, and so very little was said until they had passed the Poldarrow headland far away on their left and the *Miss Louise* finally turned and made for land. As they came into the shelter of the bay, the wind dropped and Bill lowered the sail again, and they chugged gently towards the harbour.

They drew up by the pier and disembarked, then took their leave of Mr. Gibbs and Bill with many thanks and salutations. Mr. Simpson walked with Angela back to Kittiwake Cottage.

'Thank you for a most enjoyable afternoon,' said Angela. 'I shall now go and see to my hair—although I fear that it may be beyond the capabilities of my hair-brush.'

Simpson laughed.

'Your hair looks perfectly neat,' he said. 'I shan't say anything more, as I see you are not the sort of woman who welcomes compliments.'

'No,' agreed Angela, 'better not. Are you going to telephone Scotland Yard now?'

'Yes—the sooner my men establish whether or not the Clifford Maynard we know is really Miss Trout's nephew, the better, I think.'

'And will you tell me the result of your investigations?'

'Of course,' he said, and went off.

Barbara was not there when she entered the house, and Angela had given Marthe the afternoon off, so the place was quite deserted. Angela had just regretfully decided that it was too early for a cocktail, and was hunting around for her book, when there was a knock at the door. Supposing it to be Barbara, she went to answer it, and found, to her surprise, Harriet Dorsey standing there.

'Hallo,' said Mrs. Dorsey, and smiled as an afterthought. 'I wonder if I might come in?'

'Of course,' said Angela, with great politeness. She stepped back to allow Harriet to enter and conducted her into the sitting-room. Harriet looked about her, selected the most comfortable chair and sat down.

'Lionel knows I'm here,' she said abruptly. 'In fact, it was his idea.'

'I see,' said Angela, not seeing at all.

Harriet seemed in no hurry to come to the point.

'This is a pretty cottage,' she said. 'I suppose she found it for you?'

'I beg your pardon, whom do you mean?'

'Why, Miss Trout, of course.'

'No,' said Angela, who was becoming more and more puzzled. 'I rented it from a lady in London.'

Harriet looked surprised.

'Oh?' she said. 'I thought she must have arranged everything.'

'No, not at all,' said Angela. 'I had never met Miss Trout before I came to Tregarrion.'

Harriet grimaced and shrugged.

'Oh well,' she said, 'if that's the way you want to play it, it's no skin off my nose.'

'What do you mean?'

'No matter,' said Harriet. 'I've come to make you a proposition.'

'A proposition?'

'Yes,' said Harriet. 'It wasn't my idea,' she said again. She fell silent, and Angela wondered if she would ever come to the point.

'What is this proposition?' she prompted.

'You've been searching for something at Poldarrow Point,' said Harriet all at once. 'We know you have, and we know what it is. Well, we've been searching for the same thing. We've been searching since before you arrived and we haven't found it either. The old man doesn't know anything, so it's a question of taking the place apart ourselves until we find it.'

It was useless to pretend she did not know what the other woman was talking about, so Angela saved her breath.

'What do you suggest?' she said.

Harriet examined her finger-nails.

'It's rather difficult for us to search the house at night,' she said. 'We really need to do it in the daytime, so we can move the furniture.'

'I see your problem,' said Angela.

'What share did the Trout offer you in return for finding the thing?' said Harriet suddenly.

At last, Angela understood. She hesitated, then glanced shrewdly at her visitor.

'Why, what share did you have in mind?' she said.

'We can offer you ten per cent,' said Harriet.

Angela pretended to reflect.

'That's quite a large share,' she said, 'but it's not quite as much as I was hoping for.' She paused delicately.

'I told Lionel you'd want more,' said Harriet, nodding. 'So it's no go, then?'

'I didn't say that,' said Angela. 'I shall have to think about it for a while.'

Harriet rose.

'All right,' she said. 'I'll leave you to it. But don't think for too long. They've got to leave the house soon, and then nobody will get it.'

'Very well,' said Angela. She escorted Harriet to the door and opened it. 'I shall let you know my decision very soon—but in the meantime, I suggest you have a word with your husband and ask him to raise his offer. I have expenses to meet.'

'I'm sure you do,' said Harriet, gazing at Angela's expensively-tailored sailing outfit with what might have been envy. She left the house without another word.

Angela shut the door and stood with her back to it, as though to block anyone from entering, then let out a deep breath.

'Well!' she said to herself. 'There's a turn-up!'

So the Dorseys thought that Miss Trout had paid her to find the necklace, did they? They actually believed that Miss Trout had brought her down from London and had installed her in Kittiwake Cottage for that especial purpose. And now it appeared they wanted to bribe Angela to find it and pass it to them secretly! It was almost beyond belief. Was Clifford Maynard aware of this? Harriet had said something about the old man knowing nothing—was she referring to Maynard? How extraordinary it would be if Clifford were plotting to steal the necklace from his aunt and the Dorseys were plotting to steal it from Clifford!

Angela's first instinct was to report the latest development to Mr. Simpson, but there was no telephone at the cottage, so she would have to walk to the hotel if she wanted to speak to him. On second thoughts, she decided to leave it until the next day: he had said he was going to be busy speaking to Scotland Yard that evening, and it was hardly an urgent matter. It might just as well wait until tomorrow. Besides, she did not want it to look as though she were perpetually seeking him out. She would tell him tomorrow, and ask what she ought to do: after all, she had as good as told Harriet that she was willing to be bribed, but she could not string the Dorseys along forever with a promise.

Half an hour later, Angela heard Marthe return from her afternoon off.

'Ah, *vous êtes de retour, madame*,' said the maid. 'Did you have a nice picnic with your smart friend?'

'Yes, thank you, Marthe, it was very pleasant.' said Angela.

'He is elegant, that one,' said Marthe. '*Très charmant.* He speaks beautiful French to me, which most Englishmen are too stupid to do. Have you just returned now?'

'No, I came back about an hour ago,' replied Angela, and shortly afterwards had a visit from an acquaintance which has left me feeling rather grubby.'

'*Madame?*'

'Never mind,' said Angela, 'but you might run me a bath. Perhaps that will help.'

Luxuriating in the warm water, she reflected on recent events. It had certainly been a day of surprises, starting with Barbara's account of her nocturnal adventures and ending with the most astonishing visit from Harriet Dorsey. Although she could not explain why, Angela had begun to get the feeling that she held the key to the mystery in her hands, and that if only she could catch a glimpse of the whole thing from the right angle, then all would become clear. Little snatches of conversation kept drifting into her head and whirling around, seemingly at random, mingling with her own thoughts in an increasingly frantic dance. She lay back and tried to let her mind do its own work without conscious interference, for experience had taught her that if she tried to grasp her ideas too firmly they would disappear as quickly as they had come.

Some time later, Angela sighed and sat up. The water had begun to get cold and she was still no nearer to the solution than before. Perhaps there was still a piece of the puzzle missing. Or perhaps the hot weather—or something else—had addled her brain. Well, there was no use in trying to chase after the answer. It would come in its own good time.

She wandered into her bedroom, wrapped in a silk dressing-gown. Marthe was there, attacking Angela's clothes with a brush.

'Now, I know you're going to be cross,' said Angela, 'but I somehow got a smudge of oil on my sailing-suit today. Can you do anything with it?'

Marthe pursed her lips.

'I dare say something can be done, *madame*,' she said, 'but you will not be able to wear it tomorrow.'

'Oh, no matter,' said Angela. 'The green frock will be quite suitable.'

'You are not, then, going on the boat again?'

'No,' said Angela. 'As a matter of fact, I had thought of going into Penzance. I should like to visit the library.'

'Ah.' Marthe was used to Angela's ways and made no comment.

'Have you seen Barbara today?' Angela said.

'No,' replied the maid. 'She went out shortly after you did, but I do not know where.'

'I don't suppose the wretched child really did set out to walk to Land's End?' said Angela. 'I wouldn't put it past her.'

'It will be time to eat soon,' said Marthe. 'She will no doubt be back in time for dinner.'

But dinner-time came and Barbara did not appear.

CHAPTER TWENTY-SIX

BARBARA AWOKE WITH a start and had a second's panic as she wondered where on earth she was. Then she remembered: she was in the cupboard at Poldarrow Point. She was annoyed at herself for falling asleep. Detectives were not supposed to sleep when they ought to be at work. But what was it that had awoken her? Had Clifford and his aunt returned, perhaps? She leaned forward and peered through the crack in the door, but could see nothing. She began to suspect that the cupboard was not as good a hiding place as she had imagined.

'It's no use my staying here,' she said to herself. 'How am I supposed to see what's going on everywhere else in the house if I'm stuck in a cupboard? Especially when it makes me fall asleep!'

So saying, she got to her feet and poked her head cautiously around the door. There was nobody about. She emerged quietly from the cupboard then nearly jumped out of her skin when the quiet of the entrance-hall was suddenly shattered by a great clicking and a whirring. Barbara's heart beat fast in her chest and she almost darted back into the cupboard, but then the whirring was shortly followed by the chimes of a clock striking five and she allowed herself to breathe again.

The clock fell silent and Barbara cocked an ear, but still heard no signs of life. She approached the drawing-room, trying to make no noise. The door was slightly ajar, and she pushed it slowly, then could have kicked herself as the hinges squealed loudly. What a fool she was! She ought to have re-membered about the squeaky drawing-room door—after all, Clifford had mentioned it himself the day after he had sup-posedly been attacked.

She stood still, but nobody came and there was no sound. Growing bolder, she pushed the door wide open. As she had thought, the room was empty. She took a quick look into all the other downstairs rooms but found no-one. They must be still out, then.

She returned to the entrance-hall and debated with herself as to what to do next. There didn't seem much use in hanging about here if the house were empty. Ah—but was it empty? What was that sudden noise? She lifted her head, and a thrill ran through her as she recognized the familiar sound. There it was again! The same moaning, whimpering noise she had heard before, when she saw the ghostly figure floating about on the top floor! She stood, frozen to the spot, hardly daring to breathe, and wondering whether she should make a bolt for the front door. Then she grimaced and shook herself.

'Why, you ought to be ashamed of yourself, Barbara Wells,' she thought. 'What sort of a coward are you? You know perfectly well that there are no such things as ghosts. You might have got into a funk last time you were here, but you jolly well shan't do it again this time.'

She went to the foot of the stairs and listened, and this time she heard quite a different sound. It was a voice she recognized: a voice which was usually soft and polite, but which now sounded quite different. It was harder, angrier—dangerous, even. Whoever it was seemed to be berating someone at length.

'Why, that's Clifford,' said Barbara to herself. 'Is he bullying his aunt? I may be forced to hit him over the head with something, if so.'

The whimpering noise started again, and she hurried up the stairs. It sounded as though she were just in time to rescue Miss Trout from whatever dastardly fate Clifford had in store for her. She passed the first landing and stopped to listen again, her foot on the bottom stair of the next flight.

'No, no, no,' pleaded a voice she recognized as that of the phantom-like figure she had seen the other day.

'You old horror,' said Clifford's voice. 'Don't think I don't know what you're up to. You can pretend all you like but you won't fool me. You know very well where it is—I don't know why you bother denying it.'

'No, no, no,' said the voice again.

Barbara crept up the next flight of stairs, holding her breath, and peeped through the balustrade, ready to run for her life if necessary. Her eyes grew wide at the scene before her, for there was the very figure she had seen the other day, and now she saw that it was not a ghost at all, but a wizened old man dressed in a shabby nightgown. He was struggling feebly to free himself from the grip of Clifford Maynard, who held him firmly by the arm and was pulling him along towards an open door at the end of the passage.

The old man somehow managed to tug himself free and turned as though to try and escape. Clifford grabbed him, his other hand raised as though to strike, and the man shrank back in fear, whimpering. Clifford lowered his hand slowly and made an expression of disgust.

'You try another trick like that and I'll show you I mean business,' he said.

'Please sir,' begged the old man, 'I don't know nothing. Please take me back home. I want to go home.'

'This *is* your home, you old villain,' snapped Clifford. 'Don't you remember? No—of course you don't. Not that you'll admit to it, anyway. You've lost your mind, forgotten everything, haven't you? Well, don't think I can't tell you're putting it on. One day you'll slip up, and then I'll have you, so I will. Now, get back to your room. I've told you before about wandering about up here where someone might see you.'

The change in his manner was quite extraordinary: he seemed wholly unlike the courteous and affable Mr. Maynard of before. At that moment Barbara felt afraid. For the first time it struck her that perhaps this whole thing *was* too much for one young girl to tackle alone. She had thrown herself into the treasure-hunt with enthusiasm—after all, what could be more harmless than searching for a missing antique necklace to help a dear old lady? But now it had become something more—something that she did not quite understand. That Clifford Maynard was up to no good was now certain, but who was this old man? And why was he being held here in the house, presumably against his will? Did he know where the necklace was? Clifford's words seemed to imply it.

Barbara watched as Clifford pulled his captive roughly along to the end of the passage and through the open door. She expected him to push the old man into the room then come out again immediately and go downstairs, and was preparing to make her escape, but to her surprise, the minutes passed and no Clifford appeared. She waited a little longer then, mustering her courage, emerged from behind the banister and ran silently along to the end of the corridor. The door was still open, and she approached it cautiously and peered in.

As these were presumably the old servants' quarters, she had half-expected to see a bare room with a bed and a chamber-pot, but what she saw in fact was another narrow passage, about ten feet long, with a tiny window at the end. In the left-hand wall, next to the window, was another door, which had also been left open.

Her astonishment growing by the minute, Barbara ran to this second door and saw that it opened onto a steep and narrow flight of stairs which ran parallel to the second-floor passage and led downwards into the darkness. She listened, and thought she could just hear Clifford's voice as he continued to harangue the old man somewhere ahead. Once again, she hesitated. Should she follow? What if Clifford came back this way? There would be nowhere for her to hide and then she would be caught.

At that moment, her courage almost failed her and she very nearly turned around and ran out of the house, but then she thought of the fear on the old man's face as Clifford had raised his hand to him, and she set her jaw in determination.

'They shan't write "Coward" on my headstone, at any rate,' she said to herself as she stepped with trepidation into the darkness.

She felt her way down carefully, relying on the dim light that emanated from some unknown source below, since she dared not switch on her torch lest the beam alert Clifford to her presence. The stairs ended in another door, which had been left open, and Barbara saw that beyond it was a tiny chamber with panelled walls but no windows, containing only a large armchair and a table. This room was gloomy, but benefited from a small amount of light which filtered through yet another door in the far wall. It had been left slightly ajar, so she could quite clearly hear the voices of the two men—Clifford's loud and commanding, and the old man's soft and whining.

'I know you think you can wait us out,' Clifford was saying, 'but that won't wash, d'you hear me?'

'Oh, dear Lord, dear Lord, forgive us our sins, for we who dwell on the earth are not worthy to enter the Kingdom of Heaven,' muttered the old man.

'That's enough of that! Don't tell me you've had an attack of religion in your old age, for I won't believe it.'

'Blessed are the meek, for they shall inherit the earth,' said the old man, his voice rising to a whine. 'Blessed are they which do hunger and thirst—'

'Stop it, I tell you! Stop it!'

There was a pause, and Clifford began again, in a calmer tone of voice.

'Now, listen,' he said. 'Just listen to reason. We've only got a few more days until we have to leave this place altogether —all of us, including you. And once we're out there's no saying whether we'll be able to get back in again. Now, I know it's here, and I know you know where it is but won't say, but where's the sense in that, eh? You've had it for thirty years, and what good has it ever done you? Why, none at all. You've buried yourself down here all this time, and let the place go to rack and ruin, and for what? Just for the sake of diddling your own family out of what's rightfully theirs. Well, you couldn't hide forever, and it was just your bad luck that we found you after all this time. Now you're caught, so you might as well come clean, or we'll all lose.'

'I never let the place go to rack and ruin,' muttered the old man. 'Leastways, not till you stuck me in here. I had the garden looking a treat, I did.'

'Oho, so you can talk sense when it suits you,' said Clifford. 'So, are you going to tell me where it is or not?'

'Rosie's got it,' said the old man, and gave a sudden cackle.

Clifford clicked his tongue impatiently.

'Why do you keep saying that?' he said. 'You know full well she hasn't got it. She has no more idea of where it is than I do—I'm certain of that.'

The old man cackled again and began singing 'Mistress Mary Quite Contrary' in a thin, quavering voice. Clifford gave an exclamation of disgust and gave it up.

'There's no use in talking to you, is there? I'm off, and this time I won't forget to lock the door, so don't think you'll get out again.'

The sound of footsteps could be heard approaching. Quick as lightning, Barbara ducked down behind the armchair and hid, heart beating rapidly in her chest, fearful of discovery. Clifford strode through the chamber angrily without glancing to either side. She heard his heavy tread on the narrow stairs and the bang of the door at the top, then the ominous sound of a key turning.

She was trapped.

CHAPTER TWENTY-SEVEN

BARBARA EMERGED CAUTIOUSLY from behind the chair and debated what to do next. As far as she could see, she had two choices: 1) remain hidden behind the chair in this room until Clifford turned up with food for the captive, as he would presumably do sooner or later; or 2) go into the next room and perhaps frighten the old man to death by her sudden appearance—or, at the very least, risk having him betray her to Clifford when he returned. Neither alternative was particularly enticing.

She drummed her fingers on her chin, deep in thought, then looked up and suppressed a shriek, for there was the old man, peeping round the door at her with the greatest curiosity. He saw that she had seen him and stepped fully into the room.

'Did *they* send you?' he said suspiciously.

'Nobody sent me,' replied Barbara. 'I found my way in here by myself.'

'What do you want?'

'To be perfectly truthful,' said Barbara, 'what I really want is something to eat. It's ages since I had lunch and I didn't bring any other food. Rather silly of me, now I come to think about it.'

The old man grinned impishly and beckoned to her to follow him next door. She did so with the greatest curiosity.

'Good gracious!' she exclaimed. 'Where are we?'

She glanced about her. The room was of medium size, and looked not unpleasant to live in, being furnished with a bed, a chair or two, a small table and a shelf stacked with books. There was a threadbare rug on the floor and an old-fashioned washstand in the corner. A small window looked out over the garden and the cliff top. Its panes were covered in finger-prints, as though someone had spent a lot of time with his hands against it, gazing out. But while the room looked reasonably comfortable, there was something queer about it, which Barbara struggled to define. She gazed around for a moment in puzzlement, then it struck her: apart from the one she had just come through, the room had no door. That was strange: she had come down a flight of stairs, so surely she must be on the first floor now. But why was there no door out onto the landing? She suddenly remembered something Angela had said the day they had searched Preacher Dick's bedchamber: she had observed that the room was smaller than one might have expected, given that the door to the next bedroom along was at the end of the passage. Was this, then, a secret room sandwiched between two others?

'No door here,' said the old man, as though reading her thoughts. He waved at the wall behind the bed to indicate the absence of any means of egress.

'No,' agreed Barbara. 'I wonder why they built it this way?'

The man shrugged. 'Who knows?' he said. 'They were smugglers, weren't they? They liked their little hidey-places, 'case the Customs men come. Here.'

He went to the bookshelf, on which stood a bowl of fruit that was rather past its best, and handed her an apple.

'Thanks,' said Barbara, and took a bite out of it politely. 'I'm Barbara Wells,' she said, unable to think of anything else to say.

'Barbara Wells, eh?' said the old man. 'And what are you doing here?'

'I came here because I was suspicious of Clifford—Mr. Maynard,' she said boldly. 'I thought he was trying to steal something that didn't belong to him. And from what I heard just now, when he was talking to you, I think my suspicions were correct.'

'Oh you do, do you?' said the man, glancing at her shrewdly. 'And what might this "something" be that you think he's trying to steal?'

'I think you know very well what it is,' said Barbara.

'Sometimes I do,' said the old man sadly, 'but my mind's not what it was. I forget things, you know. I'm not young any more, and my thoughts wander.'

'I'm sorry to hear that,' said Barbara. 'Should you say that they wander especially far when Clifford is shouting at you?'

The old man darted another glance at her.

'Perhaps,' he said, and gave a cackle.

'I'm trying to find the necklace before Clifford does,' said Barbara. 'I don't want him to get it. I think he's a horrid man.'

'Ah! The necklace,' he said. 'Rosie's got it.'

'You said that before. Who is Rosie?'

He raised his hands to heaven.

'"The wilderness and the solitary place shall be glad for them; and the desert shall rejoice, and blossom as the rose,"' he said.

Barbara sighed. The old man was evidently nearly ga-ga, despite occasional moments of lucidity. He was being held here because he knew the whereabouts of the necklace, and Clifford presumably hoped that one day he would remember where it was and reveal all. From what Barbara had seen of him, however, it seemed clear that there was no use in trying to bully him into telling the secret: in his senile moments he could not tell, and when he was himself he *would* not tell. Perhaps if she could befriend him then he would become more amenable.

She sat down on a chair and took another bite of her apple.

'How long have you been here?' she said conversationally.

'Here? Or *here*?' he said.

'I beg your pardon?' said Barbara.

'If you mean here, then thirty years or more. But if you mean *here*, then far too long. What month are we in now?'

'July,' said Barbara.

'Months and months,' said the old man sadly. 'They told everyone I was dead, you see. I might as well be, too. Why, look at the state they've let my garden get into! Fair breaks my heart to see it.'

Barbara came to a sudden realization.

'You're Jeremiah Trout!' she said in surprise.

'That's what they called me here,' said Jeremiah, nodding. 'I was happy, you know—happy, with my house and my garden. I came here and it was such a lovely spot I decided to retire. But then they found me and wanted to take what was not theirs.' He lapsed into silence, then looked up and said, 'Who are you? What are you doing here?'

'I'm Barbara Wells,' said Barbara. 'I'm here on holiday. I'm staying at Kittiwake Cottage. Do you know it?'

'Kittiwake Cottage,' said Jeremiah. 'There was a place I used to know in Cornwall called Kittiwake Cottage. Down Tregarrion way. Do you know it?'

'Yes,' said Barbara patiently. 'I'm staying there with my godmother, Angela Marchmont. She's a famous detective.'

'A famous detective, eh? Half my life I've spent running away from detectives. The stories I could tell!' His face grew cunning. 'There's one thing they'd all be glad to find, but they never will. I shan't let them.'

'But if it could be found, you could sell it and stay in the house forever,' said Barbara. 'The lease is going to run out on Poldarrow Point in a few days, and then you will have to leave.'

'The lease?' said Jeremiah. A light slowly dawned on his face. 'I remember them telling me something about a lease. A long time ago, wasn't it? Thirty years or more I've been here, you know.'

'Yes, but you won't be here for much longer unless that necklace can be found.'

'But then they'll take it and I shall have nothing,' he said forlornly.

'I know,' said Barbara. 'Clifford and his pals have been searching for it every night. They want to steal it from you and your sister.'

'My sister? Who's that?'

'Miss Trout, of course—Emily.'

The old man gave a great shout of laughter.

'Emily! Emily!' he said. 'That's a good one, that is.'

Barbara sighed inwardly. Talking to Jeremiah Trout was a laborious business.

'But Angela and I have been searching for it too,' she said. 'We have looked everywhere in the house, I should imagine. I have started to think that it's not here at all.'

She looked at him sideways, and he nodded.

'You're right,' he said. 'It's not here.'

'Then where is it?'

'Rosie's got it,' he said.

'Yes, but who *is* Rosie?'

He gazed at her blankly, then waved a hand expansively.

'It's a nice place this, isn't it?' he said. 'Thirty years or more I've been here.'

'Yes,' said Barbara. 'So I understand.'

She stood up and paced around the room. So Jeremiah Trout was alive after all! Alive, and being held prisoner here in his own house until he agreed to reveal where the necklace was hidden. He must have found it years ago, and hidden it somewhere safe. But why hadn't he sold it immediately? Had he done so, he might have lived here in comfort for the rest of his days, and should have been in no danger from his designing nephew. She stopped, marvelling at Clifford's cunning. He had somehow managed to keep Jeremiah hidden from Miss Trout for months. Poor thing—she thought he was dead. What a cruel trick to play on a defenceless old woman! And Jeremiah—words failed her when she thought of the evil that could lead a man to hold his senile old uncle captive for months on end. She remembered the banging noise she had heard once or twice at the house. Clifford had said it was a loose shutter, but of course it must have been Jeremiah, trying to attract attention.

There was only one thing for it: she would have to find a way to rescue the old man from his captivity, and soon. Her mind ran through the various possibilities. She had no concerns about her own escape—why, that ought to be easy enough. All she had to do was to put into effect her earlier plan to wait in the other room until Clifford arrived with food, and then slip quietly up the stairs and out of the house while he was engaged with Jeremiah. But that wouldn't work for both of them—Clifford would immediately realize the bedroom was empty and come after them.

'Mr. Trout,' she said suddenly. 'How did you escape from this room today? Clifford found you wandering about upstairs. How did you get out?'

Jeremiah looked sullen.

'Sometimes he forgets to lock the door, so I go for a walk. Not very often, though. He won't do it again today.'

Barbara had feared as much. She pondered awhile. Perhaps it would be better to make her own escape then come back with reinforcements to rescue Jeremiah. Yes, that was probably the best plan.

She slipped out of the room and crouched down behind the armchair in the tiny ante-chamber to await Clifford's arrival. Jeremiah had lost interest in her and was staring out of the window at his garden. He seemed to have forgotten her entirely, and did not even look up when she went out.

An hour went by, then another. Barbara yawned and shifted uncomfortably. She was getting awfully stiff. Surely someone must bring food soon?

Just then, Jeremiah came in and went out through the other door. She heard him plodding stiffly up the stairs. What was he doing? Was he trying to make another escape? She listened, and heard him descending the stairs again. There was a clatter of cups and plates, and to Barbara's dismay, he appeared carrying a tray of food and drink. Somebody must have left it at the top of the stairs earlier without coming down. Jeremiah went back into his bedroom and Barbara stood up in annoyance. Was this the usual way of things? Did they leave his food at the top of the stairs every day? Barbara's mouth fell open as she realized that, if that were the case, then she could be here for days before she managed to escape. She ran up the stairs and tried the door. It was locked. Clifford had been and gone and she had missed her opportunity.

Her stomach rumbled. It was long past her dinner-time, and she briefly toyed with the idea of begging some of Jeremiah's food off him, but decided against it. She was sure he would not refuse her another piece of fruit, however. She wandered back into the bedroom and found the old man eating from his knife with great relish.

'Hallo,' he said. 'You're back.'

'Yes,' she said. 'I say, would you mind awfully if I took another apple?'

'Help yourself,' he said, and went on with his meal.

Barbara ate the apple. It did little to fill the hole in her stomach and she looked enviously at the food on Jeremiah's tray.

'I came here to rescue you, you know,' she said. 'I thought you might like to get out of the house.'

'So I should,' said Jeremiah. 'The garden needs seeing to.'

'But the only way out is up those stairs,' she went on, 'and the door at the top is locked. How often does Clifford come here?'

'Clifford?' said Jeremiah. 'Why, I haven't seen him for weeks. He's left me all alone.'

'No he hasn't,' said Barbara. 'You saw him a couple of hours ago. Does he come here every day? Or does he always leave the food at the top of the stairs?'

'I don't know, I haven't seen him for weeks,' repeated the old man.

There was no getting any sense out of him, so Barbara gave it up. She went over to the bookshelf, picked up a book and began flicking through it.

'Anyway, you're wrong—it's not the only way out,' said Jeremiah, behind her.

Barbara whirled round.

'What do you mean?'

'There's another door, isn't there?' he said.

'Where?'

'I'll show you when I've finished,' he said.

She waited with barely-concealed impatience until he had dined to his satisfaction.

'Here,' he said. He rose with difficulty and led her through to the dim ante-chamber next door. 'Can't see a thing in here,' he said.

Barbara rummaged in her knapsack.

'I've got a torch,' she said. She switched it on and a beam of light illuminated the panelled walls. She moved the torch around, looking for signs of a door.

'Keep that thing still, can't you?' said Jeremiah. 'Point it here.'

He indicated a spot behind the armchair, and Barbara did as she was asked.

'There,' he said.

Barbara leaned forward and looked closely at the wall, but all she could see was a section of panelling like any other.

'I can't see anything,' she said.

'Aha,' said Jeremiah. 'That's because it's hidden.'

He reached out and placed his hand on an ornate little carving in the shape of a lion's head. To Barbara's surprise, it slid easily to one side and there, underneath it, was a keyhole.

'See?' said Jeremiah in triumph.

CHAPTER TWENTY-EIGHT

B ARBARA STARED AT the keyhole.
    'Where does it lead?' she said.

'Down to the cellars, so I heard,' said Jeremiah Trout.

'Have you never been through it?'

'Of course not,' said Jeremiah. 'I haven't got the key, have I?'

'Then who has it?'

'Nobody. It's been lost for years, as far as I know.'

Barbara could have torn her hair out with frustration. How were they ever going to get out? She went back into the bedroom and stared hard out of the window. Of course—the window! They were thirty feet or so from the ground, but perhaps there would be something she could climb down. She pulled at the catch but nothing happened. She tugged harder, and then with all her might, but it was no use: the thing was stuck fast.

She let out something that might have been described as a growl, and thrust her hands into her pockets with a peevish expression. Her right hand fell on something hard and unfamiliar, and she brought it out to see what it was. It was the key they had found the other day behind the panel in the dining-room. She had taken it from Angela to examine it, and it must have been in her pocket for days. Barbara's heart leapt, but she forced herself to remain calm. Why, it was absurd to think that this was the very key she was looking for! Still, there was no harm in trying it. She returned to the ante-chamber, where Jeremiah was gazing blankly about him.

'Let's try this key,' said Barbara, and did so. It fitted perfectly. Barbara could have sung for joy, but contented herself with merely clapping her hands together. After a little struggle, the key turned and the door swung inwards to reveal another flight of steps leading down into the pitch blackness.

'Well, there's a thing,' said Jeremiah.

Barbara turned to him.

'I'm going to see where this goes,' she said, 'and if it leads out of the house I'll come back and get you. You stay here for now. I'll be back soon.'

'All right,' said Jeremiah, and wandered vaguely back into his bedroom.

Barbara switched on her torch again and stepped into the darkness. The stairs seemed to go on for a long way, but eventually she came to the bottom and saw that she was in what looked like a cellar. She flashed the torch around the walls. The room was quite self-contained, and not apparently connected to the other cellars. But was there any way out other than back up the stairs to the secret room? The beam of the torch swept over the walls and the ceiling, and finally across the floor, where it came to a sudden stop as Barbara spotted a trap-door very similar to the one in the other cellar. It was covered in dust and evidently had not been used for many years. Could there be another smugglers' tunnel? She certainly hoped so.

Barbara dropped to her knees and pulled at the cover, which had no bolt. It gave way all of a sudden and deposited what felt like two pounds of grey dust all over her. She leapt back with a strangled yelp and spent a good few minutes coughing and sneezing, her eyes streaming with water. Eventually the attack stopped, and she brushed herself down as best she could. Wiping her eyes, she pointed the torch into the hole, and saw that iron rungs had been set into the rock in exactly the same way as in the other tunnel. Her heart beating in excitement, she tucked her torch into her sleeve and lowered herself into the hole, feeling for the top rung with her feet.

She descended for ten feet or so, and found herself in a tunnel not unlike the other one. It, too, sloped steeply downwards, and she set off to follow it. After several twists and turns she was brought to a sudden halt when she found the passage ahead of her blocked by a rock-fall. Her disappointment was severe. How provoking to get this far only to have to turn back!

She approached the rock-fall and took a closer look at it. It did not look so *very* bad. The stones at the top, in particular, looked as though they might come free with little difficulty. She sighed, and set to work, moving the rocks one at a time, while taking care not to dislodge the whole thing and bring it down on top of her. An hour or so later she stepped back to survey her handiwork, and saw that she had made good progress. Five minutes after that she breathed a sigh of relief when she tugged out a particularly difficult stone and discovered by the light of the torch that she could finally see through to the other side of the blockage. With renewed energy she set to clearing away the rocks, and within half an hour she had made a hole big enough for a man to pass through. She scrambled through it and jumped down on the other side, and immediately recognized where she was. She was in the passage that branched off the main smugglers' tunnel not far from the house. So that was where the path beyond the rock-fall led—to the hidden cellar and the secret room!

Now to go back and fetch Jeremiah, and then they could escape. Barbara sat on a rock to rest for a minute or two, then retraced her steps to the secret room. When she came to the panelled door that led into the ante-chamber, she stopped to listen carefully, but there was no sound. She went through it and tapped gently on the bedroom door.

She found Jeremiah Trout sitting in a chair with an open book on his lap, drifting into a gentle doze.

'Mr. Trout,' she said, 'I've come back to fetch you.'

His eyes opened slowly and he regarded her without enthusiasm.

'I know you, don't I?' he said.

'Yes, I'm Barbara,' said Barbara. 'I've found a way out of the house. Don't you want to leave?'

'You're filthy,' he said.

Barbara looked down at herself. It was true: her hands and her frock were almost black with dirt, and she imagined her face was the same.

'Yes, well, that can't be helped,' she said. 'Do you want to escape from the house tonight?'

'Escape? From the house?'

'Yes!' she said impatiently. 'I've found another entrance to the smugglers' tunnel and we can leave tonight, but we'll have to wait an hour or two until the tide is low enough.'

'I would like to get back to my garden,' he said wistfully.

'Then you must come with me.' She hesitated. 'Er—Mr. Trout, do you have any proper clothes you can put on?'

'Proper clothes?'

'Yes,' she said. 'You're going to look pretty conspicuous wearing just a nightgown when we come into Tregarrion, and we'll need to lie low for a while, until I can get hold of the police.'

'The police?' he said in alarm. 'No call to get the police. What do you want the police for?'

'Why, to arrest your nephew,' said Barbara. 'Even if he hasn't actually stolen anything from you yet, I'm fairly sure there are laws against holding people prisoner for months on end.'

'The police! Fetch the police!' he said. 'Now you come along with me, my lad. There'll be no more of this funny business where you're going.'

'Exactly,' said Barbara. 'That's what they'll say to him, all right. Now, what about these clothes of yours?'

After some further prompting he eventually rummaged under the bed, grumbling, and brought out a small trunk containing a variety of mismatched garments. Barbara went into the next room while he put them on, then came back in and regarded him doubtfully. In his shabby old things he looked rather like a tramp, although she was far too polite to say so.

'Well, you'll have to do,' she said. 'Now we just have to wait for a bit. The entrance to the tunnel is only uncovered at low tide, and that's not until about one o'clock, so if we set off at midnight we should arrive at the right time, I think.'

'But it's my bed-time now,' said Jeremiah. 'I'm tired.'

'Don't you want to escape from Clifford?'

'Clifford? Is Clifford here? I never liked him. I always said he'd double-cross us.'

'Yes, that's why we're leaving. Don't worry about him now. I'll tell you when it's time to go.'

She sat down to wait, chin in her hand. After an hour or so she judged it was time, and went over to shake Jeremiah, who had dozed off in his chair. He took some urging, but the promise of being allowed to see his garden again finally spurred him into action, and he declared himself ready to escape.

Together they descended the stairs into the cellar, and Barbara showed Jeremiah the trap-door that led to the second smugglers' tunnel. He was reluctant to climb down the ladder, but she persuaded him at last, reminding him all the while of his garden, and with a little assistance he eventually managed the descent. It was more difficult to get him past the fallen rocks, but Barbara cleared a few more out of the way and dragged him through somehow, although he grumbled all the while and more than once threatened to go back to his room.

After that, the journey became much easier. They passed through the barrel-chamber and into the lower section of the tunnel, and finally emerged into the cave on the beach. Jeremiah had fallen silent at last, and Barbara stopped for a moment to ponder their next move. She was getting pretty tired now, and wanted nothing more than to go back to Kittiwake Cottage and fall into bed. That was no good, though, for Clifford was sure to come after them, perhaps with Lionel Dorsey in tow, and what could three women and a frail old man do against two determined criminals who perhaps carried guns? And Jeremiah knew where the necklace was. If Valencourt— or Donati, or whatever his name was—got wind of that, the old man would undoubtedly be plunged into even more danger. No, this was a job for the police—for Scotland Yard, in fact. That meant going to the hotel to look for Mr. Simpson.

'This way,' she said, and ducked under the cave entrance.

'Where are we going?' said Jeremiah. 'I want to go to bed.'

'You shall go to bed,' Barbara promised, 'but you must come with me. It's not far.'

She grabbed his arm and pulled him across the beach towards the cliff. He mumbled and muttered but did not resist as they struggled up the steep path that led past Kittiwake and Shearwater cottages.

'Just a second,' said Barbara, stopping. It had suddenly struck her that she ought to let Angela know she was safe. She delved in her knapsack and brought out a crumpled bit of paper and the stub of a pencil. She scribbled a note, then ran up the path of the cottage and shoved it under the door. A light was still on upstairs, and she wondered whether it was Angela awaiting her return. But there was no time to stop: they must get to Mr. Simpson as quickly as possible.

'You wait here,' said Barbara to Jeremiah when they had almost reached the hotel. Given his shabby state, she thought it best that he remain in the shadows while she went to find Simpson.

'Where are we?' he said. 'I want to go to bed.'

'Soon,' she said.

She ran in through the main door. It was almost two and the whole place slumbered. The sleepy man at the desk eyed her askance as she entered, filthy and unkempt, then laughed without humour as she demanded he fetch Mr. Simpson.

'Ha! That's a good one, that is!' he said. 'What do you take me for, an idiot? Go on with you now, hop it!'

'But it's frightfully important,' said Barbara. 'I need to report a terrible crime.'

'Then why don't you go and find a policeman, 'stead of bothering our guests? But you won't, will you? I know your sort. You won't go near the police if you can help it.'

'But Mr. Simpson *is* a—' Barbara stopped and bit her tongue. Nobody was supposed to know that Mr. Simpson was an under-cover Scotland Yard man.

'Go on, get out!' said the man, coming out from behind his desk with a threatening look and picking up a broom.

Barbara made her escape. It took her a few minutes to find Jeremiah, who had wandered off and was looking up at the windows with interest.

'I've seen this place before,' he said.

'Yes, it's the Hotel Splendide,' said Barbara.

'Lots of people with plenty of money here,' said the old man. 'I bet they'd be pretty pickings.'

Barbara was not listening, for she had just spotted her friend Ginger, who was working a late night and sweeping the terrace outside the ball-room.

'Hallo,' he said when he saw her. 'What you doing out at this time of night? Shouldn't you be in bed?'

'I wanted to speak to Mr. Simpson,' said Barbara, 'but the man at the desk threw me out.'

'Mr. Simpson? What do you want to speak to him for?' said Ginger.

'It's rather a long story,' said Barbara. She indicated Jeremiah. 'This is my grandfather,' she said. 'He was hit on the head by a cricket-ball a few years ago and doesn't remember anything, so my aunt put him in the most awful nursing-home where they were horribly cruel to him and didn't give him any food or drink for days and days. Now he's escaped, but I don't want my aunt to know as she will make him go back and I'm terribly afraid they'll starve him to death. Look at the state of him!'

The kind-hearted Ginger regarded the old man sympathetically. He was indeed a sorry sight, having managed to smear dirt and sand all over his face and clothes.

'Pore thing,' said Ginger. 'What are you going to do with him?'

'I'm not sure—that's why I wanted to talk to Mr. Simpson. He's my uncle, you see. He'll know what to do.'

'Regular family party you've got down here,' observed Ginger. 'This aunt of yours seems to have caused a bit of bother. Why do you all stand for it?'

'Because she's frightfully rich, and we have nothing, and she could throw us out onto the streets if she chose.'

'Ah,' said Ginger, nodding sagely. 'There's money mixed up in it, is there? I'm glad I haven't got none myself. So, then, I suppose you want me to fetch Mr. Simpson.'

'Yes please,' said Barbara.

Ginger sighed and went off. A few minutes later he returned, shaking his head.

'There's nobody in,' he said. 'Either that or he's sleeping so soundly he can't be woken. I knocked for a good five minutes.'

Barbara rubbed her chin anxiously. It looked as though she would have to take Jeremiah back to Kittiwake Cottage after all. But Jeremiah evidently had other ideas. He sat down on a chair and refused to stir, despite all that Barbara could say to try and persuade him.

'No,' he said stubbornly. 'It's past my bed-time. You said I could go to bed.'

In vain Barbara pointed out the short distance between the hotel and the cottage. Jeremiah would not budge. Barbara was almost at her wits' end, then an idea came to her.

'Ginger, would you mind awfully doing me an enormous favour?' said Barbara. 'Is there an empty bedroom here where we can go until tomorrow? Mr.—my grandfather is dreadfully tired and just wants to go to bed.'

Jeremiah brightened up immediately.

'Yes, it's my bed-time,' he said. 'I've just escaped, you know, and when Clifford has gone away I'm going to do some gardening.'

'See?' whispered Barbara to Ginger, tapping her head with her finger. 'He's completely ga-ga.'

Ginger scratched his head.

'Well,' he said, 'there's room 402, I suppose. It's a bit small and poky so it only gets used at the busiest times, but it's empty at the moment. It's only for tonight, mind.'

'Oh, thanks awfully,' said Barbara with relief. 'Of course we'll be gone by tomorrow.'

Ginger sighed.

'This way, then,' he said, 'and for goodness' sake, keep quiet!'

He conducted them cautiously through a side door and up to the top floor, stopping only to remove a large bunch of keys from the housekeeper's cupboard.

'Here we are,' he said, opening a door at the end of the corridor. The room was cramped and tiny, and contained only a bed and a chair. Jeremiah beamed when he saw where they were. He got into bed with his shoes on and fell asleep immediately.

'Here's the key,' said Ginger. 'Put it back when you leave. And for goodness' sake, make sure you're not caught here.'

'I will,' promised Barbara, 'and thanks awfully.'

He nodded and went off. Barbara yawned. Jeremiah had taken the only bed, so it looked as though she had an uncomfortable night ahead of her. She regarded the chair with disfavour, then curled up into it as best she could and fell asleep too.

CHAPTER TWENTY-NINE

ANGELA WAITED UP as long as she could bear to, wondering where Barbara had gone and whether she ought to raise the alarm. At one o'clock or thereabouts she decided that she might as well read in bed while she waited, and went upstairs. She had just finished brushing her hair when she heard a rustling sound from the hall. Thinking that Barbara must have returned home, she went downstairs. Nobody was there, but her glance fell on a piece of crumpled paper that had presumably been shoved under the door.

Angela picked it up and gazed at it with some perplexity.

"'Don't worry, we are safe and have gone to the hotel. I will explain all tomorrow,'" she read. She turned the paper over but there was no other message. 'Dear me,' she said. 'What on earth is the child up to now? *Who* is safe? And why have they gone to the hotel?'

She pondered for a moment or two, then decided to go to bed. Barbara had evidently disobeyed her orders and gone to

Poldarrow Point with the aim of convincing Miss Trout that Clifford was up to no good. Presumably she had succeeded, and they had both escaped safely to the hotel. At any rate, the note stated quite clearly that there was nothing to worry about, so there was no need for Angela to do anything. She was relieved, as truth to tell she had not relished the idea of running about the place in the middle of the night, hunting for Barbara. She would go to the hotel in the morning and find out what was going on.

By eight o'clock the next day she had already arrived at the Hotel Splendide and was inquiring at the desk as to whether a Miss Trout and a Miss Wells were staying there. The young man at the desk was not the same as the one who had chased Barbara out the night before, and he shook his head.

'I'm afraid not,' he said. 'There's no-one of that name here.'

Angela was puzzled. Had they perhaps registered under false names? That would be like Barbara.

'I might be mistaken with the names,' she said, 'but I think they must have arrived very late last night—after midnight, in fact.'

The young man looked at the register again.

'No,' he said. 'Our last arrivals yesterday were Mr. and Mrs. Jarvis, at half-past three.'

Angela thanked him and walked away slowly. As she did so, she became aware of a boy with flaming red hair standing nearby, who appeared to be scowling at her. He looked away when he realized she had seen him, and she supposed he must have mistaken her for someone else. She left the hotel, and as she passed him she was almost sure she heard him mutter something that sounded like, 'Ought to be ashamed of yourself, you ought.' She looked at the boy in surprise, but he was staring hard at the ceiling, as though he had spotted a dirty mark up there. She walked on, assuming that he must have been talking to somebody else. Or perhaps she had misheard. At any rate, Barbara was not at the hotel, but there was no time now to wait until she chose to show herself, as Angela had a train to catch.

The little train was already puffing and blowing impatiently when she arrived at the station, so she paid for her ticket quickly and boarded, and they set off. Seated comfortably in the first-class carriage as the train chugged gently along the cliff top towards Penzance, she wanted to relax and enjoy the journey, but her thoughts insisted on intruding, and in the end she saw very little of the countryside, being occupied with the mystery at hand and her object for today.

The train drew into Penzance station with a great hiss, and Angela alighted and found a taxi.

'Take me to the library, please,' she said.

The library was a handsome white building on top of a hill, set in beautiful grounds and with delightful views over the sea. Angela entered and handed herself over to the elderly librarian, who was only too pleased to help.

'I have a fancy to read some French history today,' said Angela. 'I am especially interested in finding out more about Queen Marie Antoinette and the scandal of the diamond necklace. Do you have anything on that subject?'

The librarian beamed.

'Why, certainly,' he said. He went off and shortly afterwards returned with two or three large tomes. 'You will find what you are looking for in here,' he said.

Angela thanked him and sat down at a table to read. After half an hour or so she closed the last book and set it aside. That all seemed clear enough, although it did not prove anything. She returned the books to the librarian.

'Thank you,' she said. 'I wonder—I am also interested in the history of an old house not far from here. The name is Poldarrow Point. Do you know of it?'

'Why, yes,' said the old man. 'Poldarrow Point is very well-known in these parts. Many years ago it was the home of a famous smuggler known as Preacher Dick Warrener, and I believe the house is still in the hands of his descendants to this day.'

'I understand that there is a lease on the property,' said Angela. 'It was drawn up fifty or sixty years ago, apparently. I don't suppose you keep copies of that sort of thing here?'

'Oh, but yes we do,' replied the librarian. 'We keep copies of nearly all deeds and leases pertaining to notable and historical buildings in the area, although if the lease in question was drawn up *less* than fifty years ago it is possible that we may not have it. Let me have a look for you.'

He hobbled off, and was gone for some time. Angela waited.

'I am sorry,' he said when he returned. 'We do not appear to have a copy of the lease you asked for. Perhaps you were misinformed as to its date, and it is more recent than you thought.'

'That is entirely possible,' said Angela. 'How would one find out?'

'You would have to ask the leaseholder or, more likely, his solicitor, for a copy.'

'I see,' said Angela thoughtfully.

'We do, however, have a rather marvellous copy of the lease pertaining to Raikes Castle, just on the other side of Penzance, if you would like to see it,' said the librarian, in the manner of one offering a forbidden treat to a favourite grandchild. 'It contains the most fascinating clause which gives the tenant permission to shoot on sight any trespasser caught wearing anything other than black breeches on a Sunday.'

'Another time, thank you,' said Angela. 'You have been enormously helpful and I should like to stay here all day, but I am afraid I must go. I have just one last question: do you know of a solicitor named Penhaligon hereabouts?'

'Yes, of course,' said the librarian. 'You will find him on Chapel Street. It is not far.'

Angela thanked him and said goodbye, then left the library and set off to walk along the quaint, narrow streets of the town in quest of Mr. Penhaligon. Chapel Street was, as the librarian had assured her, very near, and she found the solicitor's office, a grey stone building by the chapel itself, without too much trouble. She went in and asked if she might speak to Mr. Penhaligon. Business was evidently quiet that morning, for she was very soon ushered into a comfortable office by a lowly clerk and invited to take a seat.

Mr. Penhaligon had presumably been taking advantage of the lull in business to have a nap, for he presently emerged from another room, straightening his tie and stifling a yawn. He was a well-fed, middle-aged man who looked as though life had treated him kindly. He straightened up when he saw Angela and darted a glance at his clerk that boded ill for the young man. The clerk suppressed a mischievous grin and went out.

'I beg your pardon,' said the solicitor. 'I had no idea anybody was here. I am Mr. Penhaligon.'

'Angela Marchmont,' said Angela. 'I'm sorry—I know I ought to have made an appointment to see you, but I just happened to be in Penzance and decided to risk a visit.'

'Oh, quite, quite,' said Penhaligon. 'How may I be of assistance?'

'Am I right in thinking that you represent the owner of the freehold of Poldarrow Point in Tregarrion?'

The solicitor stiffened.

'I believe I know the person to whom you are referring,' he said cautiously. The odd tone in his voice caught her attention.

'I am by way of acting as a representative of Miss Trout, the sister of the late Jeremiah Trout, who was the former leaseholder of the property,' she said.

'Ah, of course,' he said, nodding.

Angela paused, wondering how to proceed, since strictly speaking she had no right to demand to inquire into his clients' private matters.

'I understand the lease is due to expire on the fifth of August,' she went on. 'On that date, if Miss Trout has been unable to agree an extension with your client, she will be required to leave Poldarrow Point.'

'That is correct,' said Mr. Penhaligon. 'Or, rather, that *was* correct when I sent her my last letter.'

'What do you mean?' said Angela.

'Why, that my client has sold the freehold of the house and thus no longer has any interest in the property. If Miss Trout wishes to agree another lease then she will have to deal with the new owner.'

Angela stared in surprise. This was a fresh complication.

'Might I ask the name of the new owner?' she said at last.

'I see no harm in telling you,' replied the solicitor. 'He is a Mr. Smart, of London.'

There was a pause, then Mr. Penhaligon unbent a little.

'Had Miss Trout intended to request an extension to the lease?' he asked.

'I believe she was hoping to do so if circumstances permitted,' said Angela. 'I think she might perhaps have even considered making an offer for the freehold.'

'It is a pity, then, that she did not act sooner,' said Mr. Penhaligon.

'Unfortunately, she was not in a position to do so—is still not in a position to do so, in fact,' admitted Angela. 'But she has expectations—of a sort, at least, and—' she paused. 'Well, it doesn't matter now, I suppose, since this Mr. Smart has got there before her.'

'Yes,' agreed the solicitor. 'It does seem a shame, but this gentleman approached my client very recently and offered him a most generous sum for the freehold of the property—far more than its real worth, given that the place is almost certain to disappear into the sea in the next twenty years or so.

Mr. Warrener is very frail and infirm, and has to pay the expenses of his own care, so he was only too happy to accept the offer, given that the lease was about to expire and the property would be very difficult to sell in its current condition.'

'I beg your pardon,' said Angela quickly. 'Did you say that the name of your client is Mr. Warrener?'

'Why, yes,' said Mr. Penhaligon. 'He is a descendant of the original owner of the house, who was once rather famous in these parts for his smuggling activities.'

'But I understood that Miss Trout and her nephew were the last surviving members of the Warrener family.'

'Oh, are they part of the family too?' said the solicitor. 'I was not aware of that. They are certainly not the last, however. I know of at least two or three others. My client, Timothy Warrener, lived at Poldarrow Point for many years, until the upkeep became too onerous, then he sold the house and moved to Penzance. He did not wish to relinquish all rights over the property, however—after all, it had been in the family for many years and had many historical associations—so he retained the freehold for himself and sold the house with a lease attached. But as he grew old, the property became a burden to him, and when Mr. Smart turned up Mr. Warrener was only too pleased to accept his offer.'

Angela's frown of puzzlement was growing deeper by the minute.

'Do you happen to know when the house was sold to Jeremiah Trout?'

'Yes,' said Mr. Penhaligon. 'It was almost exactly thirty years ago, on the fifth of August, eighteen ninety-seven. The lease was a short one.'

'Thirty years ago,' said Angela, almost to herself. 'I wonder what happened thirty years ago.'

'I beg your pardon?'

'Nothing,' said Angela. 'I was just musing to myself. Do you happen to have the address of Mr. Smart? Miss Trout may wish to approach him.'

Mr. Penhaligon scribbled something on a piece of paper and handed it to her. She thanked him and rose to depart.

'Shall I tell Mr. Warrener you called?' said the solicitor.

Angela hesitated.

'Better not,' she said. 'It would only complicate matters.'

'Perhaps you are right,' he said. 'I shall not mention it, then.'

He hurried to open the door for her.

I am only sorry I couldn't be more helpful,' he said as she went out.

'On the contrary,' said Angela. 'You have been very helpful indeed.'

CHAPTER THIRTY

ANGELA CAUGHT THE noon train back to Tregarrion and sat in the carriage, thinking furiously about what she had learned that morning. The story of the lease in particular was most confusing. Miss Trout had said that her parents had sold the freehold of Poldarrow Point fifty or sixty years ago, but according to Mr. Penhaligon, that was not true. Why, then, had she lied? And why had she mentioned nothing about the existence of Mr. Warrener in Penzance? In fact, not only had Miss Trout not mentioned him, she had said specifically that she and Clifford were the last descendants of Preacher Dick Warrener, and yet, given her dealings with Mr. Penhaligon over the lease, she must have known that that was not the case.

Angela could make no sense of the mystery. The only thing she knew for certain was that Jeremiah Trout had come to Poldarrow Point thirty years ago and had lived there until his death, which had occurred not long after his sister's arrival earlier that year. Whether he and Emily Trout really were part of the Warrener family Angela could not say. But what motive could Miss Trout possibly have had for lying about it? It looked as though the whole story of Marie Antoinette had been an invention, at any rate. According to the history books she had consulted that morning, there had never been any mystery about the fate of the necklace—it had been broken up and the diamonds taken to London for sale by the Comtesse de la Motte's husband. The Warrener family legend—if indeed there were such a thing—must therefore be untrue. But in that case, what on earth were Miss Trout and Clifford and the Dorseys searching for? *Something* was evidently missing and had to be found urgently before the fifth of August, but what was it? And why bring Angela into the affair? Given all the hole-and-corner dealings of the past few days, presumably the missing thing—whatever it was—had to be kept secret, but Miss Trout had taken pains to make Angela's acquaintance, invite her to Poldarrow Point and tell her the whole story.

Angela shook her head in perplexity. What on earth was going on? And where did Edgar Valencourt fit into all this? Her theory of Clifford's being Valencourt did not quite square with the new information she had, which suggested that both he *and* Miss Trout had been telling lies all along. Was Miss Trout his accomplice?

She determined that she should tell the whole story to Mr. Simpson as soon as she got back to Tregarrion. He had the powers of Scotland Yard at his disposal, and with one telephone-call could set in motion an investigation into the residents of Poldarrow Point. Accordingly, as soon as the train drew into Tregarrion station, she jumped out and hurried as fast as she could back to the Hotel Splendide, where she asked to speak to Mr. Simpson.

Mr. Simpson was not in, she was informed. Would Mrs. Marchmont like to leave a message? Angela scribbled a brief note which, in the tumult of her thoughts, probably communicated very little, and was about to leave when a thought occurred to her, and she asked whether there was a public telephone she might use. She was directed to a cabinet installed for the use of guests, and went in.

'Put me through to Scotland Yard, please,' she said to the operator, and waited for the call to be connected. A distant voice at last announced that she had been put through, and she asked to speak to Inspector Jameson.

'Jameson speaking,' said the inspector when he eventually came on the line.

'Hallo, inspector, it's Angela Marchmont here,' said Angela. 'I'm terribly sorry to bother you, but I seem to have got mixed up in another mystery and I need your help.'

'Hallo, Mrs. Marchmont,' said the inspector. 'Where are you?'

'I'm in Tregarrion,' said Angela. 'I don't suppose you know it. It's a little place near Penzance, in Cornwall.'

'Tregarrion?' said Jameson in surprise. 'Why, yes, I do know of it as a matter of fact. What's happened?'

Jameson listened attentively as she gave him a brief account of the recent events at Poldarrow Point, ending with the revelations she had received that morning from Mr. Penhaligon the solicitor.

'I've been working with your colleague, who has reason to believe that a thief named Edgar Valencourt is also plotting to get hold of the necklace—or whatever it is that they are looking for,' she finished, 'but I can't find him, so thought that I had better call you instead, since time is of the essence, and I need someone to help me find out what exactly is going on at Poldarrow.'

'Oh, so you know all about Edgar Valencourt, do you?' said Jameson. 'I might have guessed that you would be in on the thing. Yes, there have been rumours that he is in your area at present—that's why I was surprised to hear that you were in Tregarrion. Our man has been spying out the land, but we were about to recall him since there's been nothing doing up to now. And you say you think Valencourt is masquerading as a man called Clifford Maynard—what's that, Willis? Just a second,' he said to Angela. She heard the muffled sound of conversation as Jameson presumably consulted with his sergeant. After a moment or two he came back on the line, and this time there was a note of urgency in his voice that had not been there before.

'Willis has just reminded me of something rather extraordinary. He has an excellent memory for these things and was a young constable at the time, so he may well be right. If he is, it could turn out to be the most enormous coup for us. When did you say old Mr. Trout came to live there?'

'It was exactly thirty years ago,' said Angela, 'in eighteen ninety-seven.'

Jameson turned away to say something to Willis, then came back on the line.

'It sounds as though you may be on to something,' he said. 'Mrs. Marchmont, do you ever remember hearing about the Bampton case?'

'No, I can't say I do,' she replied.

'It was a great *cause célèbre* at the time, but perhaps you are too young to remember it. I was only a child myself,' said Jameson. 'Anyway, our story starts in eighteen ninety-seven at Bampton Park, home to the Duke of Bampton and his family. In February of that year, the Duke and Duchess held a ball to celebrate the birthday of their eldest daughter, Lady Alicia Coops-Fairley. It was one of these grand society affairs, attended by all the local aristocrats, and a good number from London besides. For her birthday gift, Lady Alicia's doting papa and mama were planning to present her with a glorious diamond necklace, which they had commissioned especially for the occasion, sparing no expense.'

'Ah!' said Angela, beginning to understand.

'This necklace cost a king's ransom, apparently,' went on Jameson, 'but as it was for their darling daughter and they had plenty of money, they thought nothing of it, and no doubt congratulated themselves at the thought of her pleasure when she saw it.'

'No doubt,' said Angela.

'But of course, as you will have already guessed, they never did find out whether Lady Alicia liked the necklace, because she never received it. On the evening of the ball, while everyone was distracted, a daring gang of burglars broke into the place and stole a number of valuable items—the most valuable of these being the necklace, which the Duke had unfortunately taken out of his safe and put in his desk drawer in preparation for the grand presentation.

'Naturally, when the crime was discovered, the Duke kicked up an awful stink, and spent a week or two giving interviews to the press and asking questions in Parliament as to why the police allowed such a dangerous gang to roam at large—none of which did anything to increase public confidence, I might add.

'With the spotlight on it, Scotland Yard redoubled its efforts to find the gang, and especially its leader—one Wally Hopper, who had been well-known to them for many years. After some weeks, they succeeded in tracking down the Hopper gang to its head-quarters, and caught a number of them red-handed in possession of the stolen goods—all except for the necklace, which was missing, along with the gang's ringleader. The other gang members all insisted that Hopper had double-crossed them and escaped with the loot, and there was nothing we could do to shake their story. They were tried and imprisoned, while others were released owing to a lack of evidence. The police kept them under observation, but it seemed that the story was true: Wally Hopper had indeed made away with the necklace and left the rest of them to take what was coming to them. We kept a particularly close eye on Wally's wife, Rosie. We had nothing on her so couldn't arrest her, but we thought she most likely knew where Wally was and would go to join him when the hue and cry died down. However, we were wrong. 'Ma' Rosie soon afterwards settled down alone, and appears to have lived a perfectly blameless life from then on with her son from a first marriage, who was about fifteen at the time of the robbery.'

'Would this son of hers happen to have been called Clifford?' said Angela.

'How sharp you are,' said Jameson. 'Yes, that was his name. At any rate, as far as we know, Ma Rosie kept on the straight and narrow for thirty years afterwards, and never did go to her husband.'

'Until now,' said Angela.

'As you say, until now,' agreed the inspector. 'It looks as though she may have found him at last—too late, though, as he's dead now and can never tell where he hid the necklace.'

Angela fell silent for a moment, digesting all that she had just heard. So it had all been a lie! The Trouts were not part of the Warrener family at all—in fact, Jeremiah Trout was really Wally Hopper, the ringleader of a criminal gang who had cheated his accomplices of their booty and escaped to Cornwall thirty years ago. There, he had presumably renounced his former life of crime and gone straight, since there was no suggestion that he had done anything dishonest during his life in Tregarrion. Miss Emily Trout was in reality 'Ma' Rosie Hopper, Wally's wife, who, it seemed, had tracked down her husband after thirty years and followed him to Cornwall, presumably in an attempt to persuade or threaten him into giving up the necklace.

Everything now began to fall into place in Angela's mind. Wally had died before Rosie could induce him to tell her the whereabouts of the necklace, and with time running short and the lease about to expire, she and Clifford had needed to work fast before the house was returned to its owner. But why had they asked Angela to help in the search?

Angela thought back to the day she had met Miss Trout and Clifford for the first time. The old lady had definitely been the one to pursue the acquaintance—yes, Angela remembered now: Miss Trout had mentioned that she knew Mrs. Uppingham very well, and yet Angela had later received a letter from Mrs. Uppingham in which she mentioned that she had never met Miss Trout. Had Miss Trout recognized Angela from the newspapers and lied about knowing the owner of Kittiwake Cottage in order to scrape up a friendship? Angela remembered Clifford's surprised reaction when he heard her name for the first time, so it had not been a deliberate plan on his part.

It all made sense now: Miss Trout suspected Clifford of double-dealing, but for obvious reasons could not report her suspicions to the police, so she had cleverly appealed for protection to a woman who was known to the public as being a talented amateur detective. In that way she could kill two birds with one stone: first, Angela's involvement provided Miss Trout with a certain amount of protection from her nephew—her son, rather—since Clifford would be wary of making any precipitate moves against his mother in the presence of a woman with close connections to Scotland Yard; and second, Angela and Barbara could help with the search on Miss Trout's behalf, and save Miss Trout the exertion—no small matter, given her age and frailty. There never had been any intention to sell the necklace in order to secure Poldarrow Point, then. Presumably, once it had been found, Ma Rosie and her son would have disappeared into thin air, never to be seen again, leaving the old house to rot and eventually fall into the sea.

'Hallo?' said the inspector's voice. Angela roused herself.

'I beg your pardon,' she said. 'I was just trying to absorb what you have said. It's all most strange!' A thought struck her. 'By the way, there is a further complication in this matter. It looks very much as though Clifford is trying to double-cross his mother by finding the necklace before her, with the help of some friends of his—Lionel and Harriet Dorsey. Yesterday Harriet Dorsey offered me a bribe to hand the goods over to them instead of Miss Trout. Do you know of them at all?'

'Dorsey was the name of one of the members of the Hopper gang, who took part in the original burglary,' said Jameson. 'He died some years ago, but perhaps Lionel is his son. The presence of these Dorseys makes me more certain than ever now that there is some funny business going on down there. Perhaps the mystery of the Bampton jewels is about to be cleared up at last!'

'Let us hope so. I am certainly less in the dark than I was this morning, at least,' said Angela, 'but what am I to do now? Ought I to go to the police here in Tregarrion?'

'I shall call them myself,' said Jameson. 'We've been looking for this necklace for thirty years, and I don't want them tramping all over the place and warning the gang that we know about their plans.'

'What exactly do you intend to do?' said Angela. 'After all, as far as we know, they haven't done anything illegal yet. They certainly haven't found the necklace.'

'True,' admitted the inspector. 'If they had they'd have been away like a shot. But I want to talk to them, and find out what they know.'

'Barbara!' exclaimed Angela suddenly.

'I beg your pardon?'

'I'm sorry,' said Angela. 'I have just remembered that my god-daughter has run away with Miss Trout.'

'What?'

'Yes. She is under the romantic impression that Miss Trout is a put-upon innocent, who is being duped by her nephew, and whom she is bound to protect. She is going to be dreadfully disappointed when she finds out the truth. I should imagine they have gone to your man at the hotel.'

'All the better. Go and find him now, and tell him what is happening—discreetly, of course,' said Jameson. 'We don't want Ma Rosie getting wind of our suspicions.'

They spoke for a few minutes more, then Jameson said he must go as he wanted to speak to the Tregarrion police. Angela replaced the receiver and stared at the wall of the telephone-cabinet. She was evidently in the grip of some strong emotion, but whether it was anger or sadness was impossible to tell from her expression—perhaps a mixture of both.

She roused herself from her reverie and was about to leave the cabinet when a thought struck her. She lifted the receiver again and asked to put through another telephone-call.

CHAPTER THIRTY-ONE

A T A QUARTER past eight on Monday morning, a few minutes after Angela had inquired unsuccessfully after her at the desk, Barbara crept out of room 402 of the Hotel Splendide and set off in search of Mr. Simpson. Jeremiah Trout was still asleep, so she took the key and locked him in as she did not want him waking up and wandering around the hotel without her. She had passed an uncomfortable night in the chair, stirring frequently, and had no desire to spend any more time in the cramped room than was absolutely necessary.

She ran into the bathroom, threw some water hastily over her face and smoothed her hair, then walked down the stairs, trying to look as though she were just any paying guest—although her dirty frock rather gave the lie to that. After ascertaining that the man at the desk was not the same one as last night, she walked boldly up to him and inquired after Mr. Simpson. She was rewarded with a doubtful look and was just about to launch into a hastily-invented and colourful tale, when Mr. Simpson himself emerged from the dining-room, having evidently just finished breakfast. He greeted her in his usual friendly manner.

'Mr. Simpson!' exclaimed Barbara. 'You've no idea how glad I am! I simply must speak to you in secret. It's dreadfully important.' She grabbed his arm and pulled him outside, somewhat to his surprise.

'What is it?' he asked, once they were out of earshot. 'Has something happened to Angela?'

'Angela? No, I expect she's still lolling in bed,' said Barbara uncharitably. 'No, this is far more important.' She looked around, then hissed, 'I've rescued Jeremiah Trout!'

'What?' said Simpson.

'He's upstairs in room 402, asleep, and I don't know what to do with him. Clifford is bound to come looking for him—and he'll tell the Dorseys, and they're at the hotel too, so it's far too dangerous for him to stay here, and we can't have him at Kittiwake Cottage, as there's no room.'

'Just a minute,' said Mr. Simpson, trying unsuccessfully to make sense of this barrage of speech. 'What do you mean you've rescued Jeremiah Trout? Jeremiah Trout is dead.'

'No he's not,' said Barbara. 'He's a bit ga-ga but he's definitely alive. Clifford Maynard has been keeping him prisoner in a secret room at Poldarrow Point for months, trying to get him to tell where the Queen's necklace is. I rescued him last night and we came here, but we couldn't find you so we had to wait until morning and try again.'

He still looked blank, and she related the story of her night's adventures. He eyed her as though he could not quite believe it.

'But what do you want me to do?' he asked.

'Why, arrest Clifford, of course!' said Barbara, as though it were obvious.

'I?'

'Yes,' said Barbara. 'I know who you are, you know: Angela told me.'

'Did she indeed?' said Mr. Simpson thoughtfully.

'She didn't want to, but I forced it out of her,' said Barbara. 'I—er—may have overheard your conversation the other day—' she stopped, and reddened at Mr. Simpson's look. 'Well, it can't be helped now,' she went on quickly. 'The important thing is to catch Clifford. Miss Trout is still at Poldarrow Point, in danger. What if he decides to imprison her too?'

'Why should he do that?'

'To get her out of the way while he looks for the necklace, of course! Now that Mr. Trout has escaped he has lost his only source of information, so he will simply have to buckle to it and start searching properly, but his aunt stands in his way.'

It looked as though Simpson were starting to believe her at last.

'Do you think Jeremiah Trout really knows where the necklace is?' he asked.

'Yes, I think he does,' said Barbara, 'but he can't always remember, and when he *can* remember he won't tell. He might tell us, though, if we can only get him to understand how important it is.'

Mr. Simpson rubbed his chin and reflected. After a few moments he seemed to come to a conclusion.

'You have done very well to rescue Mr. Trout,' he said, 'but now I think it is time for me to take charge. First of all, we must get him to a place of safety.'

'But where?'

'My room will have to do for the present. We can move him elsewhere later on. Where did you say he was now?'

'Room 402,' said Barbara. 'We'd better go soon. I have to give the key back this morning, before we are discovered. We're not really supposed to be there, you see,' she said in response to Simpson's inquiring glance.

He laughed and shook his head.

'I admire your flexible approach to life,' he said. 'In a few years' time, I expect you will run rings around whichever young man is brave enough to marry you.'

'I certainly hope so,' said Barbara, flattered. They went back into the hotel and she led him up to the fourth floor.

Jeremiah was still asleep, and Barbara went over to him and shook him gently.

'Wake up!' she said. 'We have to leave now.'

'Eh? What's that?' said the old man, awakening with a snort. He sat up with an effort and looked about him. 'Where am I?' he said.

'You're at the Hotel Splendide,' said Barbara. 'I rescued you.'

He looked at her with disfavour.

'I know you,' he said. 'What's your name?'

'Barbara,' said Barbara. 'We have to go to a different room now and hide you from Clifford.'

'I want my breakfast,' said Jeremiah. 'I want some eggs. I always have eggs for breakfast.'

'You shall have some eggs as soon as we have got you out of here,' said Barbara.

'My room is much more comfortable than this one,' said Mr. Simpson. 'You will be much better off there.'

'Who are you?' said Jeremiah rudely.

'My name is Simpson,' said Mr. Simpson. 'I am a friend of Barbara's. I should like to help you get away from Poldarrow Point if you will let me.'

'But I don't want to get away from it,' said Jeremiah. 'The garden needs doing.'

'Yes, yes,' said Barbara impatiently. 'You shall work in the garden as soon as you like, but we need to hide you just for today, until Mr. Simpson has arrested Clifford.'

He was finally persuaded to leave, and was escorted grumbling all the way down to Simpson's room, which was a rather grand corner one on the second floor. As soon as he arrived, he started demanding eggs again, but permitted himself to be satisfied with some day-old rolls provided by Mr. Simpson.

'Are you going to Poldarrow Point now?' asked Barbara of Simpson, when they had ensconced Mr. Trout in a chair by the window and given him a newspaper to read.

Simpson shook his head.

'Not yet,' he said.

'Oh, but you must!' said Barbara in dismay. 'You have to arrest Clifford before he does something desperate.'

'I don't think he will do anything desperate,' said Simpson. 'Besides, I cannot act without first receiving orders. This is a very delicate case, and one false move could ruin everything.'

'But—'

'You have done extremely well, and I shall make sure that you receive all due credit, but you must leave it all to me now.' He spoke with finality and she saw that he was resolute.

'All right,' she said, 'but please hurry.'

'I shall phone Scotland Yard now and get my orders,' he said, and smiled at her disappointment. 'What? Did you expect me to rush off immediately with my gun and wrestle Clifford to the ground?'

'I did, rather,' admitted Barbara.

'Well, I'm afraid that police work is not so exciting as that,' he said. 'Lucky for me, as I am not sure I could stand it. Now, I will look after Mr. Trout. You be a good girl and go back to Kittiwake Cottage. I am sure you need some sleep—and I imagine Mrs. Marchmont will be very worried about you too.'

'I sometimes think Angela doesn't notice whether I'm there or not,' said Barbara, a little sadly.

'Of course she does. She is very fond of you.'

'Do you think so?' said Barbara, brightening.

'Oh yes. She talks about you often.'

'Oh! Well, then,' said Barbara, 'I suppose it can't do any harm to show my face at home.'

'Good girl,' said Mr. Simpson approvingly. 'Stay out of trouble, and I shall let you know as soon as there is anything to tell.'

'Do,' said Barbara, and ran off.

There was no-one at home when she arrived at the cottage, so she went upstairs and threw herself down on her bed, calculating that there was just enough time for two or three hours' sleep before she had to be up again to catch low tide.

For Barbara had plans. Disappointed that Mr. Simpson seemed so unwilling to act, and worried about what Clifford might be capable of, she had decided that she would go back to Poldarrow Point that afternoon and rescue Miss Trout herself. She had done it once with Jeremiah, and could do it again, she was sure. She would go back through the tunnel, find Miss Trout and lead her to safety. Then the police would arrest Clifford, they would find the necklace, and the Trouts would remain happily at Poldarrow Point for the rest of their days.

She was just drifting off to sleep with these pleasant thoughts uppermost in her mind, when her eyes suddenly snapped open as she remembered that she had not told Mr. Simpson about Mr. Donati. Donati had as good as admitted to being Valencourt, but she had forgotten all about him in the excitement of finding Jeremiah and the secret room. She sighed and shifted into a more comfortable position, and her eyes closed again of their own accord. The news would just have to wait until another time.

Five minutes later she was asleep.

CHAPTER THIRTY-TWO

B Y ONE O'CLOCK, Barbara was hurrying across the sand towards the smugglers' tunnel. Neither Helen Walters nor Mr. Donati was anywhere to be seen today, and she had the beach to herself. The tide was out, and the cave entrance was clear. She scrambled inside, switched on her torch and followed the familiar route up to the cellars at Poldarrow Point. The trap-door was still unbolted, and she was relieved, since she had half-expected that Clifford would have bolted it during his search for Jeremiah. She pulled herself out of the hole, ascended the cellar stairs and went through the customary routine with the hair-pin after first listening to make certain that nobody was on the other side of the door. Having reached the hall safely, she considered hiding in the cupboard again, and had actually got as far as opening the door, when her attention was caught by the sound of voices issuing from the half-open door of the drawing-room. Her heart beat fast and she stole across to listen. An animated conversation appeared to be in full flow. Barbara's eyes opened wide.

'—far as I know he never had any friends in Tregarrion,' a voice was saying. Barbara recognized it as Clifford's. 'He could be anywhere. For all I know he fell into the sea and was drowned. We'd be well rid of him if he did. Months, we've kept him here—months, and has it done us a ha'porth of good? No, 'Course it hasn't. He's more cracked than he ever was. I don't think he knows where it is any more than we do.'

'He's a close one, all right,' agreed another voice, which Barbara eventually identified as Lionel Dorsey's. 'Well, we'll just have to get on without him.'

'I don't think you quite understand, Lionel, dear,' said a third voice. Barbara jumped. It was unmistakably that of Miss Trout, but there was a steely note to it that was quite unlike her usual gentle tones. 'It's not just a question of getting on without him. What if someone finds him? He may have had few friends in the area, but he was well-known by sight to many people. Somebody is bound to recognize him and then the fat will be in the fire. We must find him, and fast. Clifford, how many times have I told you about leaving that upstairs door open?'

'I can't always be remembering everything,' said Clifford petulantly. 'I told you, I've had a lot on my mind.'

'Like cheating your poor old mother out of her rightful property, perhaps?' said Miss Trout sweetly.

'I never would've, you know that.'

Miss Trout snorted.

'You and Lionel, and that wife of his,' she said. 'The three of you together haven't got half a wit between you. Did you think I had no idea? I'm not stupid, you know. I heard you, night after night, knocking on the walls and shuffling the furniture about.'

'You were supposed to be asleep,' said Clifford.

'And so I would've been if I'd been fool enough to drink that hot milk you brought me every night. Don't think I don't know what you put in it. Poisoning your own mother, Clifford? For shame!'

'Don't say that, Ma,' said Clifford. 'I would never poison you. You know I'm fond of you. It was just supposed to make you sleep better, that's all.'

There was another snort.

'Well, it didn't,' said Miss Trout. 'I knew exactly what was going on all the time, so you might as well have saved your efforts. Anonymous letters, indeed!'

'That was Harriet's idea,' said Lionel. 'I told her it was stupid but she said we might as well try it anyway.'

'Yes, it was stupid,' said Miss Trout. 'I was hardly going to leave, was I?'

'I thought she'd given it up,' said Dorsey, 'but then she went and sent one to that snooty Marchmont woman.'

'What on earth was she thinking?' said Clifford. 'Angela Marchmont has the ear of Scotland Yard. She could have the whole boiling on top of us as quick as winking if we don't watch our step.'

'We didn't know that, did we? Not until you told us,' said Dorsey. 'What did you have to bring her in for anyway?'

'Because, you ninny, like Clifford said, she has the ear of Scotland Yard,' said Miss Trout acerbically. 'I'm not as young as I was, and my own son was plotting against me, and I could hardly go to the police themselves, now, could I? But someone like Angela Marchmont, now—well, that's a different thing altogether, isn't it? She's the law but she's not the law, if you catch my meaning. I thought you might behave yourselves if you knew she was keeping an eye on you.'

'Did you invite her here, then?' said Dorsey. 'What did you tell her?'

'No, I didn't invite her. I saw her one day and recognized her from the papers, and thought she might be useful to me if I could only tell her a good enough story. Luckily she and that girl of hers fell for it easily enough and I felt a bit safer after that. Queer, though, isn't it? Who'd've thought that I'd need protecting from my own family?'

'Funny—isn't that what Wally said?' said Dorsey with a snicker.

'Wally's no use to himself or anyone else,' said Clifford, 'and he's double-crossed us enough times. He got what was coming to him, that's all.'

'Except he didn't, did he? He's escaped, and made fools of us all once again. He's got more lives than a cat, has Wally.'

'Not this time,' said Miss Trout. 'We're going to find him— or shall we say *you're* going to find him, and when you do we're going to settle for him once and for all. As you said, he's no use to us. He's been in that room for months and never yet come up with the goods, so I reckon it's a pretty safe bet that he never will.'

There was a note of cold determination in her voice that made Barbara shiver, and she took an involuntary step back from the door. She could hardly believe her ears. It had all been a lie then, from beginning to end! Miss Trout was not the innocent little old lady she had purported to be at all. Quite the contrary, in fact: she was one of the instigators of the plan to hold her own brother prisoner while they tried to pry the whereabouts of the necklace out of him. Miss Trout had known all along that Clifford had been plotting against her in turn, and had scraped an acquaintance with Angela in the hope that Angela's fame and close association with Scotland Yard would give her some protection against him. And it had worked, too! Barbara and Angela had fallen for the lies, and had given up their time willingly, coming to Poldarrow and turning the place upside-down in search of the necklace because Jeremiah could not or would not reveal its hiding-place.

There were many things Barbara still did not understand, but it looked as though Jeremiah's escape had led to a certain *rapprochement* between Miss Trout, the Dorseys and Clifford, and they had agreed to work together to catch the old man. Who knew what they would do to him if they found him? The old lady had said they were going to 'settle for him once and for all,' which sounded very sinister indeed. Barbara thought with relief of Jeremiah, safe in the hands of the police. That was one difficulty solved, at any rate. They could look for him all they liked but they would never find him, locked safely away as he was in Mr. Simpson's hotel room.

Barbara wondered what she ought to do now. She had come here with the intention of rescuing Miss Trout from her designing nephew, only to discover that the designing nephew was in fact her son, and that Miss Trout had no need of rescuing at all! A hurt look crossed her face as she thought of how she had been deceived.

'If one can't trust a sweet old lady, then whom can one trust?' she thought. 'She has been stringing us along all the while with her sob-stuff. And how sly she was, too! How clever of her not to ask us to help her, but instead make us volunteer as though we had thought of the idea ourselves. And we fell straight into her trap, just as she meant us to. It's too bad of her. I should like to give her a jolly good piece of my mind, but I suppose it would make more sense to get out of here now and tell everything to Mr. Simpson.'

She did neither, but instead moved closer to the door to listen again. The gang appeared to be discussing the best way to go about searching for Jeremiah.

'—through the tunnel,' Miss Trout was saying. 'But if it was high tide when he escaped then he couldn't have gone that way. Has anybody had a look to see whether he went out through the trap-door?'

'He didn't go that way, surely?' said Clifford. 'How would he get down the ladder? He's far too old for that kind of thing.'

'All the same, I think someone should go and see,' said Miss Trout.

'Oh, very well,' said Clifford reluctantly. 'I'll go and have a look. Where's the torch?'

Barbara sprang away from the door and darted, quick as lightning, into the cupboard. She was just in time, for almost immediately she heard the squeak of the drawing-room door as someone came out. A thrill of fear ran through her as she remembered that she had left the door to the cellar unlocked, but it was too late to lock it now.

She heard the sound of footsteps descending the stairs slowly and carefully, and waited with bated breath. She had left the trap-door open too, and Clifford was about to discover it. Would he immediately assume that Jeremiah had escaped that way? After what felt like an age, she heard footsteps climbing the stairs, and the click of the door being shut. The drawing-room door squeaked again and she waited a few seconds, then emerged from her hiding-place as silently as possible. The first voice she heard was that of Miss Trout.

'Well you'll just have to go down there after him, won't you?' came the voice. There was a harsh edge to it, and Barbara wondered why she had never noticed it before.

'But he won't be there, will he?' said Clifford. 'He's probably in Penzance by now. Or if he caught the early train he could even be in London already.'

'Don't be ridiculous,' said Miss Trout. 'How would he get to London with no money?'

'He could have taken the necklace,' said Clifford.

'And used it to pay for a train ticket? No,' said Miss Trout, 'you mark my words—he's hiding in that tunnel. I'll bet my life on it. You'll just have to go down and look for him.'

'I can't,' said Clifford. 'You know I've got—'

But what he had Barbara never found out, because at that moment she felt a hand on her shoulder and almost jumped out of her skin.

'What do you think you're doing?' said Harriet Dorsey.

CHAPTER THIRTY-THREE

BARBARA GASPED AND looked about her for a means of escape, but Mrs. Dorsey had her arm in a steely grip and, try as she might, she could not pull free. The older woman wrenched her round and stared hard into her face.

'What do you mean by listening at doors?' said Harriet.

'Oh, thank goodness you're here!' began Barbara. 'I've just seen a suspicious man wearing an eye-patch climb through the kitchen window. He was carrying a hatchet, and—'

'Can it!' snapped Harriet. 'I know your sort. That funny stuff won't work with me. I saw you come out of that cupboard just now. Don't try and come the innocent. You're here spying for that woman, aren't you?'

'Who, Angela? Of course not,' said Barbara truthfully. 'I'm not spying for anybody.'

'Then why are you here?'

Barbara was about to speak, when the drawing-room door opened.

'Oh, it's you, is it?' said Miss Trout, without notable enthusiasm, when she saw Barbara. 'I might have known you'd be
nosing around here.'

'I'm only doing what you asked me to do,' said Barbara, stung.

'Yes,' said Miss Trout. 'I shall be more careful next time.
You'd better come in, hadn't you?'

Harriet pushed Barbara into the drawing-room and pointed to a chair.

'Sit,' she said.

Barbara sat reluctantly. Clifford, Lionel, Miss Trout and
Harriet all regarded her with expressions ranging from surprise to mistrust.

'How much did she hear?' asked Lionel of his wife.

'I don't know. I was walking downstairs when I saw her
come out of that old cupboard and start listening at the door.
I don't know how long she'd been there.'

'I don't know myself,' Barbara said. 'What time is it? I
thought I'd left my umbrella here, you see, and I got into the
cupboard to look for it and fell asleep—ow!'

She broke off with a yelp as Harriet slapped her hard in the
face.

'I said can it!' said Harriet.

'What did you do that for?' said Barbara, rubbing her flaming cheek and biting back the tears.

'Now, Harriet, dear, there's no need for that,' said Miss
Trout. 'I'm sure Barbara will tell us the truth of her own accord. Won't you, Barbara?'

Barbara scowled.

'Tell that woman to stop hitting me,' she said mutinously.

'But indeed, we must treat our guests kindly, Harriet,' said Clifford. 'Now, Barbara, I'm sure you have been taught that children ought not to listen at doors. In the normal way of things, a little girl caught eavesdropping would be punished very severely. We shan't do that, of course, but you must tell us exactly what you heard.'

Barbara pressed her lips tightly shut. Lionel Dorsey clicked his tongue impatiently.

'Why won't she talk?' he said.

'Perhaps she has nothing to tell,' said Clifford.

'Of course she has,' said Harriet. 'I saw her listening, I tell you.'

'We haven't got time for this,' said Miss Trout suddenly. 'We still don't know where Wally is. We have to find him, and quickly. Clifford, take the girl to Wally's room for now. You go with him, Lionel. We don't want her escaping. We can decide what to do with her later. And don't forget to lock the door this time.'

'I won't, Ma,' said Clifford.

He and Lionel rose and bore Barbara away between them. Barbara had a good idea where they were taking her, and her spirits rose within her as they crossed the hall and ascended the stairs to the top floor.

'Who is Wally?' she asked, although she thought she could make a pretty good guess.

'Never you mind,' said Clifford.

He opened the door at the end of the second-floor passage and motioned for her to enter.

Barbara was almost starting to enjoy herself. She opened her eyes wide.

'What are you going to do with me?' she said, with a note of hysteria in her voice. 'Oh, *please* don't lock me up! I couldn't bear it! They warned us about white slavers at school, and said it was a fate worse than death. Oh, please let me go! Please! I shall die, I know it!'

She sank to her knees and clutched at Clifford's jacket, sobbing dramatically. He shook her off in disgust.

'Don't be ridiculous!' he said. Barbara howled and lunged at Lionel, who leapt back in consternation.

'I knew she'd try some funny business,' said a woman's voice behind them. It was Harriet Dorsey, who had followed them upstairs. Barbara, her cheek still tingling from the slap, closed her mouth at once, jumped to her feet hurriedly and ran through the door.

'That's better,' said Clifford. He followed her to the end of the hidden passage and unlocked the door at the end. 'Down you go,' he said brusquely.

Lionel and Harriet stood guard at the top of the stairs while Barbara descended, followed by Clifford. They went through the dark ante-room and emerged into the familiar surroundings of Jeremiah Trout's bedroom.

'Why, it's a secret room,' said Barbara, feeling that she ought to make some show of surprise.

'That's right,' said Clifford. 'That door at the top of the stairs is the only way out, and I have the key, so don't bother trying to escape.'

'How long are you going to keep me here?' said Barbara.

'That all depends,' said Clifford ominously, and departed. Barbara heard him climb the stairs and exchange a word or two with the Dorseys, then the door was shut and there was the unmistakable sound of a key turning in the lock.

Barbara waited a few minutes then pulled out her torch and ran into the ante-room. It took her a little while, but she eventually found the lion's head on the panelling which hid the keyhole, and slid it aside. The gang were evidently unaware of the hidden door, and had assumed that Jeremiah had escaped up the stairs. How angry they would be when they discovered that she had gone too! Barbara smiled to herself at the thought of their furious faces, then fumbled in her pocket and brought out the key, and was soon on her way down to the cellar.

The trap-door was still open. She clambered through it and down into the tunnel, then set off down the steep passage-way. Very soon she reached the rock-fall and scrambled through the little opening that she had laboured so hard to create the previous night. She had just jumped down to the other side when she heard the sound of voices, and her heart leapt into her mouth. Of course! Lionel and Clifford had come to search the tunnel for Jeremiah! How could she have forgotten?

She very nearly turned tail and ran all the way back to the secret room, but immediately recollected herself. No, that was no good: if she waited any longer, she would miss the tide and have to wait here for hours, and that would never do. What if the gang decided she was too dangerous and made away with her? What Barbara wanted more than anything at this moment was to get as far away from Poldarrow Point as possible and tell Angela or Mr. Simpson all that she had learned. She had great faith in her own abilities, but there were times when only a grown-up would do. Someone had to come and arrest the gang as soon as possible.

Gathering all her courage, she crept along the tunnel to where it joined the main passage, and stopped to listen. It sounded as though Clifford and Lionel had passed the fork and gone on towards the barrel-chamber, for she could hear muffled footsteps to her left. She peered out and saw the beam of torchlight moving away from her. Swiftly, she followed it, keeping as silent as possible, and was soon within ten yards of the two men.

'I don't know how Ma thinks Wally could have got himself all the way down here,' grumbled Clifford. 'It's hard enough for us, and we're younger.'

'Yes, but he wouldn't think sensibly like that, would he?' replied Dorsey. 'He's cracked in the head. Who knows what he might decide to do?'

'Cracked in the head is right,' said Clifford, with a humourless bark of laughter. 'With any luck he *has* cracked his head—on a rock, to save us any more trouble!'

They were now entering the barrel-chamber, where it was slightly less dark. Barbara stayed well back, in the pitch black of the upper tunnel, and watched as the silhouettes of the two men moved about uncertainly in the dimness.

'What's this?' said Lionel, his voice echoing around the walls of the cave.

'It's where the old smugglers used to store their goods, years ago,' said Clifford.

'Could come in useful,' said Lionel.

'Too late for that now,' said Clifford. 'We've got to find the thing and get out by the fifth.'

'Mightn't it be down here?'

'I hope not. I shouldn't much fancy going through this place with a tooth-comb, should you? Besides, why hide it in a tunnel that anyone can get into at low tide, when you can keep it safe in your own house, close at hand?'

'Just a minute,' said Lionel. 'You said the tunnel leads down to the beach. Surely, then, even if you do have to leave the house, we can still come in here and search, can't we?'

'We *could* have,' said Clifford, 'until that little brat cottoned on to us. Now we'll have to find the necklace as quickly as we can and then disappear sharpish.'

'Can't we make her disappear instead?'

'That's for Ma to decide. I don't know what plans she's got for the girl, but it's not all that easy to get rid of someone without drawing people's notice.'

'I know that, but there are ways,' said Lionel. There was an unpleasant tone to his voice. In the tunnel, Barbara shivered.

'Well, whatever we do, we'll have to be careful, or that godmother of hers will be sticking her nose in—and she'll most likely bring the police with her.'

'True enough,' said Lionel. He waved his torch around the chamber. 'Well, Wally's not here. Shall we go on?'

'Not yet,' said Clifford. There's another branch of the tunnel back there. We'd better take a look before we go any farther.'

Barbara retreated hurriedly back up the passage, but in her haste tripped over a loose stone and nearly fell. The stone rattled down into the barrel-chamber with a loud echo, and Barbara froze in terror.

'What was that?' said Lionel.

'Well I never!' said Clifford. 'The old devil must be down here after all. He's been following us all this time. He's got more tricks than a monkey!'

The two men directed the beams of their torches into the upper tunnel and advanced slowly. Keeping out of the light, Barbara retreated quietly, then turned and fled as fast as she could—which was not very fast, given that she dared not turn on her own torch. She heard Clifford and Lionel approaching behind her and quickened her pace. Her breath came fast in her throat and it was a struggle to keep silent.

'Stop!' came Clifford's voice behind her. 'I know you're down here, you old villain. You didn't really think you could escape, did you?'

Barbara heard the panting of the men as they toiled up the steep passageway behind her. Their torches were powerful ones; another minute and they would see her. She stumbled and gasped, then picked herself up and ran on blindly. She passed the fork in the tunnel. That way was no good—it led back to the secret room and then she would be back where she started. She half-ran, half-scrambled along the last few yards of the tunnel, and finally came up against the iron ladder. She began to climb, but before she had got more than four feet off the ground the light grew bright and they were upon her.

'Here!' said Lionel. 'It's not Wally after all, it's the brat! How did she get out?'

He started forward and clutched at her ankles. She kicked out and caught him hard in the stomach.

'Oof!' he said, winded. He staggered backwards and Barbara scrambled further up the ladder, trying to reach the open trap-door.

'Why, you little terror,' said Clifford. 'You'd better not try that on me.'

He grabbed her legs and pulled with all his weight. Barbara had no choice but to let go, and they both fell down in a heap onto the hard ground. Barbara scrambled to her feet and made a dart to escape, but Lionel was too quick for her. He grabbed her and boxed her ears soundly, and she whimpered and attempted to shield her head with her arms.

'Try that again and it'll be the worse for you,' he said angrily.

Clifford had risen to his feet with difficulty, and now regarded Barbara grimly.

'How did you get out?' he asked.

Barbara pressed her mouth shut, and Lionel boxed her ears again.

'Ouch!' she cried. 'Stop it!'

'Answer the question, then,' said Lionel. He made as if to hit her again, and she ducked.

'All right!' she said sulkily. 'If you must know, I came out along that tunnel.'

She pointed towards the second passage that led to the rock-fall.

'But it's blocked,' said Clifford.

'Not now,' said Barbara. 'I unblocked it. It leads to the secret room.'

'What?' said Clifford, astounded.

Barbara nodded.

'Maybe that's how Wally escaped,' said Lionel.

Barbara would have liked to boast triumphantly of the part she had played in Wally's flight, but her ears were still ringing so she held her tongue.

'Come on,' said Clifford. 'We'll go and take a look. Don't let her go.'

Dorsey gripped Barbara's arms firmly and they set off towards the fork in the tunnel. The two men gazed in surprise at the rock-fall, with its hole just big enough for a man to climb through.

'Where did you say it goes?' said Clifford to Barbara.

'It leads into another cellar, then up some stairs and through a hidden door into the little dark room with the armchair,' she replied.

Clifford nodded to Lionel.

'Go and take a look,' he commanded. 'I'll hold the girl.'

Lionel approached the rock-fall and shone his torch through the hole.

'All I can see is another tunnel,' he said.

'Yes, but then there's a ladder that leads through another trap-door into a different cellar-room,' said Barbara.

Clifford shifted his grip on his torch, and Barbara seized the opportunity to kick him in the shins as hard as she could. He yelled and dropped the torch, and Barbara wrenched herself out of his grasp and darted off down the passage. There was no question of creeping about secretly in the dark now—she was concerned only with getting away as fast as she could, so she pulled out her torch and switched it on, shining it on the ground before her as she went. She turned into the main tunnel and half-ran, half slid down the steep passage, hearing the shouts of the men behind her as she went. Soon she reached the barrel-chamber, and sprinted across it and into the lower tunnel. Here she had the advantage over her pursuers, as she had been through it several times in the past few days, and she heard the sound of their voices behind her grow fainter as they slowed down and stumbled along the unfamiliar route.

Barbara slackened her pace slightly and began to breathe again, but her relief was short-lived as she rounded a bend and ran straight into a pool of water. Aghast, she realized that it must be later than she had thought: the tide must have advanced some way into the cave already. She pointed her torch at the ground and saw that the water was not as deep as it had been when she had been caught by the tide the other day. The sound of the men's voices was growing louder again. It looked as though she were trapped.

A beam of light approached.

'There she is!' growled Lionel's voice. Barbara blinked into the light and made her decision. She took off her shoes then turned and ran straight into the water. It was freezing cold but she paid no heed and pressed on doggedly, and was soon up to her knees.

The men had paused, evidently not relishing the thought of following her into the sea, but after a hasty conference they took off their own shoes and came after her. Barbara was up to her waist now. She glanced behind her and saw them, but continued determinedly. The passage ran level here, for the water remained at the same depth for some way, but then she felt the ground dip beneath her, and suddenly the icy water was up to her chest. Wading was too slow now, so she discarded her torch and began to swim. Ahead of her, she could see a dim light, and realized it must be the cave entrance. She redoubled her efforts, and to her joy felt the ground rise beneath her and the water grow shallower.

Gasping and panting, she emerged into the outer cave and blinked at the bright light that came in from the outside. Here, the water was only up to her thighs, and she began wading towards the entrance. She was halfway across the cave when Lionel and Clifford emerged. She squealed and stumbled, then recovered herself and pushed on. The tide had not yet quite covered the cave opening, and she ducked underneath it and emerged squinting into daylight, then started wading towards the beach as quickly as she could. But Lionel Dorsey was too fast for her: he was younger and fitter than Clifford, and was now almost upon her. She shrieked as he lunged at her, and wrenched herself away, but he caught up with her easily and brought her down. The water was knee-deep here and the current was strong, and she coughed and spluttered as she swallowed a mouthful of salt water.

'I'll teach you a lesson, you little beast,' he said harshly, then grasped her by the shoulders and held her under the water. Barbara thrashed about frantically, and he pulled her back up, gasping and whooping for air. He waited until she had caught her breath, then ducked her again. This time, Barbara was ready for him. She went limp in his grasp, as though unconscious. Lionel relaxed his hold in surprise and Barbara bit him hard on the hand. He yelled and let go of her, sucking his bleeding thumb, and Barbara was up like a shot, splashing desperately for the shore, choking and sobbing. The water stung her eyes and she could hardly see where she was going, but she pressed on, her one thought to reach land.

Panting, she ran blindly into an obstacle. A pair of arms caught her and she shrieked, thinking for a second that it must be Clifford.

'Quick, take her to the shore and make sure she's not hurt,' said a strange, foreign voice. She was aware of the shouts of other voices around her but was too exhausted and confused to understand what was going on. She was handed over to someone else, who picked her up, carried her out of the water and set her gently down on the sand.

'Are you all right, miss?' said someone. Barbara looked up, shivering, and saw what looked like a struggle going on in the water between Clifford, Lionel and several policemen.

'I think I'm going to be sick,' she said, and was.

CHAPTER THIRTY-FOUR

ANGELA MARCHMONT SAT on the terrace of the Hotel Splendide, gazing into space absently, a glass of chilled lemonade standing untouched on the table before her. At last she seemed to come to herself, for she looked about her with a slightly surprised expression, then sighed and brought out a gold cigarette-case from her handbag.

'Allow me,' said a voice. It was George Simpson, holding out a cigarette-lighter. Angela turned her eyes towards him and advanced her cigarette to the flame. Simpson sat down, lit one of his own and regarded her quizzically.

'I was just gathering my thoughts,' she said. 'I have lost Barbara. She didn't come home last night, but sent me a rather extraordinary message saying that she was safe and that they had come to the hotel—whoever "they" may be. However, I have inquired several times at the desk and nobody seems to know anything about her.'

'I think I can help you there,' said Mr. Simpson. 'I saw her this morning. She was looking for a place to hide Mr. Trout.'

Angela looked up.

'Mr. Trout?' she said.

'Yes,' said Mr. Simpson thoughtfully. 'It appears that Jeremiah Trout is not dead at all, but has been held prisoner at Poldarrow Point for the past few months. Barbara found him and smuggled him out through the tunnel, and he is now here at the hotel—in my room, as a matter of fact.'

Angela's look of astonishment was almost comical.

'I beg your pardon,' she said at last. 'I thought I heard you say that Jeremiah Trout is still alive.'

'That is exactly what I said,' he replied, amused. 'It appears he knows the whereabouts of the necklace, but is rather—er— vague in his mind these days and can no longer remember where it is. According to Barbara, Clifford Maynard has been keeping Jeremiah captive in a secret room, with the purpose of trying to extract the information from him. So far, he has been unsuccessful.'

'What on earth has that child been up to?' said Angela. 'I can't turn my back for a moment without her getting into some scrape or other. Ah,' she said, as understanding came to her, 'so it was *Jeremiah* Trout she was talking about in her message, not Emily Trout. I thought she had taken it upon herself to rescue Miss Trout from the clutches of her nephew.'

'It seems not,' said Simpson. 'I should warn you that she wanted me to go and arrest Clifford immediately and was not terribly happy when I said it should have to wait. I did not like to tell her that Miss Trout was presumably in on the plot too, and so she is still convinced of the old woman's innocence.'

Angela nodded.

'Yes,' she said, 'I am afraid that she is in for a sad disappointment. All the more so, because I have found out Miss Trout's real identity. I did a little investigating of my own in Penzance this morning, and was coming to tell you the results, but I could not find you so I telephoned your colleague, Inspector Jameson.'

He looked up sharply.

'Oh yes?' he said.

'Yes,' she said, 'and I found out something rather interesting.'

She told him about the Bampton case and the Hopper gang, and he whistled.

'Yes, I remember hearing about the case, although it was long before my time,' he said. 'So Jeremiah Trout is really the elusive Wally Hopper! And he has been living blamelessly for all these years down here at Poldarrow Point.'

'With only his priceless stolen necklace for company,' added Angela dryly. 'I wonder why he gave up his life of crime.'

'He seems to have developed a passion for gardening since he moved here,' said Simpson. 'Perhaps that is what decided him. I don't suppose he had much of an opportunity to indulge the hobby in London.'

'I suppose not,' agreed Angela. 'You say he has no memory of where he hid the necklace?'

'I think in his lucid moments he remembers very well,' said Simpson, 'but he is a wily old thing and won't tell. I tried to get it out of him myself not half an hour ago, but there was nothing doing. I wonder—perhaps you would like to try and persuade him?'

'Why not?' said Angela. 'I should like to meet this Wally Hopper and see what a famous criminal looks like.'

The famous criminal turned out to be an unprepossessing elderly man wearing a filthy, ill-fitting suit. He leered at Angela when they were introduced, then sat down again and seemed inclined to forget about her immediately.

'Mrs. Marchmont wants to thank you for helping her god -daughter escape from Poldarrow Point,' said Mr. Simpson.

Angela took her cue.

'Oh yes,' she said. 'I was very worried about Barbara, but Mr. Simpson tells me you were very kind to her and helped her get out of the secret room.'

'Barbara?' said Wally. 'Who's Barbara?'

'She's the girl who brought you here,' said Simpson.

'Oh, that one,' said Wally. 'Very polite, she was. Who are you?'

'I'm her godmother,' said Angela. 'I hope you're not too tired after your adventure last night. I understand you came out through the smugglers' tunnel.'

He glanced at her sideways.

'You're another one, aren't you?' he said. 'You're all the same. You want to take what is mine.'

'But it's not yours, Mr. Hopper,' said Angela. 'It belongs to the Duke of Bampton.'

'Oh, so you know about that, do you?' he said. 'I suppose you think you're clever, working it out. Well, don't bother trying to find it, because you won't. Rosie's got it.'

'Are you sure Rosie has it?' asked Angela. 'She seems to think you have it. Why should she have held you prisoner all these months if she knew where it was?'

'Not *Rosie*,' he said. 'Rosie.' He snickered and began humming tunelessly. It sounded like a nursery rhyme.

Simpson turned to Angela and shrugged.

'You see?' he said. 'I don't know what he means.'

They left Wally and went back downstairs.

'I ought to go and make certain that Barbara is all right,' said Angela.

'May I come?' said Simpson. 'I promised to tell her if I had any news.'

They left the hotel and walked the half-mile or so back to Kittiwake Cottage. Barbara was not there, although she had evidently been back to the house, for her bed had been slept in, according to Marthe.

'She must have come back for a nap and then gone out again,' said Angela. She looked worried.

'Do you think she has got into another scrape?' asked Simpson.

'You said she was not pleased when you refused to arrest Clifford,' she replied. 'I am a little concerned that she may have taken it upon herself to go back to Poldarrow Point and attempt to resolve the matter in her own way—whatever that may be.'

'I see,' said Simpson. 'Knowing Miss Barbara, that is certainly a distinct possibility.'

Angela came to a decision.

'It's time to put an end to all this,' she said. 'I am going along to the house now. I have the feeling she may be in danger.'

Simpson hesitated.

'Then let me come with you,' he said.

Angela gave him an odd look.

'Very well,' she said.

They left the cottage and walked quickly along to the headland on which stood the dilapidated old house.

'What do you intend to do?' asked Simpson.

'Why, I intend to knock at the front door and ask for her,' said Angela firmly.

Simpson looked a little alarmed.

'Are you sure that's a good idea?' he said. 'You will alert them as to our suspicions.'

'Inspector Jameson has already informed the Tregarrion police about the goings-on at Poldarrow Point,' said Angela. 'They will be here shortly, but by that time the gang might have hurt Barbara, or worse. I intend to forestall them before they can do any more harm.'

There was no quarrelling with that, and Simpson fell silent.

Very soon they arrived at the house, and Angela walked purposefully up the front path and knocked on the front door. There was no answer.

'They must have gone out,' said Mr. Simpson.

Angela said nothing but walked around to the back of the house and began peering through the windows. Simpson followed her.

'Mrs. Marchmont,' said a voice behind them. They whirled round. Miss Trout was standing there with Harriet Dorsey. Angela stared at the dainty little pistol in the old lady's hand.

'Hallo, Miss Trout,' said Angela warily. 'I am looking for Barbara. I don't suppose you have seen her?'

'Funny way of looking for someone,' said Miss Trout, 'sneaking around in people's gardens.' There was no trace of her formerly friendly manner. She looked at Mr. Simpson and then back at Angela. 'Well, well,' she said. 'That explains a lot. I never should have thought it.'

'Thought what?' asked Angela.

Miss Trout did not reply directly, but looked hard at Mr. Simpson.

'I know you,' she said.

'I don't think so,' said Simpson politely. 'I am Inspector Simpson, of Scotland Yard.'

Miss Trout laughed mirthlessly.

'Oh, so that's the story, is it?' she said.

'I'm not here to make trouble,' said Angela. 'As far as I am aware, nobody has done anything illegal. All I want is Barbara.'

'What makes you think she's here?' said Harriet. She was her usual sullen self.

'She is a romantic child and she still believes the story you told her, Miss Trout,' said Angela. 'I think she has some idea of protecting you from Clifford.'

'It's a bit late for that,' said the old woman. 'And you can stop calling me that. You must know what my name is if you're here with him.' She nodded towards Simpson.

'Very well, Mrs. Hopper,' said Angela, and Ma Rosie sniffed with grim satisfaction.

'You see?' she said to Harriet. 'I told you she was no fool.'

'Is Barbara here?' said Angela. 'Why don't you just send her out? Then we shall let you on your way without interference.'

'Ah, but you forget one thing,' said Ma Rosie. 'We haven't found what we're looking for yet, have we? We've got until the fifth of August before we have to leave, and I mean to find it by then. I've waited thirty years to get my hands on that necklace, and it'd be silly to let a little thing like this get in the way of it now I'm so close, don't you think? If I let Barbara go—or you, for that matter, we'll have to disappear sharpish. No, I've got other plans for you.'

Angela glanced again at the little gun in the old woman's hand. It was tiny, but she had no doubt of its lethal potential. Ma Rosie saw her looking at it and smiled.

'You're wondering whether I'm going to shoot you, aren't you?' she said.

'The question had crossed my mind,' said Angela.

Ma Rosie regarded her with narrowed eyes.

'It's a shame you're far too clever for your own good,' she said. 'You're dangerous. I was going to lock you up for a while, but perhaps I will shoot you after all. What do you think, Harriet?'

'Look here,' said George Simpson, 'this simply won't do. Do you really think you can get away with shooting us both in cold blood?'

'You never know until you try,' said Rosie, 'and I'm an old woman. They might look kindly on me—that is, if they ever find your bodies. There are plenty of places to hide them around here.'

She started to raise the gun, but before she could point it at anyone her arms were pinioned to her sides from behind and someone wrenched the little pistol from her hand. Ma Rosie shrieked in surprise, and Angela had just time to recognize Mr. Donati before a voice shouted, 'Police!' and four or five uniformed men swarmed into the garden and overpowered the two women.

''Ere, what are you doing, attacking a pore old woman?' snapped Ma Rosie, all pretence at gentility gone.

'I haven't done anything,' cried Harriet shrilly. 'It was all this old cat's idea!'

'Shut your mouth, you—' said Rosie, as she struggled in the grip of a young constable, who seemed rather embarrassed at having to arrest a little old lady.

'Now then, the both of you,' said a burly sergeant. 'You'll have plenty of time to explain yourselves down at the station. You can't just go waving guns around, you know,' he said. 'You might hurt somebody.'

The two women were borne away, struggling and protesting.

'I hope you are not hurt,' said Mr. Donati. 'I am sorry it took us so long to arrive. We had a little more difficulty than we anticipated in arresting Clifford Maynard and Lionel Dorsey.'

'We are quite all right, thank you,' said Angela. 'But where is Barbara?'

'Barbara is safe and well at Kittiwake Cottage,' said Donati. 'She got rather wet, but your maid is looking after her.'

'Thank goodness for that!' said Angela. 'I was starting to get quite worried. Thank you for turning up just in time!'

Donati nodded, and prepared to depart.

'Please excuse me,' he said. 'I must go and help the men with the prisoners. We will speak later, yes?'

He grinned briefly and ran off, leaving Angela and Mr. Simpson alone in the garden.

'Quick!' said Angela. 'We must hurry, before the police come back and start searching the house!'

CHAPTER THIRTY-FIVE

W HAT?' SAID SIMPSON.
Angela did not reply but hurried over to a little wooden hut that stood to one side of the garden and pulled the door open.

'There must be something here,' she said.

'Just a minute,' said Simpson. 'Did you know that Donati was a policeman?'

Angela was peering inside the shed. She reached in and brought out a spade.

'I knew Wally would have some gardening tools,' she said in triumph. 'Yes,' she said in reply to Simpson. 'Inspector Jameson told me this morning. Mr. Donati is a very highly-regarded officer in the Swiss Sûreté, no less.'

'I see.'

'Weren't you informed?'

'No, it appears I wasn't,' he said.

'Well, never mind that,' said Angela. 'We've just time to get the necklace.'

'Do you mean you know where it is hidden?'

'I don't know for certain, but I have a fairly good idea,' she replied, then smiled at his puzzled face. 'Didn't you hear what old Wally said? He knew where it was all along.'

'But he said his wife had it,' said Simpson.

'He said Rosie had it, yes, but he wasn't talking about his wife,' said Angela. 'Look here.' She indicated the gnarled old rose-bush outside the study window, in which Barbara had hidden on the night she followed the Dorseys. 'What do you think?'

'Do you mean he buried it under a rose-bush?' said Simpson in surprise.

'Yes. It's the perfect place for someone who loves his garden as Wally does, don't you think?'

'By Jove, it's certainly a thought!' said Simpson eagerly. He took the spade from her and went over to the bush.

'That looks a likely spot,' said Angela, pointing.

Simpson set to work, but after half an hour stopped and rested upon the spade.

'Are you quite certain it's here?' he said.

They stared at the empty hole he had dug.

'It must be there, I'm sure of it,' said Angela. 'Here, let me try.'

He shook his head reprovingly and went back to work. Finally, the spade hit something solid.

'Ah!' he said. He dug round the obstacle and levered it up. It was a small tin box.

'Open it!' said Angela.

'It's locked,' he said. 'No matter, though.' He lifted the spade and brought it sharply down on the lock, and it burst open.

Angela bent and brushed the earth off the box, then opened it. Inside was an oilskin package. She took it out. It felt heavy. She looked up at Mr. Simpson and saw him staring intently at it.

'Go on,' he said.

She unwrapped the package delicately, then let out a little gasp as she saw what was inside it.

'Well, I'll be damned,' said Simpson softly.

They stared at the thing for a moment, then Angela reached into the package and picked it up. The necklace glittered in her hand.

'I don't think I've ever seen anything so beautiful,' she murmured. She let the diamonds trickle through her fingers like water. There must have been three hundred of them or more—small ones and large ones, tumbling over each other in her hand, twinkling like stars. 'How could anybody bury such a thing for thirty years?' she said.

Simpson was as mesmerized as she was, seemingly unable to take his eyes off it. Angela held up the necklace, and it gleamed in the sunlight. They gazed at it in silence, then their eyes met for a long moment. There was no sound but the rushing of the waves and the crying of the seagulls.

'You know, don't you?' he said at last.

'Yes, Mr. Valencourt,' said Angela. 'I know.'

He smiled ruefully.

'I ought to have realized you would telephone Jameson,' he said. 'He was bound to give the game away.'

'Yes,' said Angela. 'He told me that they did have a man down here looking for Valencourt, but that he was from the

Swiss police force, not Scotland Yard. Obviously he meant Mr. Donati. A telephone-call to Mr. Penhaligon in Penzance told me the rest.'

'Ah, yes,' he said. 'I met Penhaligon several times while I was completing the purchase of this place. I hope he described me in flattering terms.'

'He described you in enough detail to make me quite certain that you were Edgar Valencourt, at any rate,' said Angela. 'I congratulate you on a very cleverly thought-out plan. It really required very little effort on your part. Why, all you had to do was to keep an eye on the house and make sure nobody found the necklace before the fifth of August, then you could step in as rightful owner and search the place at your leisure.'

'It certainly seemed worth the trifling expense required to buy the freehold of Poldarrow Point,' he agreed. 'I thought Ma Rosie and Clifford were highly unlikely to find the necklace— although of course, I didn't know that Wally was still alive until today. It was rather a shock to me, I can tell you. Had he chosen to reveal all, he would have spoilt everything.'

'What should you have done then? I mean, if Ma Rosie had found the necklace?'

'Why, I should have taken other steps to get it,' he said. He saw her expression and said simply, 'I am rather fond of diamonds, you see.'

'So I understand,' said Angela. She dropped the necklace into one hand and then into her pocket. 'That is unfortunate for you.'

There was a short silence.

'I do hope you're not going to be difficult,' he said. 'I have, in spite of what you say, put myself to some trouble to get my hands on that necklace, and I should hate to be thwarted at the last minute—even by *you*, pleasant as our association has been.'

Angela felt the anger rise within her. Her eyes flashed and she took a step towards him.

'Listen to me, Mr. Valencourt,' she hissed. 'I don't like being made a fool of. If you think I am just going to hand it over like a lamb, you are very much mistaken.'

'I never meant to make a fool of you,' he snapped back. 'As a matter of fact, I nearly abandoned the thing altogether because of you. You were never part of my plans. You caught me completely by surprise. You—well, if you must know, you rather bowled me over. I never expected something like this to happen.'

She was by no means mollified.

'But you didn't abandon it, did you?' she said. 'You kept on deceiving me—deceiving us all. Why, there was no end to the lies you told. And I fell for them hook, line and sinker! What an idiot I was to believe your stories! I went along to Poldarrow Point like a good little girl and spied on the Hoppers for you, convinced I was helping the police—but all the time I was doing nothing but furthering the ends of a common thief!'

'Don't call me that!' he said fiercely. They were very close now, glaring furiously at each other.

'Then what *are* you, if not that?' she said.

He clenched his fists and breathed heavily, but said nothing as he tried to master his anger. At length he succeeded. He closed his eyes briefly, then sighed and spoke more calmly.

'I want that necklace, Angela,' he said. 'What does it matter to you if I get it? It's been missing for thirty years. The Duke of Bampton has claimed the insurance-money and bought other trinkets for his daughter since then. Nobody cares about it any more.'

'*I* care about it,' said Angela.

'Oh, I see,' he said. 'It's just your pride that's hurt.'

'Whatever my reasons, I am still not going to give you the necklace!'

Her breath was coming rapidly. He moved still closer until they were almost touching.

'I could take it from you, you know,' he said meaningfully.

'You could,' said Angela, 'but you won't. You're not that sort.'

The appeal to his better nature seemed to startle him. He looked down into her upturned face, his eyes searching hers.

'Shall I tell you exactly how much of a fool I've been?' went on Angela. 'I could have told Donati who you are, but I didn't. I didn't tell Inspector Jameson either. Nobody knows except me. You're free to leave whenever you choose. No-one will stop you. Tell me, then—will you take the necklace from me by force?'

Her voice held a challenge. He caught his breath and stepped back.

'Put it on,' he commanded suddenly.

'What?'

'The necklace. Put it on. I want to see you in it.'

Angela stared at him for a long second, then slowly put her hand into her pocket and brought out the necklace. She lifted it up and fastened it around her neck, her heart thumping in her breast. The sun reflected off the hundreds of stones and lit up her face and hair as she stood there, splendid and defiant. He gazed at her, drinking in the sight, then stepped forward and, before she could stop him, caught up her hand and kissed it.

'You ought to wear jewels, Mrs. Marchmont,' he said, and then he was gone, leaving Angela standing alone in the sunlight.

CHAPTER THIRTY-SIX

'BUT WHY DIDN'T you come and fetch me?' wailed Barbara for perhaps the twentieth time. She was sitting on the sofa, having refused to remain in bed a second longer.

'I've already told you,' said Angela. 'I didn't know where you were.'

Barbara pouted.

'You could have waited for me,' she said. 'After all I've done, I didn't even get to help dig up the treasure!'

'No,' said Angela. 'It was just your hard luck and I'm very sorry. But at least you got to try it on.'

Barbara's eyes gleamed.

'Wasn't it simply gorgeous, though?' she said. 'I've never seen anything quite like it. I never used to understand all those women who think of nothing but jewels, but now I've seen the necklace I think I could quite easily become one of them.'

'I know what you mean,' said Angela.

'I wonder you didn't try it on yourself,' said Barbara.

Angela examined her fingers.

'I didn't care to,' she said. 'It looked dreadfully scratchy.'

'And so Mr. Simpson wasn't a detective at all, but was really Edgar Valencourt all along!' said Barbara. 'I must say, he fooled us all rather neatly—and you, especially.'

'Yes, thank you, there's no need to rub it in,' said Angela crossly.

'Mr. Donati must have been furious when Ma Rosie told him that Valencourt had been there under his nose all the time,' said Barbara. 'I only wish I'd seen his face when he went to Mr. Simpson's hotel room and found that he'd skipped. Although he did catch Wally instead. I suppose it was a fair exchange—one jewel-thief for another. I wonder what will happen to Wally now. They can't keep the poor old thing in prison, can they?'

'I shouldn't have thought so,' said Angela. 'I know he's a dreadful old reprobate, but he's hardly in his right mind. They couldn't possibly try him now. I expect they'll put him in an institution of some kind.'

'Well, you're not the only person who was fooled,' said Barbara glumly. 'I really believed Miss Trout—Ma Rosie—was a sweet old lady who needed our help.'

'Don't feel too bad,' said Angela. 'She was very convincing.'

'But what made you suspect her in the first place?'

'Why, I'm not sure. But I must say the whole story did seem to get more and more complicated, until eventually I thought that someone *must* be telling lies. Miss Trout seemed such a sharp old lady that I didn't see how Clifford could possibly have pulled the wool over her eyes so effectively. It was obvious, therefore, that if there were any funny business going on, then she must be up to her neck in it too. And I caught her out in one or two lies—for example, her story that she knew Mrs. Uppingham well, which was not true. There was also the fact that she said she had never been into the tunnel, because she was too old—but if Poldarrow were really her family home, then surely she would have explored it in her younger days, even if she were no longer capable of doing so now? And where had she been living for the past thirty years if, as she claimed, she had only come to live with her brother a few months ago? These things were all fairly innocuous in themselves, but they seemed to add up to something rather more suspicious.'

'And then you found out the story of Marie Antoinette's necklace was a lie,' said Barbara. 'I wonder we didn't think of checking the history books earlier. That would have told us that the Queen's necklace was broken up and sold.'

'I don't know that it would have helped,' said Angela. 'After all, the history books don't prove whether or not a legend about the necklace exists in the Warrener family.'

'True,' said Barbara. 'When did you start to doubt it yourself?'

'It was the missing page in the memoirs,' said Angela. 'Someone had clearly torn it out recently, and who else was likely to have done that but Clifford or Ma Rosie? Mr. Simpson—Valencourt, I should say, pointed me in the right direction when he said that presumably the page contained proof that the necklace existed. That made me wonder: what if, in fact, it contained proof that the necklace *didn't* exist? The memoirs break off just before they reveal the contents of the parcel that the dying man left with Richard Warrener. I imagine that if we could read the next page, we should find that it mentions something that is not a necklace at all!'

'I hadn't thought of it like that,' said Barbara, considering.

'But if Ma Rosie could make us believe in the story of the Queen's necklace, then it would be all the easier to persuade us to help her find the real object of her search: that is, the necklace stolen from the Duke of Bampton.'

'So that was why the Dorseys were searching Jeremiah's—Wally's writing-desk,' said Barbara. 'They knew Wally himself had brought the necklace to the house, and so it was quite as likely to be hidden in a new desk as it was to be stuffed behind a secret panel. How did they find him here in Cornwall after all these years, by the way?'

Angela began to laugh.

'Poor Wally,' she said. 'His love of gardening proved his undoing. Last year he won a trophy for "Most Beautiful Garden In Cornwall," or some such nonsense, and his photograph appeared in the *Times*. Ma Rosie happened to see it, recognized her missing husband immediately, and set off for Tregarrion to claim her share of the loot. I don't know how Valencourt got wind of it, but he knew Ma Rosie—she recognized him when she saw him with me—so I imagine that some rumour or other must have got abroad, and he saw his chance to steal the necklace from under their noses.'

'Did he really buy the freehold of Poldarrow Point? That seems an awful lot of trouble to go to.'

'Not really, when you consider the possible reward,' said Angela. 'The house is falling into the sea and so was virtually worthless. I imagine he snapped it up for a song.'

'Well, it's no use to him any more, is it?' said Barbara. 'It's a shame to think that it will be allowed to go to rack and ruin now.' She shifted uncomfortably on the sofa. 'Oh, do let's go into the garden,' she said. 'I feel as fit as a fiddle now, truly I do!'

'Very well,' said Angela. 'I don't see why not. I suppose the doctor was only being cautious.'

Barbara jumped to her feet with alacrity and threw open the French windows. The tabby cat immediately ran towards her and started winding in and out of her ankles.

'Have you missed me, Puss?' she said, bending down to scratch under its chin.

'Hallo, Barbara,' called a voice. 'Are you feeling better now?'

Barbara looked up and saw Helen Walters and Mr. Donati passing the gate. They had evidently just returned from a walk along the beach. Barbara approached them.

'Hallo,' she returned. 'Yes, I'm much better now, thank you.' She blushed a little. 'I'm sorry I accused you of being Edgar Valencourt, Mr. Donati,' she said, all in a rush. 'I didn't realize you were actually a policeman.'

Donati bowed and smiled. He looked much less eccentric now that he was no longer wearing his absurd scientist's outfit.

'Think nothing of it,' he said. 'You could not have known.'

'I'm sorry he got away from you,' said Barbara.

Donati waved a hand.

'I will catch him one day,' he said, 'but in the meantime, I have caught myself a much greater prize.'

He looked fondly at Helen. Barbara wanted to laugh at his quaint way of expressing himself, but saw that Helen was blushing with pleasure, and so merely smiled politely instead.

'Have you told your mother?' asked Barbara, lowering her voice lest Mrs. Walters hear her from next door.

Helen nodded.

'How did she take it?'

'Badly, at first,' replied Helen, 'but I told her that she would simply have to accept it. I'm sure she'll come round at last. Pierre has determined to win her over, and I should hate for us to fall out permanently. I am very fond of her, you know.'

'Helen!' came a voice from next door. Helen looked at Donati, then at Barbara, and then grinned.

'Coming, Mother!' she called. She grasped Donati's arm and pulled him towards the gate of Shearwater Cottage. He followed with a bemused air and they walked up the path to the house together.

'What was all that about?' said Angela, who had just come into the garden.

'The worm has turned, I believe,' said Barbara.

'Oh, I am glad,' said Angela.

'I think Mrs. Walters is upset,' said Barbara. 'You will have to comfort her. You can comfort each other, in fact.'

'Thank you, but I don't need comforting,' said Angela with dignity. She sat down and buried herself pointedly in her book. Barbara smiled to herself and began playing with the cat.

A short while later, Marthe came into the garden bearing an enormous bouquet of red and pink roses.

'I say!' said Barbara, impressed.

'These have just arrived for you, *madame*,' announced Marthe. 'Is it that you have an admirer?'

Angela looked taken aback. She read the card that came with the flowers, then put it in her pocket without saying a word.

'What does it say?' said Barbara eagerly.

'Nothing,' said Angela.

'You're blushing!' said Barbara.

'Nonsense.'

'They're from Edgar Valencourt, aren't they? I knew it! He's in love with you, isn't he? Oh, Angela, you'll simply have to marry him!'

'Don't be absurd!' said Angela, laughing.

'Well if you don't, then perhaps I shall when I'm old enough. He's awfully good-looking, isn't he? And nice, too.'

'Hardly a catch, though,' said Angela dryly.

'I shall be a bridesmaid at the wedding,' said Barbara. 'I should like a pink dress.'

'I admire your romantic notions,' said Angela, 'however little they may be grounded in reality. Let me remind you that

Edgar Valencourt is a wanted man, who is on the run from the police. I dare say I'll never see him again.'

Barbara snorted.

'Oh yes you will,' she said. 'He'll be back. I'd bet my life on it!'

Mrs. Marchmont shook her head and went back to her book.

New Releases

If you'd like to receive news of further releases by Clara Benson, you can sign up to my mailing list here: smarturl.it/ClaraBenson.

We take data confidentiality very seriously and will not pass your details on to anybody else or send you any spam.

ClaraBenson.com

Books in This Series

Made in the USA
Middletown, DE
15 March 2019